There was something magical about tonight.

Until now, Nicole had been more comfortable around Jake because he was like one of her brothers, always teasing, keeping her off guard. And Peter, well, she certainly hadn't thought of him as her brother, and anytime they veered away from subjects like the mayor's race or city council business, her words stuck in her throat.

She glanced up, right into his blue eyes, and her heart fluttered. No, definitely not like a brother.

She yanked her gaze away. Her feelings were still reeling from being trampled by her last boyfriend, and she refused to go there. *Keep it light.*

Focusing forward, Nicole helped Peter load the presents for the shelter's kids into his truck, hoping she'd be able to follow her own advice.

Dear Reader,

We all want to win and we all want to be chosen. It starts in childhood when we want to be picked first—not last—for a team and continues into our adult years when we want to be chosen by someone special.

And when it comes to winning, it's a given that no one wants to lose. But what happens when winning becomes more important than anything else?

My characters in *The Christmas Campaign* struggle with these issues. Nicole never worried in high school about being chosen for a team—being a great athlete, she was always the team captain and the one doing the choosing, but when it came to dates...well...her brother took her to the senior prom. And then when someone finally does choose her, after four years it suddenly ends. So when cousins Peter Elliott and Jake O'Neil start paying attention to her, she is more than a little leery.

All their lives, Peter and Jake have competed against each other, and that doesn't change when they get reacquainted with Nicole. Not only that, they are in a contest with half a million dollars at stake.

I loved writing this story and hope you enjoy it, as well.

Patricia

Connect with me at patriciabradleyauthor.com and let me know what you think about the way Nicole, Jake and Peter dealt with their struggles.

HEARTWARMING

The Christmas Campaign

—

Patricia Bradley

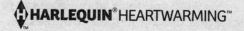

ISBN-13: 978-0-373-36748-1

The Christmas Campaign

Copyright © 2015 by Patricia Bradley

Printed in U.S.A.

HARLEQUIN®
www.Harlequin.com

Patricia Bradley lives in north Mississippi with her rescue cat, Suzy. She presents workshops on healthy relationships and writing. But her heart is tuned to writing stories of love and hope with happily-ever-after endings. When she's not writing or presenting workshops, she likes to throw mud on a wheel and see what happens. She loves to connect with readers on Facebook.

Books by Patricia Bradley

Harlequin Heartwarming

Matthew's Choice

To check out Patricia's books,
visit the Author Profile page at Harlequin.com.

To my friend Joyce Dickey. You have overcome.

Thank you, Kathryn Lye, for your awesome work sharpening this story and catching my many mistakes. And to the wonderful team at Harlequin Heartwarming—thank you. You are the best.

CHAPTER ONE

It had been Monday morning all day, and it was after three on the last day of November. Not even the soft music or small Christmas tree Peter Elliott's assistant had placed in the corner of his spacious Social Services office lessened the tension in the room.

Peter tented his fingers and searched for the most diplomatic way to say no to the man across from him. No matter what he came up with, Cal Sheridan would not be happy. He decided to go with direct.

"I appreciate that as a foster parent, you and your wife would like to take Logan, but I'm not separating the twins."

Sheridan locked his jaw in place. "It looks to me like it'd be better if at least one of the boys was in a decent home instead of the shelter."

A dull headache throbbed in Peter's head. Cal Sheridan had twenty years on him, but no one could make his blood pressure spike like this man, whether it was in Cal's capacity as truant officer for the city schools or voting against him on the Cedar Grove city council. "The shelter is not the abyss. Sarah Redding provides a warm and loving environment, and they've been with her for two years now. She's like a mother to them."

The fifty-four-year-old's face turned red. "I didn't say it wasn't a good place, but it's not the same as being in a family." His tone challenged Peter.

"But therein lies the problem." He stared Sheridan down. "The only family the twins have left is each other. Do you want to take that away from them? Especially at Christmastime?"

Sheridan's jaw softened, and he sighed. "Put that way, no, I suppose not. They're both good kids, but I've gotten closer to Logan working with him in the after-school program."

"I hope you'll continue working with him. Lucas, too. Until they came to Cedar Grove, they had it pretty rough." Cal knew that the twins' mother had died at the hands of their abusive father, who'd used his sons to deliver drugs. The two young boys had ended up in Cedar Grove when the state placed them in protective custody.

Cal ran his hand over the side of his face. "It's not that I don't want to take both of them, but little Emily needs a lot of care."

Peter nodded. Even though Cal was opinionated and set in his ways, the man had a good heart. After his two sons married and moved out, Cal and his wife had become foster parents. Just last year the state had placed an infant born with a cocaine addiction with the Sheridans.

Peter cocked his head. "Have you thought about taking Tyler Bennett? He's fifteen and extremely bright."

Cal shook his head. "Are you joking? I've seen that boy with my granddaughter a few times, and I don't like his attitude. In fact, he was just suspended from school today."

Peter stifled an inward groan. Sarah hadn't called and told him about that, yet. "How do you know?"

"I was in a meeting with the principal when Coach Dawson brought him into the office. Seems he unscrewed the pepper shaker at the teachers' table and ruined Dawson's lunch, not to mention the sneezing fit it caused."

Peter doodled on a paper on his desk. "You never did that?"

Cal averted his gaze, but didn't answer.

Peter crossed his arms. "When I was a freshman in high school, I remember hearing this legend—seems like there were these senior boys who put the football coach's Jeep in the school lobby. If I'm not mistaken, that's when you were a senior. Know anything about that?" He knew very well Cal Sheridan was the ringleader.

Cal at least had the grace to grin. "That was then and this is now. Tyler's different, and I'm afraid if the boy doesn't change, he'll end up in juvie."

"You didn't end up there, and maybe with an understanding hand—"

"Can't do it, Elliott. I have a granddaughter who's already defending him every time he does something. Sure don't want to give them even more opportunities to be together."

"Well, talk to your wife before you totally rule him out." Peter's phone buzzed, and he picked up the receiver. It was his secretary reminding him of an appointment with his grandfather's lawyer. He checked his watch as he replaced the receiver. If he didn't hurry, he'd be late. "I'm sorry, Cal, but I have a meeting. I'll walk out with you."

Peter grabbed his briefcase. "Seriously, give some thought to fostering Tyler. The boy is hurting after losing his mother and dad and his grandparents."

"I'll think about it."

"Think about something else, too. I want to start a youth center similar to a Boys and Girls

Club, and I'll need your help tomorrow night with the city council."

"Youth center?" Cal rubbed the back of his neck. "You're talking big money that the city doesn't have."

That wasn't news to Peter. He sighed. If only his grandfather hadn't died two weeks ago, the money would not have been a problem, and he wouldn't be on his way to the reading of the will.

PETER TURNED INTO his grandfather's tree-lined drive. He'd always loved the way the magnolias stood sentry at the old home. He parked in front of the Tudor-style house and walked to the front door where magnolia and pine boughs formed a huge Christmas wreath.

He was glad the tradition continued even though his grandfather wasn't there. The housekeeper ushered him into the foyer.

"They've gathered in the den," she said.

"Thank you, Millie. How are you?"

She sniffed. "Tolerable."

He patted her on the shoulder. "It's going to be okay, Millie. I'm sure grandfather made provision for you and Gunner to remain here."

"I'm not worried about that. I just miss the old buzzard."

Peter laughed out loud. Millie and his grandfather had been at odds ever since Peter could remember, but each of them would defend the other against the world.

"How's your momma?" Millie asked. "Is she still in Georgia with your grandmother?"

He nodded. "She sounds good when I talk to her, and my grandmother has almost recovered from her surgery. Mother should be coming home soon."

But not in time to be here today. He glanced toward the den, not looking forward to the next hour.

When Peter entered the room, he nodded to his grandfather's attorney, Robert Corbett, and then spoke to his aunt Amelia before he took a seat in one of the wingback chairs. His cousin Jake had commandeered his grandfather's leather recliner.

"Now that everyone is present we can begin," Corbett said. "First I want you to understand that although the will is in Richard's wording, it is legal."

Heads nodded and he began. "To my daughter, Amelia, and my daughter-in-law, Deborah, I leave half of my personal property to be divided equally between you, except for the house. That goes solely to my daughter. Robert will put all the *hereby* and *wherewiths* in later if they are needed."

His grandfather's verbiage sounded strange in the lawyer's hushed tones. Peter glanced at his cousin, then his aunt, fearing they might resent Grandfather leaving so much to his daughter-in-law. But no frowns appeared.

Peter hadn't expected to receive the house. In fact, he didn't expect to receive much of anything. He was here because his mother had delegated him to represent the family at the reading of the will since she couldn't come.

Robert Corbett continued, "The other half goes to my two grandsons with the exception of the following bequeaths."

Peter blinked back his surprise. Sitting across from him, Jake did the same thing. Even though Peter and his grandfather had put their past differences behind them, he hadn't expected to be left a quarter of the estate.

Not that he ever wanted any of Richard Elliott's money, but he had wanted his approval—something he wasn't sure he had until now. That's what a will was—a person's final judgment of his heirs. He took in a satisfied breath and released it.

The attorney went on to list the few people his grandfather had left personal items to, including Millie and Gunner. They would remain in their little cottage behind the main house along with a nice pension.

While the attorney searched his papers, a mantel clock chimed four times. Peter slipped his grandfather's pocket watch out and flipped it open. Four o'clock. Right on the money.

He closed the watch and ran his thumb over the smooth case, remembering how his grandfather had given it to him after he'd won a race against Jake, using less than honorable tactics. But instead of admonishing Peter, he'd simply said that winning wasn't everything, and he hoped the watch would remind him of that. It was a lesson Peter wasn't sure he'd learned yet.

He would deeply miss his grandfather, miss the long talks even though they usually disagreed, miss the challenges, and even the contests his grandfather came up with.

And Peter would miss sitting with him in his walnut-paneled den. Correction. The house now belonged to his aunt, something his cousin already seemed comfortable with as he leaned back in the leather chair and propped his ankle across his knee.

Jake, like Peter, had taken his lanky, six-foot-one frame from the Elliott side of the family. Height and blue eyes were the only physical traits he and Jake shared. Jake had more of the Irish in him from the O'Neils, with his dark hair and somewhat darker complexion, than Peter who had the fairer Scottish coloring and blond hair. But they both had the Elliott competitive spirit.

The attorney cleared his throat. "Now, to the business end."

Amelia stood. "Is there any need for me to stay for this?"

Corbett looked up. "No, it deals with the two grandsons," he said. "If you wish to leave while we conduct this part of the will, you are welcome to do so."

She glanced at Jake, her eyes questioning him.

Color flooded his face. "I can handle this, Mother."

"Good. I have a house to show at four-thirty." She kissed her son and hugged Peter. "Come to dinner later this week."

"Thank you, Aunt Amelia," he said. "Let me know which night."

He'd always liked his aunt—she'd had fun games for them to play when they were growing up and never tried to get him and Jake to compete against each other. In fact, she'd tried to get her father to stop his games. To no avail.

After the door closed behind Amelia, Robert Corbett shifted his gaze back to the document while Jake maintained an air of indifference, and Peter studied the dark red carpet.

He didn't understand why Corbett said this

part of the will dealt with him and Jake. Jake, he understood. His cousin was already operations manager at the furniture factory, and it was only natural that he would step into his grandfather's shoes.

Peter would be surprised if he were mentioned at all, since his grandfather never got over his spurning the family business to gallivant around the world and then choose a government career.

"The reins to Elliott Manufacturing will pass to the winner of the following contest."

Peter jerked his head up. "What?"

"What?" Jake's indifference evaporated as he echoed the question.

Corbett peered over his glasses. "I assume your questions reflect surprise rather than an inability to hear or understand, so I will continue rather than repeat myself."

He resumed reading. "I can hear both of you squawking about right now, but it will do you no good. At the time of this writing, Robert will attest to the soundness of my mind."

Peter and Jake exchanged glances, and Peter knew his cousin was thinking the same thing he was. *Not another one of Grandfather's crazy contests.* For as long as Peter could remember, Richard Elliott loved to pit his two grandsons against each other. "Iron sharpens iron," he'd always said. Trouble was, it sometimes sharpened it to a nub.

"I tried to talk him out of this, but he would not be dissuaded." Corbett placed the will on the desk and handed each of them an envelope. "The terms of the contest are laid out in these papers. If you will take your—"

"Is this some kind of joke?" Jake asked.

"I can assure you, Mr. O'Neil, it is not a joke. Your grandfather put a lot of time and thought into this. It was his belief that the director of Elliott Manufacturing needs all of the skills this contest will require. Now, I will give you a minute to look over the instructions and terms."

Peter opened his envelope and slid out the papers. As far as he was concerned, the contest was over. He had no desire to run the company and would gladly cede the directorship to Jake.

He liked his life just the way it was, much preferring his involvement with the children's shelter and his job as head of the Department of Human Services in Cedar Grove to running a furniture manufacturing business. And he looked forward to starting the teenage community center he'd mentioned to Cal. Getting it approved by the city council and obtaining the funds needed to run it was all the challenge he wanted.

Peter skimmed the papers and abruptly stopped, frowning.

A half million dollars. He blinked and looked again. No, he'd seen right. He raised his gaze to the lawyer, who sat with his hands clasped together on the desk, his face unreadable. Peter sneaked a glance at Jake. His wide eyes indicated he'd seen the figure, too.

"Now, if you are ready, I'll go over the broad points of the contest. You can read the fine print later at your convenience. You are welcome to make notes on the papers I gave you."

Without waiting for an answer, he began reading.

"Okay, boys, you both know that for several years, it's been in my heart to start two things in Cedar Grove. A place for senior citizens to meet and another one for teenagers. A year ago I purchased a building that would be suitable to house either of these projects. I'm assigning the youth project to Peter and the senior citizen project to Jake.

"You have ninety days to form a nonprofit organization and to come up with a five-year business plan, as well as obtain approval and backing from the city, which will include twenty-five thousand dollars a year to help run the operation. The rest of the money to run it will come from the half million dollars the winner receives. Whichever one of you is the first to get approval gets the building and the half million dollars. He also becomes CEO of Elliott Manufacturing.

"However, in obtaining city backing, neither this contest nor the subsequent funding can be mentioned. If the city doesn't believe in the project enough to invest in it, you don't have their support.

"As for a director for your project, it can't be either of you. If you can't get someone to volunteer to head it initially, you haven't done your job. Whichever of you wins will then have the pleasure of hiring a director."

Jake leaned forward. "I don't think it's fair that Peter has the advantage of being on the city council."

Peter snorted. "That's no advantage when I have two people who almost always vote against me, no matter what it is."

Getting this project through wouldn't be a slam dunk. He could probably count on two other members to vote his way, and the mayor if there was a tie. Then there was Cal and his crony, George Bivens—the two picked apart any proposal presented to the city council that didn't come from either of them. That left G. Nicole Montgomery.

While she didn't *always* vote against him, she asked hard financial questions. Which shouldn't surprise him, since she was the bookkeeper in her dad's small family-run company. Of the six council members, Nicole was the one who focused more on the money aspect of a project. Everything would have to be in order, and the numbers would have to add up, for her to vote for it.

If he couldn't sell her on the city spending twenty-five thousand dollars a year, she would sway the other members to vote against the proposal. Even the ones who usually voted with him.

"It's still not fair," Jake shot back. "And I don't think you should vote when I present my proposal to the board meeting."

"Didn't plan to. Or on mine, either," Peter replied. He turned to Corbett. "When do the ninety days start?"

"And who will run the company until the winner is declared?" Jake asked.

"The ninety days starts now, and Jake will continue to run the day-to-day operations."

Corbett took two letter-sized envelopes from his briefcase. "This is from your grandfather and to be read in private."

Peter took the envelope, and his breath hitched at his grandfather's large, flowing scrawl. It was hard to believe he was really gone.

AFTER PETER AND the attorney left, Jake wandered around the den, mentally forming a plan to win the contest. Becoming CEO of Elliott Manufacturing had been his lifelong dream. He couldn't believe his grandfather hadn't left it to him outright, instead of making him jump through hoops.

But, if it took jumping through hoops, he'd do it. He stopped in front of the bookcase and ran his fingers over the spines of a few of the books. *The Hunt for Red October, The Firm...* He paused to count a series collection and smiled. Every one of the Jack Reacher books was there.

Yeah, his grandfather was a man's man, and for as long as Jake could remember, he'd wanted to be like him. On another shelf above the books were several of his grandfather's carvings, and Jake slipped a small whittling knife from his pocket.

Out of everything Richard Elliott had ever given Jake, the knife meant the most. *It's my favorite knife,* he'd told Jake. *It's small enough to carry with you—that way, if you can find a piece of wood, you'll never be bored.*

Like everything else, the knife was an object lesson. Jake no longer remembered what underhanded thing he'd done to Peter, but his grandfather had caught him at it. *Winning is good, but it's not the most important thing. How you win is much more important, and I want this knife to be a reminder that win or lose, it's all about honor.*

He wished he could say he'd always followed his grandfather's words. If the truth were known, probably the opposite was true, especially when it came to women...or Peter.

Jake crammed the knife back in his pocket. He didn't know why he still carried it, unless it was to remind him of his connection to his cousin.

He and Peter were so different, even down to their styles of running businesses. Peter, a textbook type A personality, liked having his finger on the pulse of every aspect of a project, where Jake usually took a more relaxed stance. And while it might look like he wasn't really doing anything, the job always got done.

He looked up as Millie entered the den.

"Oh! I thought everyone was gone. I'll come back later." She turned to leave.

"Don't go," he said, suddenly tired of his thoughts.

Millie hesitated. "You miss him, don't you?"

"Yeah. It helps that you and Gunner are staying on, though."

"Mr. Elliott was a generous man, and Gunner and I want to help keep this place like he wanted it."

"I know what you mean." Jake sat behind his grandfather's desk in the leather chair.

Millie's fingers fluttered to her face. "Oh, my goodness, how you remind me of him."

"Me?" Jake had never thought he looked like his grandfather. That honor went to Peter.

"Except for your dark hair, you could almost be him sitting there."

Jake sat a little straighter. He'd always been told he favored the O'Neils, especially his father. Not something he liked to hear since Keith O'Neil was the poster child for wild living and divorce after leaving Jake's mother.

"Are you going to do it?"

He frowned. "Do what?"

"Build the senior center Mr. Elliott wanted."

"You know about that?"

She nodded. "Your grandfather and Gunner and me used to talk about it. He—your grandfather—drew up a plan…" She glanced toward the walnut file cabinet in the corner of the room.

His heart speeded up. He and his grandfather had discussed the senior center he wanted built, but Jake had no idea there was a plan. If he could get his hands on it, he'd be light-years ahead of Peter.

"Do you know when the city council meets?" he asked Millie.

"The first and third Tuesday. They'll be meeting tomorrow night."

His mind whirled. If he worked at it, he could present his proposal to the city council at tomorrow night's meeting. But he needed a director…or maybe two.

He eyed Millie. "You and Gunner are pretty familiar with what Grandfather wanted, right?"

She beamed at him. "We are."

The couple might not have MBAs, but they knew what the senior center needed. He raised his eyebrows. "How would you and Gunner like to be the directors of the Richard Elliott Senior Center?"

"Why, that's exactly what your grandfather suggested," she said.

"Good. It's settled, then. In the beginning, there won't be any pay, though."

She put her hand on her hip. "Wouldn't take it if there was any." Then she frowned. "But how will you get the city council to put money into it? Your grandfather was worried about that."

Jake was as well, especially since he wasn't that familiar with the council members. The only member he knew was the one for his district, Boyd Anderson. He wished now that he had attended a meeting or two. But at least the mayor was a good friend.

"Isn't that nice Nicole Montgomery on the city council?" Millie asked. "I know you could charm her into voting for it."

He searched his memory. He wasn't familiar with her as a council member, but he'd gone to school with a Nicole Montgomery. The image of a dark-haired teenager floated to the surface—could that be her?

"Do you know where I could find her tomorrow?"

"She's the bookkeeper for her daddy at Montgomery and Sons Construction Company," Millie said. "And her mother is in my book club—we meet tomorrow night. I'll work on her."

He stood. "Good. Now, let's see if we can find Grandfather's plan for the center."

If he could get Nicole Montgomery on his side along with the mayor, Peter wouldn't have a chance.

CHAPTER TWO

NICOLE MONTGOMERY CAREFULLY put the sixtieth candle on her father's birthday cake, and wondered which of her brothers would make a crack about Daniel Montgomery not burning down the house. "Do you want the cake in the dining room?"

"On the buffet." Her mother turned to get something from the refrigerator.

Nicole pushed open the dining room door and couldn't keep a grin from sliding across her lips. She shook her head. As usual, her mom had gone all out. Blue and white streamers hung from the ceiling and birthday balloons floated up from their tethers, competing with Christmas decorations that had been up since the day after Thanksgiving.

While normal people hit the stores at 5 a.m. on Black Friday, her mother decorated the family home, inside and out. It never seemed to faze her that a week later, she would add birthday decorations. If it'd been Nicole, she would have simply waited on the wreaths and Christmas trees.

Back in the kitchen, she peeled the Idaho golds that would soon be her mother's award-winning creamed potatoes.

"Look at this."

Joyce Montgomery pushed her smartphone under her daughter's nose. Nicole leaned back so she could see what was so important, but the words blurred. "It's too close, I can't read it."

"It's a text from Sarah Redding, the director of the children's shelter. Volunteers are needed this Saturday to help get the place ready for state inspection. I'm sure Peter Elliott will be there."

Her mother was matchmaking again. Maybe she'd drop the subject if Nicole ignored her.

"You should plan on going. Your brothers, too. I'll tell them as soon as they get here for dinner."

"It's Pop's birthday. You might want to wait until the celebration is over." Nicole scratched her nose with the back of her hand. She wished her mom would quit trying to fix her up. She'd done the relationship thing, and it hadn't worked out.

And it wasn't as if men didn't ask her out. She'd simply gotten in the habit of preferring her own company to the dreaded dating scene. The nervousness of that first date. Making small talk. Shake hands or kiss at the door? Nope. Been there, done that, had the broken heart to prove it.

She could count on one hand the men she trusted, and they were all family members. "What do you want me to do after I finish the potatoes?"

"I want you to promise me you'll help at the shelter this Saturday. I know you don't have anything planned."

"I might. There are a lot of Christmas parties happening already." It was only Monday afternoon. Anything could happen in four days and seven hours.

"Pff," her mother huffed. "You never go out on Saturday."

Nicole washed the diced potatoes and put them on to boil. "You never know, I might have a hot date. Besides, Peter Elliott doesn't notice me any more now than he did in high school. So don't try to find ways to throw us together."

Nicole was surprised she hadn't mentioned Jake. He was another of her mom's men-you-could-date-if-you-wanted-to subjects since Nicole's breakup with Stuart two years ago.

"But you both serve on the city council. If you'd just practice flirting a little—"

"Mom! Really." She bent down and hugged her five-foot-four mother. "I'm not his type. All during high school and in college, he only had eyes for Allie Carson. She was cute and dainty—something I'll never be.

"And don't start with his cousin Jake. Neither of them are into someone who can look them straight in the eye, or outshoot them on the basketball court...or who walks like a heifer plodding across cotton rows."

Nicole's reference to a comment made twenty-one years ago brought a frown from her mother. "You do no such thing. And that dance instructor never said that was the way you walked."

Nicole might have been only twelve, but she knew what she'd heard. And she'd never gone to another class.

Her mother wasn't one to let a subject die. "I mean, you might not have been asked to dance the lead in a ballet, but you were...very graceful on the basketball court."

And that was the only place she was graceful. Nicole's size-ten feet and five-ten frame were not made for dancing, no matter what her mother wanted to believe.

"She could've been another supermodel,"

said her brother Sam as he entered through the back door. He handed Nicole the two-year-old in his arms, and then turned to take a shopping bag from his very pregnant wife.

"With my feet, I'd probably stumble on the runway." She nuzzled the baby's soft blond hair as Sam tenderly guided Amy to a chair. Her oldest brother, who'd just turned forty, had it good, and he knew it. No biological clock ticking for him. Or Amy, who at thirty-six was only three years older than Nicole. With the birth of their son in two months, Amy would have her family complete. At least that was her plan.

"I'll take Grace, and you can put this wherever Mom has the other presents stashed," Sam said.

Her brother held out the prettily wrapped package Amy had brought in. Nicole glanced at the silver bow and embossed paper. All that fancy wrapping was wasted on her dad. Now, her mother on the other hand…

"No, I'm good." She so seldom got to hold her niece, and she wasn't ready to give her up yet. "Put that in the dining room and then go drag Pop out of his wood shop and tell him dinner will be ready in twenty minutes. Chris and Aaron should be here by then." It would take that long for Sam to pry their dad away from whatever special project he was working on and get the sawdust brushed off his clothes.

Just as she'd predicted, twenty minutes later when the two men came in from the shop, her other two brothers arrived with their families. When it came to celebrating birthdays, or any holidays for that matter, no one did it up any better than the Montgomerys, and an hour and a half later, the house rocked with the sound of conversation and laughter.

With the meal finished, Nicole leaned back in her chair and glanced around the dining room table, lingering on each face, especially her dad's at the head of the table. He sat with his steepled fingers against his chin, a contented smile on his lips. She glanced down at her matching long fingers. She'd always been fascinated that his large hands could tease a delicate dolphin out of a block of wood or set a bird's broken wing. He was probably the reason she hadn't married—she hadn't found any man who could measure up to him.

Her mom set the candle-laden cake in front of him, and Sam said, "Where's the fire extinguisher?"

Daniel Montgomery raised an eyebrow. "Better be careful what you say—you'll be here one day."

Then he took a deep breath and blew all the

candles out while everyone cheered. Nicole sighed, wishing her empty apartment had a little of this warmth and hominess. Except celebrations like this also served as a reminder of what she didn't have.

On days like this when the whole family was together, she felt like an outsider, the only one without someone special and without children. *Oh, good grief.* Being single wasn't the worst thing in the world. It wasn't like she didn't have friends. She traveled when she wanted to and controlled the TV remote—what more could she ask for?

"I neef potty!" Her niece's yell broke her thoughts.

Thank you, Grace. Nicole pushed her chair back and threw her brother a smile. "I'll take care of this."

Sam glanced at his brothers. "Now, that's the way to train your sister."

She whacked him on the shoulder as she led Grace toward the bathroom.

"Tank you, Aunt G.," Grace said a few minutes later as Nicole helped her with the Pull-Ups. All of her nieces and nephews had trouble saying "Nicole," so the problem was remedied by calling her by her first initial.

"You're welcome, honey. Let's wash your

hands." When she finished drying Grace's hands, she asked her, "Having fun today?"

The golden curls bobbed, and Nicole swept the tiny girl up in her arms, marveling at how light she was. With her dainty frame, no doubt she would become the ballerina her grandmother always wanted. A good thing, since the other three grandchildren were boys.

As Nicole neared the dining room, her mother's voice carried through the open door.

"Samuel, I want you to make sure your sister goes to the children's shelter cleanup Peter Elliott is doing Saturday. And Aaron and Chris, I expect you to encourage her and to be there, as well."

Nicole stopped midstride as heat raced up her neck to her cheeks. She should have known her mother wouldn't listen to her. She counted to ten, giving her heart time to still, then, setting Grace down, she slipped her phone from her pocket and texted her best friend. Invite me to lunch and Christmas shopping Saturday? PLEASE.

Less than a minute later a message pinged. Sure. But why the PLEASE?

Explain later. Nicole put her phone back in her pocket. Then in a voice loud enough to carry, she said, "Okay, Gracie, let's get you back in your booster seat."

Silence greeted her as she reentered the dining room and slid Grace into the high chair. "Did I miss anything?"

"Nope," said her brother Aaron.

Nicole caught the look her mother gave him.

"Oh, by the way," Aaron said. "I'm volunteering Saturday to help Peter Elliott fix up the shelter. What time do you want me to pick you up?"

"Pick me up for what?"

"Aren't you going to help?"

She shook her head. "Sorry, I have a lunch date, but I hope you have fun."

"Lunch date?" her mom repeated. "You never said—"

"Cheryl sent me a text a few minutes ago. We're doing lunch and then we'll pick up some Christmas presents." Which wasn't a lie. She glanced at her brothers, and the sympathy in their eyes burned her insides. Burned enough to make her blink back tears.

Her dad cleared his throat. "Hey, Nic, if you're finished eating your cake, come see what I'm working on in the shop."

She cut a sharp glance at him. No sympathy, just love in his face. She nodded.

Her dad crooked his arm for her to slide her hand through. "We will be back directly, unless Nicole decides to sand a little on that book-case she's making," he said over his shoulder.

"Don't either one of you dare!" her mother called after them. "You still have your presents to open."

"Yes, ma'am."

As they stepped out of the house, her phone alerted that she had a text, and she glanced at it. It was from Cheryl, already canceling their lunch date because she'd remembered a prior commitment. With her boyfriend, no doubt, but Nicole would keep the cancellation to herself.

She strolled with her dad to his workshop.

"Can you believe it's almost the first of December and seventy degrees?" he said.

Thank you, she replied silently. "I think it's supposed to turn cold this weekend."

One thing about her dad—he didn't push her to talk about something she didn't want to discuss. The fragrant smell of cedar washed over her when she stepped through the door. "You're making a cedar chest."

"Yep. It's over here." He led her to the chest, which was finished except for attaching the hinges.

She ran her hand over the smooth wood, admiring the red lumber that seemed to glow. "You never did make me one."

"You know what they say about the cobbler's children having no shoes," he said with a laugh. "Except that's no longer true. This one's yours."

Tears sprang to her eyes. She had so not expected this. "Oh, Pops, thank you. It's beautiful!"

"Like you."

"Stop that. You're going to make me cry."

He hugged her. "It's true."

Nicole laid her head on his shoulder. She knew better. Her mouth was too wide, and her hair too straight, just like her body. Guys never seemed to give her a second look.

She squeezed him and then walked over to the bookcase she'd been working on, half tempted to pick up her sanding paper. "Thanks for feeling sorry for me and getting me out of the house."

"What are you talking about?"

"I heard Mom when I was in the hallway."

"Oh." He rummaged in his toolbox and handed her a sheet of garnet sanding paper. "She means well—she knows how much you want a family, and we've both seen the way you look at Sam and Amy. And little Grace." He put his arm around her. "Honey, I know it was bad after Stuart married what's her name—"

"Tiffany."

"Yeah, her. But the point is, eventually you'll have to risk your heart again."

If only her heart wasn't a block of ice. Nicole wasn't sure she'd ever be willing to trust another man.

"Your mom just wants you to be happy."

She quirked her mouth in a wry grin. "And Jake O'Neil and his cousin Peter Elliott are at the top of her list of eligible men in Cedar Grove."

Her dad laughed. "Could be worse."

"But pushing me on Peter isn't the answer. I spend two hours a month with the man at the city council meetings, and not once has he indicated he might be interested in me. Other than to get my vote on one of his pet projects."

"Speaking of votes, I talked to Hugh yesterday. He's talking about not running for the mayor's office again in the next election."

Her heart kicked up a notch. She hadn't heard that. "Really? Why not?"

"He said he'd been having a few health problems. If he doesn't run, that would get rid of one of the obstacles you mentioned when we talked about you running for mayor."

Her mind raced. She'd known and respected Hugh Gordon all her life, but he wasn't the most effective mayor Cedar Grove could have.

If he didn't run, and if she could win the election, she could implement a plan she'd been working on with Judge Connors, an old friend of her dad's.

"Whatever you're thinking, I like it," her father said. Then he wrinkled his nose. "Except if you become mayor, I'll have to get someone to run the office."

The family-owned company was small, and Nicole did it all, from bookkeeping to answering the phone. "Do you really think I could get elected?"

"I don't know why not. You handily won the city council seat, and the mayor's office will be a cinch, too. But you need to start campaigning now, let people see you helping out at places…like the children's shelter. I doubt Cheryl would mind if you canceled your outing."

"Pops!"

"I'm serious, Nic. You know as well as I do that you would have jumped on helping out if your mom hadn't been the one to suggest it. I've heard you say a dozen times the shelter is a good thing for Cedar Grove. If you're seriously considering the mayor's race, you need to get your name out there and quit hiding your light under a bushel. And who knows, you and Peter might just hit it off."

She stared at him. "Not you, too."

He raised his eyebrows. "You never know—"

She put her hands on her hips. "I know this. South Mississippi will freeze over before Peter Elliott ever asks me for a date."

Or his cousin Jake.

CHAPTER THREE

THE SUN HUNG low on the horizon as Peter walked to his car. He'd tucked the letter from his grandfather in his briefcase to read later tonight. Right now he had to answer a text from the director of the children's shelter. Call me.

As he dialed Sarah Redding's cell phone number, he shrugged out of his suit coat. It was unseasonably warm weather for the last of November. That was one thing he'd enjoyed since returning home—the odd days of warm weather in fall and winter. Of course, tomorrow it could be thirty.

Sarah answered on the first ring. "We have a problem."

"We always have a problem, Sarah," he responded.

"Well, you know that recent storm damage we had, it's more extensive than I first thought. And we have the state inspector coming next Monday. I'm afraid we won't be ready in time. I've put the word out for volunteers this Saturday, but—"

"Just hold on, I'll be there in five minutes. We'll figure out something."

That was another good thing about Cedar Grove. A person could go anywhere in town in less than ten minutes. Sarah met him at his car. "I don't see how they can expect us to get all this done in seven days."

"Did you call them and explain?"

"I tried to, but they wouldn't budge."

He took the list of repairs from her hand and scanned it. Whoa. The roof needed repairing, windows needed to be unstuck, shutters replaced or repaired, leaves were too close to the foundation, holes needed to be filled in the yard, receptacles...the list went on. No way could they get all this done without hiring a crew, and *that* they didn't have money for.

"Have you contacted Mr. Davis?" Davis was a handyman the center used for repairs.

"He's in the hospital with a broken leg—he fell off a roof. I've called a few other contractors, but with this warm weather they're all busy trying to beat the rain predicted for this weekend."

"Show me what needs to be done inside."

He followed her through the back door into the kitchen where Tyler Bennett sat at the table. Peter had almost forgotten the trouble the boy had gotten into. "Hey, Tyler. Did something happen at school today?"

The teenager brushed a mop of brown hair away from his forehead, revealing defiant blue eyes.

Sarah folded her arms. "He's suspended for three days."

Peter struggled to keep disappointment from his voice. "What was it this time, Tyler?" Even though he knew the answer, he wanted to hear the boy's side.

Tyler's mouth twitched. "Nothin' important."

Sarah said, "Nothing important? He—"

Peter put his hand on her arm. "Let him tell me what he did," he said gently.

The hand the teenager had been dealt the past few years was one most adults would want to walk away from, and Peter hurt for the teenager. But the kid had his whole life ahead of him, and in this particular circumstance, having him own up to what he did was the only way Peter knew to help him.

Tyler drew circles on the paper in front of him. Peter waited. When the boy looked up, Peter raised his eyebrows, but said nothing.

Tyler huffed. "I unscrewed the top of the pepper shaker at the teachers' table. One of the *basketball* players ratted me out. Shoot, Coach Dawson doesn't even taste his food before he grabs the salt and pepper."

Peter clamped his jaw to keep from grinning. "Why?"

The teen looked down. Finally, he lifted a shoulder in a half shrug. "Coach wouldn't let me even try out for the team. Said I should've come three months ago with everybody else. Not my fault I wasn't here, yet."

"Did you tell him that?"

He shook his head. "He's the coach, he ought to know."

"Well, he might not," said Peter. "So, you don't see anything wrong with what you did?"

The teenager averted his gaze. Again the half shrug. "Maybe it was a dumb thing to do."

"Maybe?"

"*All right*. It was a dumb thing to do, and I won't do it again."

"That's better. Have you written the coach an apology?"

Tyler slid an envelope from the papers on the table. "Along with five pages of 'I won't unscrew the top of the pepper shaker again.'"

Peter took out the paper and looked over the apology.

I'm sorry I unscrewed the pepper shaker and ruined your lunch. It won't happen again.
Tyler Bennett

"You'll give it to him tomorrow?"

"I can't go back to school until Thursday."

Maybe Peter could do something about that. "Okay."

He turned to Sarah. "Show me what needs fixing."

They walked into the living room first, and she pointed out the light switches and receptacles that needed replacing. "Like I said, I put out a call for some volunteers this Saturday. The warm weather is supposed to hold until late afternoon before it rains and turns cold. If enough people show up, maybe we can knock out every bit of this."

Peter looked at the list again. He could replace the receptacles, but it'd probably be faster to hire an electrician. Everything else could be done by the volunteers. "You're a genius. How many people did you contact?"

"I started with our regular volunteers, and a couple of people I know from church."

"Good. I'll see if I can find an electrician for the wiring."

She tilted her head toward the kitchen. "Do you have time to shoot a few baskets with Tyler? You can turn the floodlights on."

A mound of paperwork waited for him back at his office, not to mention he'd like to read his grandfather's letter. But those things could wait. If there was a chance that shooting a few baskets with the teenager might soften those stony blue eyes, he'd give it a try. "Sure." He turned and raised his voice. "Hey, Tyler, do you have time to shoot a few baskets?"

"Are you kidding? Sure."

The boy was waiting with his basketball by the back door when Peter walked into the kitchen. "You sure you can play basketball?" Tyler looked skeptical.

"Our team won the state championship when I was a senior."

"But did *you* play?"

"I was cocaptain." Matthew Jefferies was the other cocaptain. "Still want to take me on for a game of HORSE?"

"Sure. You can even go first," Tyler said.

"That sure of yourself, huh?"

Overhead lights lit up the concrete pad and goal. When he bought the property for the shelter, one of the first things he did was have the pad built and a hoop installed so the kids could at least shoot baskets. He bounced the ball a couple of times and sank the first shot from ten feet away.

"Is that your best shot?" Tyler hooted and easily dropped the ball in the hoop.

Peter backed up a few more feet and missed.

"Too bad." The teenager dribbled the ball

to the edge of the concrete pad and shot from twenty feet away, easily sinking the ball.

Now Peter had to make the same shot. Which he missed, earning himself an *H*. Grinning, Tyler hooked the ball over his head, once again making the shot. And once again, Peter missed.

The boy was good, no doubt about it. Peter knew Dawson, had gone to school with him. It wouldn't hurt to talk to the coach and ask if he'd give Tyler a chance, since he'd arrived too late for the tryouts.

"How are things going at school, other than the pepper shaker incident?"

Tyler half shrugged. "Okay, I guess."

The kid was the king of half shrugs. Peter made a mental note to check his grades tomorrow. "You're a freshman, right?"

"Yeah." He bounced the ball back and forth in front of him, then made another three-point shot.

Once Peter had the ball, he took his time and pictured himself making the goal. *Swish.* He grinned at Tyler.

"See if you can make this one." Tyler dribbled in and executed a layup shot.

When Peter tried, the ball rolled around the rim and bounced out. "That puts you up to *R*. Two more and you're out." Tyler hooked another shot over his head, using his left hand this time.

"I'll catch up." Peter bounced the ball, getting a feel for it, focusing. No way could he make that shot. "What are you planning to do after high school?"

"I don't know. I want to get a basketball scholarship to State, but I don't figure I'll stay at any school long enough to play on a team. I'm too short anyway." He cocked his head. "You going to shoot or not?"

Peter arced the ball over his head, and it landed behind the goal.

The teen retrieved the ball. "Good try. One more miss and you're out."

Tyler bounced the ball and stood a little taller, his shoulders a little straighter, and for the first time since the boy had come to the shelter two months ago, he actually looked happy.

"You're pretty good," Peter said. He'd like to see what Tyler could do on an actual basketball court. Too bad the youth center was still just a dream. If Peter won the contest, though, it'd be a reality, and the building that went with it would house a gym with a basketball court and a workout area.

Tyler moved to within ten feet of the basket and bounced the ball off the backboard and through the hoop. He handed the ball off to Peter. "Think you can do that?"

It was a throwaway shot. The kid had purposefully handed him an easy shot—he wasn't sure if it was to prolong the game or for Peter to save face. He took his time and completed the throw. Tyler high-fived him, and then the teenager turned around and made a perfect three-pointer.

"You really handle the ball well."

"My dad used to practice with me."

He nodded, not quite sure whether to pursue the subject. Tyler's parents had been killed in an automobile accident two years ago, and he had shifted from one foster home to another until he landed at the children's shelter in Cedar Grove in September.

"He taught you well," Peter said, and just as he shot the ball his cell phone rang. He missed by a good three inches.

"*H-O-R-S-E*!" The teenager pumped his fist in the air. "You lose."

"I would've made that one if my phone hadn't gone off." He fished his cell from his pocket and glanced at the ID. His office. He'd call them back when he left.

"Yeah, right." Tyler bounced the ball a couple of times, then put it under his arm. "Anytime you want a rematch…"

"I definitely want one, but I better get back to work."

As he walked away, Tyler said, "Thanks, Mr. E., and I won't be doing any more stupid stuff."

Peter looked over his shoulder. "Good. And I'll talk to the principal and see if you can go back to school tomorrow."

Tyler rewarded him with a groan.

PETER STARED AT the envelope with his name scrawled on it in his grandfather's handwriting. He'd purposely left reading the letter until bedtime and smiled, imagining Grandfather penning the words.

Richard Elliott had always been "Grandfather," never "Gramps" or "Granddad"—those names simply didn't suit him. He'd had such a strong personality, although the death of his only son a few years ago had tempered it some.

His father's death had been a blow to Peter as well, and it'd been hard to withstand his grandfather's insistence that he join Elliott Manufacturing. He was certain Grandfather devised the contest for the sole purpose of drawing Peter into the company, and he was equally certain the letter would confirm his suspicions.

He unfolded the paper and began reading.

Dear Peter,

By now you have learned what is in the will and are probably scratching your head. I hope you'll take the contest seriously. I know how much you want the youth center, and I'm sure you don't like the strings attached, but I hope you will take the challenge.

You probably are thinking I could have just given you both the money, but there is one last lesson for you to learn.

On a personal note, I want you to know how proud I am of you. You are a lot like your father, and that's quite a compliment. While I don't agree with your desire to serve the citizens of Cedar Grove in your capacity as director of Social Services, I see what a wonderful job you are doing. You are to be commended. Still, I would rather that you had joined the family business.

It was a joy to be a part of your raising. And never forget, winning isn't the most important thing—it's how you win or lose that matters—it all comes down to honor. Remember that whenever you look at the pocket watch I gave you.

I love you, Grandson, and I realize I didn't say it often enough.

Your Grandfather

Peter stared at the last sentence. His grandfather had only told him one other time that he loved him. The day his father was buried.

A lump settled in his throat. He was going to miss them both.

CHAPTER FOUR

TUESDAY MORNING JAKE slowed to make the turn into the Montgomery and Sons Construction Company. He'd looked up Nicole Montgomery in his high school yearbook last night. The girl in the photo was rather plain, and he couldn't place her at all.

He parked his Lexus in front of the brick building and went in, the bells over the door making Christmas sounds. The Christmas effect didn't end there. "Frosty the Snowman" played from stereo speakers, and he smiled, thinking of the seventy-degree weather outside.

"May I help you?"

He turned, looking for the speaker. She stepped out from behind the freshly cut cedar in the corner, and he caught his breath. Oh, wow. He'd never seen a Greek goddess before, but this had to be what one would look like. Surely this wasn't the girl in the yearbook. Her black hair was caught up in a French braid and green eyes the color of Ireland looked him over. "I, ah, I'm looking for Nicole Montgomery."

She hung the ornament on the tree before walking toward him. "I'm Nicole."

Jake held out his hand and was surprised at the firm grip. For the first time he could ever remember, he couldn't think of anything to say.

She tilted her head, puzzlement in her eyes. "Do you want to hire our company to do a job for you?"

"Did we really go to high school together?" He did not remember anyone looking as good as Nicole Montgomery.

"What?"

Heat burned his face. He surely did not just say that. "Forgive me, but I think your beauty has caused me to take leave of my senses."

She leaned back, and crossed her arms. "Jacob O'Neil, you were full of yourself in high school, and you still are."

A memory niggled in the back of his mind. Yeah…they'd been in chemistry class together, except the younger Nicole had been rail thin and wore glasses. That hadn't stopped him from trying to charm her, and he'd gotten the same response as today.

"Strike two, huh?"

A smile played at the corner of her mouth. "One more, and you're out."

"Then I better be on my best behavior."

"Try it. You might like it." She unfolded her arms and walked to her desk.

He checked her out while he had the chance. The silky braid draped over her shoulder. A plaid shirt, skinny jeans that fit nicely and midcalf boots—the girl he remembered would never wear anything so fashionable. Her style had changed, for sure. She turned, almost catching him.

"Now, did you have a purpose for coming in here, or is it just my lucky day?"

But not her sassy lip. Just thinking of it made him stare at her full lips. Which she promptly licked. He glanced up to focus on her eyes instead. "I came to see you about a city council proposal."

Understanding seemed to click into place. "And you need my help."

"No! I mean, yes." If he'd known what a pretty woman she'd blossomed into, he'd have been there a long time ago.

She checked her watch, and he quickly did the same and groaned. Nine thirty. He had an appointment with the mayor in thirty minutes. He'd wasted what little time he'd allotted for talking to her. "Would you have lunch with me today?"

"No."

Jake regrouped. He hadn't made a very good impression. He held up his hand. "Hang on for a minute."

He hurried out the door, turned around and came back in. "Hi, Nicole. I can't believe we haven't seen each other since high school. But I'd truly like to rectify that. Is there a snowball's chance in South Mississippi that you'll have lunch with me at Norma Jean's?" He held out his hand.

A strange look crossed her face, and then she swallowed and slipped her palm in his. "I, ah, well, since you put it that way, I guess so. Noon?"

"How about eleven thirty? Would you like me to pick you up?"

"No! I'll meet you there."

"Great." He started to leave and turned around. "You look really—"

"Don't mess it up O'Neil."

He grinned. "Well, you do."

Jake whistled as he drove across town to city hall. Getting Nicole Montgomery's vote was going to be much more interesting than he'd thought. But something about her name didn't seem right.

He remembered now…it was G. Nicole Montgomery in the yearbook. He couldn't remember what the *G* stood for, but given time, he'd find out.

Jake pulled into a parking space in front of city hall, and grabbed the packet that contained copies of the senior center proposal for each city council member. He would leave them with Betty Atkins, the city clerk, when he added his name to the agenda for tonight's meeting.

Betty looked up as he entered her office and closed the door.

"What can I do for you, Jake?"

He handed her the envelope. "I'd like to appear before the city council tonight to request a permit for renovating a building on Washington Street and to submit a proposal for a senior center. I'll also be asking for funding."

"I see. How much?" she asked.

"Twenty-five thousand."

"You can't run a center on twenty-five thousand dollars."

"That will just be the city's part. I'll come up with the rest. I'm going up to see Hugh now, and get his support."

"I'll put you down."

"Thanks." He turned to leave and she followed him.

"I'm going after coffee. Care to join me?"

"No, I told him I'd be there at ten, and it's almost that time now."

A CONFERENCE CALL about the children's shelter kept Peter from getting to city hall when he wanted to, but at least he had a better understanding of what the inspector would be looking for next week. It was now nine forty-five as he took the stairs to the city clerk's office two at a time.

He'd managed to get by the city inspector's office before they closed yesterday, so his application for a renovation permit for the building was in process. Now he needed to get the youth center proposal and the New Year's Eve teen dance he wanted to hold on tonight's agenda.

"Is Betty in?" he asked her secretary.

Treva Fisher looked up from her typing. "She has someone with her right now. Do you want to wait?"

"Do you think they'll be long?" He wanted to catch the mayor before he got too busy.

"It's your cousin Jake. What do you think?"

His heart sank. Surely Jake didn't have his proposal ready for the council. Peter was almost finished with his own except for a volunteer director. The door to Betty's office opened, and his cousin stepped out behind the city clerk. When he saw Peter, a smug grin spread across Jake's face.

"You're just getting here?" Jake said.

"Yeah, I heard it's the early worm that gets eaten."

Jake laughed. "We'll see, cuz. We'll see."

Peter ignored him and turned to Betty. "I need to put something on the agenda for tonight."

"And, I need a cup of coffee. How about walking with me to Cups and More. We'll discuss it there."

He checked his watch. "I wanted to see Hugh before it got much later."

"Whatever you want to see him about can wait. I want to talk to you."

"Let me give him a call and let him know I want time with him." Peter dialed the mayor and Hugh gave him an eleven o'clock appointment. He'd changed his plans without hesitation because everyone at city hall knew that since the mayor's heart attack, Betty Atkins ran the office. "He said I'm to bring him a white chocolate mocha."

"Don't you dare. Do you know how many calories there are in that drink? Over three hundred, not to mention the fat." She peered at him. "He doesn't know you're with me, does he?"

"I didn't actually mention your name." Peter tried not to grin. She not only ran the office, she ran the mayor. The two had been an item for years now, and everyone wondered why they didn't get married.

"We'll get him a plain coffee," she said grimly.

The aroma of fresh ground beans met them at the door. As usual the shop was full of customers, some already at tables with their coffees and others waiting in line.

He spied a table by the window. "You stake out our table, and I'll get your coffee."

"Sounds good to me. I'll take a skinny caramel latte."

He wasn't surprised the health-conscious city clerk ordered something low calorie. As he walked to the counter, several people greeted him, and he stopped to chat briefly with Mrs. Palmer about her health. The white-haired retired English teacher had been his favorite in school. When he turned to get in line, he bumped into another customer, making him almost spill his coffee.

"I'm sorry," he said, and then he recognized Allie Carson's brother. Make that Allie Jefferies. He didn't know why her new last name was so difficult to remember. Peter held out his hand. "Clint, what are you doing in town?"

"I live here now," Clint said with a smile.

He transferred his cup and shook Peter's hand, then nodded toward the counter. "I think she wants your order."

"Don't leave, yet." He turned to the barista. "I'll take a small Kona-blend, black, and a large skinny caramel latte," he said, then shifted his attention back to Clint. "I thought you were the director of the Boys and Girls Club in Memphis."

He shook his head. "I've taken over the farm since Dad decided to retire, and he and Mom hit the open road."

"You're kidding." Why had he not heard about this before now? "Will you still be in town this afternoon? I'd like to pick your brain about something."

"I have an appointment, but I'm free later in the week."

"Sounds good. I'll call you tomorrow." Peter paid for the drinks and took them to the table where Betty waited.

She scooped a spoonful of foam off the top, tasted it and closed her eyes. "Now, that's good." Then she looked at him. "So, what do you want to put on the schedule?"

"I'm not sure. I'd like to hold a dance for teens New Year's Eve. What do I need to do?"

"Apply for a permit tonight at the city council meeting. Where do you plan to have it?"

"In a building my grandfather owned. It's part of the estate now."

Betty sipped her latte. "Is it the same building Jake plans to use for a senior center?"

Peter nodded. So Jake *had* finished his proposal, and he would have left a copy of it with Betty. "Any chance I can look over his paperwork?"

She eyed him over her glasses, her green eyes boring into him.

"I'll wait until tonight."

"I think that'd be a good idea. So, do you want me to put your request for a permit on the docket?"

"Yeah, and I want to submit a proposal for a teen recreational center."

"Got it." She took another sip of her latte. "Don't you two ever get tired of competing against each other?"

He'd like to explain that this time, it wasn't his idea. Instead he said, "My grandfather always said iron sharpens iron."

"Just don't get the mayor all wrangled up in your deal—he hasn't been feeling that well." She hesitated, pressing her lips together. "That's what I want to talk to you about."

Peter resisted checking his watch while he waited for her to continue.

"I don't think Hugh is going to run for office when the election rolls around."

"Oh?" He didn't know what that had to do with him.

"In fact, I know he wouldn't if you would agree to run."

"Me?"

"Yes, you. You'd make an excellent mayor."

Him, mayor? He'd never considered the possibility before.

"I see I've taken you by surprise, but I wish you would think about it. I really don't want Hugh to run, but he will unless someone he admires steps forward."

"You're serious. But why me?"

"You have all the qualifications. First of all, you're electable. Everyone knows the Elliott name. And with a master's degree, you're well qualified, and your work in Washington, DC, speaks for itself. And here—you've done an excellent job with Social Services and getting the children's shelter set up here. And then there's your council seat. In fact, I'm surprised you haven't thought about it yourself."

Now that the shock had worn off, he had to admit the job appealed to him. "I'll think about it."

She squeezed his arm. "Good. Now go get Hugh's coffee. I have to get back to work."

Peter saluted and did as he was told.

A few minutes later, he handed the mayor his coffee. "Sorry it isn't what you ordered, but I was with Betty."

Hugh Gordon sighed. "That woman will be the death of me. It isn't enough that she runs this office, now she's telling me what I can drink."

"She's worried about you." Judging by his pallor, Betty had good reason to be worried. And the mayor could stand to lose a few pounds. Peter considered telling Hugh about their conversation regarding the election, but in the end, he simply said, "It's Kona-blend."

"That's a plus." Hugh took the top off and sipped the still-steaming coffee. "Now, what can I do for you?"

Peter hesitated, remembering Betty's admonition. Better that he be prepared for tonight. "I want to start a youth recreational center in a building my grandfather owned."

"I suppose it's the same building your cousin wants to put a senior center in."

Jake was going to give him a run for his money. Peter nodded. "Can I count on your vote?"

"Same thing he asked."

"What'd you tell him?"

"At the time, I didn't know you were going to be submitting a proposal in opposition to him, so I said yes, and I'll give you my support, as well. But if you're looking for funding, only one of you *might* receive it. Money's tight, and there's no guarantee either of the projects will be funded, though both do seem worthwhile."

Peter should have realized Jake was on his way to see the mayor when he left Betty's office. "Thanks. I'll see you tonight."

AT THE LAST MINUTE, Nicole had to call her mother to cover for her at the office after an expected shipment of lumber failed to arrive before noon. She paused just outside the front door of Norma Jean's to collect herself.

If only she could lie. *Really?* But she couldn't, not to her mother, anyway, not even little white lies about the person she was having lunch with. As soon as Joyce Montgomery discovered Nicole was meeting Jake for lunch, she would be off and running, practically planning an engagement party.

Not even if South Missi— Nicole broke the thought off. That's what got her into trouble in the first place. She'd had no intention of accepting Jake's lunch offer, but when he used that phrase, her mouth said yes even as her brain said no.

She straightened her shoulders and pushed

the door open. Might as well get it over with. Besides, he'd only asked her in order to get her help. *Keep that in mind.* She scanned the room and spotted him in a corner booth, talking to one of the waitresses.

Nicole walked toward the booth, dodging harried servers and catching snatches of conversation. Not even noon yet, and Norma Jean's was booming. Yet their waitress had time to stand and talk to Jake with a dreamy look on her face.

The man was too good-looking for his own good. When he came into the office this morning, she'd almost dropped the ornament in her hand. And then all that blarney about how she looked—he was probably telling the red-haired waitress the same thing. Her cheeks flushed just thinking about it.

"Sorry, I'm late," she said and scooted into the booth. From the frosty look the waitress gave her, Nicole had arrived too early.

He checked his watch. "You're not really late, more like right on time."

"Water, with lemon?" Red asked.

The waitress already thought she had Nicole pegged. "I think I'll have iced tea with the lemon."

"Sweet or unsweetened?"

It was on the tip of her tongue to say she

didn't know Norma Jean's served anything but sweet tea. Instead she smiled pleasantly. "Sweet."

Red turned to Jake, and her smile stretched wide. "I'll be right back with your coffee, hon."

When the waitress was out of hearing range, Nicole gave him a sideways glance. "What did you tell her? That you were having lunch with the troll who lives under the bridge?"

He laughed. "There's no use in having charm if you're not going to spread it around."

Jake was very good at that. His photo was often in the Jackson paper for various galas, and he never had the same woman on his arm. "Well, I'm immune, so don't waste your breath."

He laughed. "I can see this is going to be an interesting lunch."

Oh. My. Goodness. He thought she was flirting with him. She wasn't. Before she could say anything, Red brought their drinks and whipped out her pad and pencil.

"Are you ready to order?"

Jake leaned forward. "Nicole, do you know what you want?"

"I'll take the lunch special." It didn't matter what it was, Norma Jean's special was always good.

"I'll take the same," he said, winking at the waitress.

"Be right back with your meatloaf and English peas and baked apples."

Nicole shook her head at his flirting, and before he could turn his charm back on her, she said, "So, exactly what do you want to discuss about tonight's meeting?"

"No more fun and games, huh?"

"Nope."

"But I haven't found out what the *G* stands for in your name."

"And you never will." She should have known that was bound to come up. She gave him her most serious stare. If only her mother hadn't named her Giselle. Even as a child she'd known the name didn't fit her. It'd taken her father's intervention to get everyone to call her Nicole. "The meeting tonight…"

"Oh, okay," he grumbled. "Tonight I'm submitting a proposal to open a senior center in Cedar Grove, and I'd like you to support it."

"That's no problem. I'll be glad to support that."

He unwrapped the napkin from around the cutlery. "I also need twenty-five thousand dollars from the council."

"That puts a different spin on it." There was very little money in Cedar Grove's coffers to spend on nonessential projects. She should know. She'd been going over the budget since last week. "Why do you need twenty-five thousand from the city?"

He leaned forward, his casual air gone. "Primarily, so the city will get behind the center. No money invested equals little interest."

She saw his point. "How about you? Are you investing in it?"

"Yes, time and money."

"Do you have a budget?"

He nodded and reached in his briefcase. "You'll get another copy tonight, but I brought this in case you wanted to look over the proposal before the meeting."

Jake was prepared, and she didn't know why that surprised her. She flipped through the pages, and then set them aside. "Why do you want to do this?"

His blue eyes darkened as he caught her gaze and held it. "Because there's no longer one here. The previous center closed because it wasn't well run and the director lined his pockets instead of providing services." He leaned back.

"I remember that," she said. "I believe he's now spending his time in a state-run prison facility."

"Yep. And even with a new director, the

center couldn't regain its momentum, and government funding was cut, effectively closing it."

"How will your center be different from that one?" Nicole asked. "How will you get senior adults to come?"

"There won't be anyone stealing money, for one thing. And they will be running it, or at least an advisory board made up of senior citizens will be. I've talked to a lot of the senior adults in town, and they've told me they'd support a center if it provided what they needed.

"Several of them pointed out that they'd like to have a place to exercise without being intimidated or hurried by younger people. I want it to be a place where seniors can be comfortable."

He sat up straighter. "Last of all, but probably the most important, it's something my grandfather wanted. It's a way I can honor his memory."

Their waitress appeared and set their plates in front of them. Jake's personality instantly moved into charm mode. "Thanks, sweetheart," he said, dazzling her with a smile.

Nicole focused on her food. If passion were enough, Jake would make a success of this senior center. Her problem with the project was sustainability—his. If she agreed to help him to the tune of twenty-five thousand dollars of the city's money, she'd first have to believe he'd stick to the project. Even though she really had no reason to believe he wouldn't.

He can't stick to one woman.

That was not a measuring stick, and she couldn't let how he lived his personal life override his reputation for being a good businessman.

They ate in silence for a few minutes, and then he put his fork down. "Well, what do you think?"

She sipped her tea, trying to find a diplomatic way of saying what was on her mind. "I think it's a good idea…"

"But?"

"Are you sure you're the person to do this?" She'd feel much better about it if his cousin Peter were the one asking. "A month ago I saw in the *Gazette* that you were in Paris and before that, in the wine country in Italy. Do you really have time for this?"

Two red dots appeared on his cheeks. "Are you questioning my ability?"

"Not exactly. More like your focus or ability to commit. It's a practical concern. And, if it's something your grandfather wanted, why isn't your cousin helping you with it?"

The red dots grew to splotches. He crossed

his arms. "We don't work too well together, and I assure you, if I get the go-ahead, I'll make time for it."

She'd hit on a touchy subject by the tone of his voice. "Tell you what, I'll look at your proposal and see how the numbers add up when I get back to the office. I'll let you know if I can support the center."

He flashed her another of his high-wattage smiles. "You will. It's a worthwhile project."

She didn't doubt that.

CHAPTER FIVE

NICOLE TOOK HER seat in the conference room. They were going over the agenda before tonight's open city council meeting. Often, problems could be worked out before the actual meeting convened in the adjacent room. It was also a time for minor requests to be moved to the front of the line.

Jake sat along the wall next to Rebecca Caine, a reporter from the *Cedar Grove Gazette*. Nicole had looked over his proposal this afternoon and had been impressed with how professional it was. Jake winked when their eyes met, and she looked away. The problem was, he was never serious for long.

All the city council members were present except Peter, which was strange, as he was usually the first one at the meetings. But then the whole day had been strange, starting with Jake coming into the office and asking her to lunch.

Peter entered the room and slipped into the chair next to her. She sneaked a look at him and noticed how a lock of his blond hair fell over his forehead.

"Thanks for saving me a seat," he whispered.

She turned to protest she hadn't, but before she spoke, he asked if she wanted to grab a cup of coffee after the meeting.

The request caught her off guard. The day had just gotten even stranger. "Coffee?"

The blue pin-striped shirt he wore deepened the blue in his eyes and melted the *no* forming in her brain. *He's like Jake and only wants your help. Maybe not...* The rap of Betty's gavel kept her from answering.

"We'll talk later," he said as Betty handed out the agenda.

Nicole faced the head of the table as Mayor Gordon called the meeting to order. She frowned when he then turned it over to the city clerk. Hugh usually conducted the meeting, but tonight, he looked tired, and more than a little pale.

Nicole scanned the list of people who were on the agenda. She expected Jake's name, and skimmed further down. *Peter was on the agenda, too?*

She glanced toward Jake, and amusement glinted in his eyes. Evidently he'd been watching her. She ducked her head and finished reading the list. Maybe Peter was here to support his cousin.

But that couldn't be it. He wouldn't be on the agenda unless he was asking for something. What was wrong with her? She looked up as Betty asked Peter to explain his reason for requesting to address the council.

"I'd like a permit for a dance on New Year's Eve. It's for a building my grandfather owned, and then I want to present a proposal for a youth recreational center in the same building."

He passed around a sheet of paper. "This is a brief overview of what I want to do and the funds I'm requesting from the city. All I want tonight is the permit for the dance and a motion to consider the proposal."

Nicole scanned the paper. A youth center at 1453 Washington Street. Wasn't that where Jake planned to house his senior center? She lost whatever else was said as she read the outline Peter had provided. Nicole had long believed the town needed a place for older teens to gather. In fact, it was part of her long-range plans for the city—if she ever became mayor.

Betty called on Jake to explain his reason for being there, and Nicole turned her attention to him.

"I'm here to submit a proposal to the council, asking for approval and financial support for a senior center," Jake said. He handed each member an envelope. "I realize you'll need time to look this over, but I'll be glad to answer any questions."

Nicole had already read the proposal, but she wanted to see his five-year business plan and budgets. She found the address of the building: 1453 Washington Street. She hadn't been wrong on that.

A slow burn started in the pit of her stomach. If Jake had drawn her into some sort of contest between him and Peter, she'd throttle him. She looked up as Boyd Anderson cleared his throat.

"Jake, how do you propose to get the rest of the money to run your center?"

Jake turned to address the oldest member of the council. "Boyd, I intend to form a nonprofit and have already applied for tax-exempt status. That way I can apply to foundations for money. I also applied for my first federal grant, getting it in just under the deadline. I'll know in April if I'll receive it. In the meantime, I have backers who will help fund it until the grant money starts coming in." Beside her, Peter stiffened. She'd bet he hadn't applied for tax-exempt status.

"This is a grassroots-type thing," Jake continued. "Until I receive funding, we'll start small and see where it goes. The first step will be renovating the building on Washington Street. I applied for a permit this morning."

Peter raised his hand, and the city clerk nodded. "If you would all look at item four, you'll see I applied for a renovation permit on the same building late yesterday afternoon, which supersedes Jake's."

Mayor Gordon nodded.

Cal Sheridan folded his arms across his chest. "Looks to me like you two need to get your ducks in a row."

Nicole winced. When Cal used that confrontational voice, it meant they were in for a long meeting.

"That's why I'm here tonight," Jake said.

Peter leaned forward. "Same here. Item five is for the permit and the proposal for a youth center, and item six is my request for a permit to host a dance on New Year's Eve."

Mayor Gordon usually voted for whatever Peter proposed, but she knew he was a good friend of Jake's, as well. She turned to see the mayor's reaction.

He shook two tablets from a bottle and popped them in his mouth, and then shed his jacket. "Is anyone else in here hot?"

The room was warm, and the head of the

transportation department got up and adjusted the thermostat. In minutes cool air circulated around them.

"At least it's not just me." Hugh loosened his tie and glanced around the table. "We're not going to settle this in the work session. We may as well table it until the council meeting." He nodded to Betty. "Put them together as the last point of business, and let's move on to other matters."

The remaining items listed on the agenda were quickly dealt with. "Okay, let's adjourn until five o'clock in the boardroom."

Nicole checked the time. Only ten minutes before the meeting was scheduled to start. Enough time to get some answers. She hunted Jake down. "Are you and Peter working together, or competing for the same building?"

He grimaced. "Competing, unfortunately."

"Why didn't you tell me before you recruited me for help?"

"He'd mentioned a youth center, but when I asked you to help me, I didn't know he'd present something tonight."

"You still should have mentioned it."

"I'm sorry. You're right. I'll try to remember that for the future. Will dinner after the meeting make up for it? Maybe Venelli's... they have great pizza."

She rolled her eyes. "Charm won't get you out of this one. And for the record, my support for your project will depend on numbers and your long-range plans, not dinner at Venelli's. Now, if you will excuse me, I need to get to my seat." She started to walk away. "Oh, by the way, Peter asked me to go for coffee with him when we're done here."

Ouch. Had no one ever turned Jake down for Peter? One would think not from the look on his face. In a blink, he was back to his usual self with twinkling eyes and sideways grin. "It's only fair to warn you I always get my way…eventually."

She laughed and walked out of the boardroom, almost bumping into Peter.

"I'm sorry."

Peter ran his fingers through his blond hair, catching the lock that had fallen over his forehead. The one she'd been tempted to brush back herself because it was so uncharacteristic of him. She'd never seen Peter anything but put together.

He glanced past her, and his shoulders stiffened. "Jake has a good proposal," he said. Then he looked at her. "I really would like to have coffee afterward. I'd like to talk to you about the youth center."

At least he was being honest. *That wasn't*

fair. Jake had been up front about why he'd wanted to have lunch with her. "I think I can spare you a few minutes."

"Good. Have you ever written a tax-exempt application? Because I haven't even looked at what's involved."

"I helped write one for the art guild. I might be able to give you a few pointers."

"Thank goodness." He nodded toward the mayor. "I need to see him a minute."

Jake approached her again as she climbed the podium to take her seat. She couldn't help but notice that the cousins had the same blue eyes. Yep, Jacob O'Neil was every bit as good-looking as Peter, but in a different way.

With his Irish features, he was really more handsome than Peter, more dangerous in a sense. Like the bad boy in movies that always got the girl. Peter had more of the California surfer look. She wasn't sure which of the two might be more trouble to her heart.

Nicole drew in a deep breath. No way was she setting herself up for another Stuart. Neither Jake nor Peter would cause her a problem as long as she remembered why they had suddenly started paying so much attention to her.

"I really do want to apologize," Jake said. "And if you won't go out with me tonight, how about some other time?"

And the game was on. She crossed her arms. So this was the way a deer felt in the crosshairs of two hunters. "Call me tomorrow."

"I don't have your cell phone number." He cocked his head. "How about giving it to me and then agreeing to go to dinner tomorrow night? Unless you want to ditch Peter and grab something to eat tonight."

Her mother would be ecstatic if she knew both Jake and Peter were trying to get dates with her. Too bad she wasn't telling her. Nicole fished a card from her purse and handed it to him.

"That takes care of question one, and for the second question, I'm not ditching Peter or anyone else. It would be the wrong thing to do. You see, I have a conscience." Nicole almost laughed at the way his shoulders drooped.

His grin was back instantly. "I was only joking. I knew you wouldn't do it. But I really would like to take you out tomorrow night."

"Look, you don't have to take me to dinner to get my vote. If it's something I think will benefit the city, and we can afford it, I'll vote for it. On the other hand, if I don't like it, I'll vote against it, dinner or no dinner."

He pressed his hands to his chest. "You know, you've totally wounded me. I'm not trying to influence your vote. My proposed senior center stands on its own merit. Unlike my cousin, I simply want to get to know you better. You've flown under my radar way too long."

Evidently, he'd inherited the Irish blarney from the O'Neils, as well.

PETER TOOK HIS regular place to the right of the mayor for the open city council meeting. At least the agenda was light tonight, other than his and Jake's proposals.

He glanced across at Nicole on the end. Her cheeks were flushed, and she seemed to be looking at someone in the audience. He followed the direction of her gaze to his cousin, who was definitely flirting with her.

An overpowering impulse to protect her from Jake rose in his chest. She was out of her league with his cousin, much too innocent for the likes of him. He was a love 'em and leave 'em type of guy, and had probably dated every eligible woman in Cedar Grove except Nicole. The last Peter heard, Jake was dating someone in Memphis.

With a start, he realized the city clerk had rapped her gavel, and they all stood for the invocation and the Pledge of Allegiance. After everyone was seated, Betty explained that the first item on the agenda had been moved to the end of the meeting and called the next person to the front.

It didn't take long to work through the points of business and the reports from the different department heads. When Betty called his name and Jake's, Peter raised his hand.

"Can we dispense with the permit to hold the dance before we address the other items?" he asked when she acknowledged him.

Betty glanced at Jake, and he shrugged. "Go ahead."

Peter presented his request for the permit, and Betty asked if there were any questions.

Cal Sheridan doodled on the notepad in front of him. "Why do we need a New Year's Eve dance for teenagers?"

Peter turned to him. "Last year two teens were involved in a wreck coming home from Jackson. They'd gone there because there were no dances in Cedar Grove. The parents came to me last summer, asking if we couldn't do something about getting more youth activities here."

Sheridan held up the agenda. "One of the things you're asking for is a permit to renovate the building. I'd like to know exactly who owns the building and will it be up to code for a dance?"

"The building belongs to my grandfather's

estate, and it's up to code now. It already has offices that can be used for mentoring and other kinds of classes. The renovation permit is to put in a basketball court and dressing rooms, that sort of thing. It has nothing to do with the dance."

Boyd Anderson spoke up. "I, for one, would like to see it approved. I think we need a place around here for the teenagers on New Year's Eve." He turned to Peter. "How many chaperones will you have?"

"I have commitments from at least fifteen people. And the police chief said he'd send over a few patrolmen."

Nicole leaned forward. "I move that we grant the permit for the dance."

"Second," Anderson said.

When it came up for vote, Cal abstained and the others voted yes. Peter relaxed. One down.

Mayor Gordon fanned his face as the city clerk looked down at her agenda. "We have the last two points of business. Jacob O'Neil's proposal for a senior center, and Peter Elliott's proposal for a youth center. Each of you has five minutes. You want to go first, Jake?"

"Before I begin, I want to make sure I don't need a permit for a noon get-together for a few of the seniors who are helping me on the center. It'll be on New Year's Eve, as well, but it'll be over long before Peter's soiree. Besides that, it'll be in a different part of the building."

Peter agreed with the general consensus that no permit was needed, and Jake thanked them and began his presentation.

As Peter listened to his cousin's proposal, he acknowledged it sounded like a worthy project, and any other time, he'd be happy to support it.

Jake echoed Peter's feelings as he closed his presentation. "I wish the city had the money for this project and the youth center, but I feel we owe it to our senior citizens to do something for them. And a place to gather and play dominoes or cards and have a hot meal is something we can do. Are there any questions?"

George Bivens raised his hand. "Why do you need twenty-five thousand dollars from the city?"

"To ensure your support. If the city doesn't invest in this, there won't be an incentive to promote it," Jake said with a smile. "I'm not asking for a vote on it tonight. Just take a look at the proposal, and I'll be back at the next meeting to answer more questions."

The vote was unanimous to take Jake's proposal under consideration. Betty eyed Peter. "You want to stay where you are and tell us about your project?"

"Sounds good to me." He remained seated and glanced at the other members. Sheridan and Bivens sat with their arms folded. David Carr and Walter Thomas, who usually voted with Peter, leaned forward. He'd already talked with them, and they were enthusiastic about the project.

Nicole nodded her encouragement, and then he glanced at the mayor. Sweat beaded his forehead and his color was terrible. Tomorrow he'd say something to Hugh about seeing a doctor.

He cleared his throat. "The dance I proposed is only the starting point. Cedar Grove needs a place for older teens to gather. A place where they can feel safe. A place to participate in athletic activities. And that's what the Richard Elliott Youth Center will be.

"You have my proposal in front of you, and like Jake, I'd like you to take it under advisement. We can—"

"Cedar Grove already has a youth center," Cal said.

Cal never disappointed him. "That one is for younger kids. The center I'm proposing is for teens old enough to drive." Peter shuffled his papers. "For the sake of getting out of here in the next five minutes, could we just vote tonight for the city council to take a look at the project?"

Sheridan unfolded his arms and leaned forward. "I've looked at it. And I like Jake's project better. He—"

The mayor rapped his gavel. "Come on, you two. Can't you— Oh!" Groaning, he clasped his chest. "I, I—"

Hugh Gordon keeled forward.

Peter leaped from his chair as the room erupted in activity. "Nicole, call 9-1-1!"

Betty reached Hugh first, and Peter pulled her away. "Let me help him."

He leaned over the mayor, trying to get him upright. "We need to get him on the floor!"

"You get one side. I'll get the other."

It was Jake.

Peter nodded and the two of them maneuvered the mayor to the floor. Peter worked feverishly to remove Hugh's tie and unbutton his shirt. His chest was turning blue.

"An ambulance is on the way," Nicole said. She pressed her fingers against the mayor's wrist, then felt around, indenting the fleshy skin. "I can't find a pulse."

Peter glanced up at Betty. Her eyes begged him to save the mayor. Placing two fingers on Hugh's carotid artery, he shook his head. "Get the defibrillator!"

Using the heels of his hands, he started CPR and kept the rhythm going until Nicole attached the leads from the portable defibrillator to Hugh's chest.

The screen showed no rhythm, just waves.

The automated voice blasted, "Clear! Do not touch the patient. Analyzing."

Peter stopped compressions while the defibrillator analyzed Hugh's heart rhythm. "Shock advised. Charging. Stand clear."

"Get back, everyone," Peter ordered. He pressed the flashing button, delivering the shock. Hugh's body came up off the floor, and then Peter began another series of compressions. Where were the paramedics?

"Did someone call 9-1-1?" he shouted.

"I hear the sirens," Jake said. "Do you want me to take over?"

"I'm good."

Suddenly the machine spoke again. "Stop CPR. Do not touch patient. Analyzing."

He backed off. Hugh groaned and tried to move at the same moment the paramedics burst into the room.

CHAPTER SIX

THURSDAY MORNING PETER stepped off the elevator at the second floor and walked into the ICU waiting room. Yesterday a heart cath found blocked arteries, and surgery was scheduled for the following morning.

Hugh had refused to have it right away, saying he had business to take care of...in case he didn't make it. As if that was going to happen. But he was adamant, and Betty had called early this morning with a message that Hugh wanted to talk to him.

He scanned the room. Families sat in clusters, talking among themselves or just sitting quietly, waiting. Betty stood and motioned him to join her.

"Good, you're here," she said when he reached her.

"How is he?" Peter asked.

"He had episodes of chest pain during the night, but he seems better this morning."

Dark circles ringed Betty's eyes, and her

clothes were rumpled. "Have you been here all night?"

She glanced toward the stainless steel doors that led to the patients' rooms. "I thought he might need me, and these chairs recline. They did let me back to see him around one this morning when he couldn't sleep."

"Are you two going to get married now?" They'd been a couple for as long as he could remember, and he never understood what held them back.

"My momma always said, if it ain't broke, don't fix it," she said with a smile. "But I didn't ask you to come here and discuss our relationship. They'll let us go see him in a few minutes. It's important that you say yes to whatever he asks, even if you don't agree with him. Got it?"

"What's he going to ask me?"

She hesitated. "He didn't want me to tell you because he didn't want you to have time to think of a reason to say no. But I don't think you will."

He frowned. "What are you talking about?"

"He wants you to run for mayor, and if you agree, he's going to resign. You'll be a shoo-in."

"What? Why? After his surgery, he'll be as good as new."

"He knows if he stays in the mayor's office, he won't focus on getting healthy. He'll do just what he's doing now."

Peter stared at the floor. Run for mayor? He hadn't given it any thought since Betty brought it up yesterday. But with Hugh's endorsement, he probably would get elected.

He tried to think of anyone else who might be interested. No one ran against Hugh in the last election, but Cal Sheridan had a few years back. Peter figured he could beat Cal. *Mayor Peter Elliott.* He liked the way it sounded.

She touched his arm. "It's visiting time."

He nodded and followed her through the steel doors. When they reached Hugh's room, the mayor was sitting up in bed with an oxygen mask over his nose and mouth.

"You look much better than you did yesterday," Peter said. Hugh's color was still pasty.

"You're a great liar. Make a good politician," Hugh croaked.

"Probably." Peter touched his throat. "What—"

"The doctors had to put some kind of tube through his nose to his stomach because of nausea," Betty explained. "But they took it out early this morning." She turned to the mayor. "I told him what you wanted."

"I told you not to." Hugh turned to Peter, his gaze boring into him. "What do you think?"

Looking at Hugh, he knew two things. One, Betty was right. Hugh needed to resign and take care of himself. And two, that he was going to run for mayor.

NICOLE WAS GOING over Jake's proposal one more time and had it spread out on her desk when her cell phone rang. She glanced at the number and quickly answered when she saw Betty Atkins's name. "How is Hugh?" she asked.

"He's still having chest pain. Surgery is in the morning at seven." Betty sounded tired.

"I'll be there."

"Thanks. I'm phoning because Hugh wants a special called meeting before he goes into surgery. He'll be on a speakerphone from his room. I know this is last-minute, but can you meet at city hall this afternoon? I've contacted everyone else, and they can make it."

"Sure. What time?"

"Four thirty."

In forty-five minutes. Her brothers and dad were on a job an hour away. She would have to ask her mom to close up the office. "I'll be there."

Nicole hung up and called her mother, and after she agreed to come, Nicole began gathering up Jake's papers. She'd have to admit it was an excellent proposal. The office door opened, jingling the bells.

When she turned, Jake was standing just inside the doorway. He never had called today, and she assumed her ten minutes of fame with him had ticked off.

"Hi," he said, giving her that slow smile he was so good at. "I meant to call earlier and then things got crazy at the factory. I had to run an errand in the area and decided to just stop by."

She'd almost forgotten he managed Elliott Manufacturing. "No problem," she said, thankful she sounded normal.

"Well, what's your answer?"

Nicole glanced at the papers still on her desk. "It's a good proposal. And if the city coffers can come up with the twenty-five thousand dollars, I'll support it wholeheartedly. I just don't know where the money will come from."

He laughed. "I meant about going out with me tonight."

"Oh." *Take your foot out of your mouth, Nicole.* "Ah… I don't know. A special meeting for the city council has been called for four thirty, and since I don't know what it's about, I have no idea how long it will take."

She glanced at the clock on the wall and

caught her breath. Her mother would be there in the next few minutes. Nicole had to get him out of the office. "Why don't we make it another night?"

"Is it a closed meeting?"

"Not that I know of."

"What if I went to the meeting, and then we could get something afterward?"

"Perfect." *Now go.* She edged toward the door, hoping he'd take the hint.

"If I didn't know better, I'd think you were trying to get rid of me."

"Of course not."

"Good. So why don't I hang around here until it's time to go?"

"No! I mean…" She swallowed. "Look, Jake, my mom is on her way. If she finds you here…" Nicole shrugged. "Let's just say, she'll read more into the situation than there is. Especially since we had lunch together yesterday."

He grinned. "Are you making it less than it is?"

"Please, Jake!" She held her hands out. "Just go. I'll meet you downtown in thirty minutes."

"Okay, but it will cost you. Dinner tonight and a movie tomorrow night. Unless your Friday night is booked."

"Fine. We'll talk about it later."

Her heart had barely settled down when her mom's red BMW convertible pulled into the parking area. With the top down, no less. Joyce Montgomery stepped out of the car finger-combing her hair. Not that it needed it—the wind had simply given her a casual, tousled look.

Nicole had never been a girly-girl, and looking at her mom now, she had trouble believing she had even one of Joyce's genes. Early in her teen years, she'd tried to mimic her mom and be more like the girls who had the damsel-in-distress attitude that attracted the boys, but she'd discovered she didn't have what the boys seemed to crave. Plus, there was her tomboy figure to consider.

A rail-thin frame and muscles instead of soft curves served her well on the basketball court, but not in the world of dating. While she'd filled out somewhat as she matured, she was still more comfortable on the basketball floor than the arena of guy-girl relationships. *Thank you very much, Stuart Langford.*

She smiled as her mother entered the office. "Thanks for coming."

Joyce waved her off. "Duty calls. Do you know what the meeting is about?"

Nicole shook her head. "We never wrapped up the one Tuesday night..."

"I sure hope Hugh will be all right."

"Well, as soon as I know something, I'll call."

"Are you still coming to dinner?"

She froze. She'd forgotten about telling her mother she'd eat with them tonight. "I don't know what time the meeting will end, so don't count on me. In fact, let's just make it another night."

"But you have to eat, so just come by when you've finished."

Nicole's heart sank. "Actually..." maybe if she said it very quickly "... Jake-asked-me-to-dinner."

She cringed as a slow smile spread across her mother's face. "Lunch yesterday and now dinner tonight? I—"

"Mom, don't go there. Jake has a project he wants me to vote for. That's all it is."

She eyed Nicole and frowned. "You're not wearing *that*, are you?"

Nicole glanced down at her white blouse and jeans. "What's wrong with what I have on?"

"Honey, you need to dress up a bit. Put on some makeup."

Nicole picked up her purse and walked to the door. "I don't have time. I have to be there *now*."

"At least put on some lipstick," her mother called before Nicole shut the door behind her.

Nicole glanced in the rearview mirror as she pulled away from the office. Maybe a little lipstick wouldn't hurt, she thought, fishing a tube from her purse.

Several people were in the vestibule and inside the meeting room. Peter stood beside the podium.

"Nicole," Jake called before she stepped inside.

She turned. "I didn't see you, but I need to get in my chair."

"I think I know why Betty called the meeting."

She stopped. "Why?"

"I think Hugh is going to resign."

Surely not. People had bypass surgery every day. A month at the most, and he could return to work. "I doubt it."

"I heard it pretty straight. And I figure you should run for the office."

Run for mayor? Background noises faded as she focused on that thought. She'd been preparing for the possibility for the past couple of years, and she had a good plan. Nicole took a deep breath to clear her head. "I'd never win."

"Don't sell yourself short," Jake said. "We'll talk about it over dinner at Venelli's."

"I'm not dressed for Venelli's. Let's just get a sandwich somewhere."

"They don't have a dress code, and you're fine."

Nicole wasn't so sure, but she didn't have time to argue with Jake. Boyd Anderson and Peter turned as she neared the podium, and once again Peter's blue eyes distracted her. She shifted her gaze to his attire. Tonight he wore a classic blue windowpane shirt with a jacket that fit him to a T. Obviously tailor-made.

"Is... H-Hugh still going to join us by phone?" She couldn't understand what it was about Peter that made her stutter.

"Yes," Boyd said. "Betty is at the hospital with him, and his nurse agreed he could make the call—after he threatened to cancel the surgery unless she allowed him to."

Boyd left to prepare for the meeting, and Nicole stared at the floor, tongue-tied. Words just didn't come easily when she was around Peter, not the way they did with Jake.

"Thanks for being so quick Tuesday night with the defibrillator," he said. "It probably saved Hugh's life."

She looked up. "You did all the work."

"We're a pretty good team," he said and raised his eyebrows. "We never did get our coffee. How about grabbing something after the meeting?"

After months without a single date, she was suddenly having to turn them down? She glanced to the back of the room where Jake sat. "I'm afraid I already have dinner plans."

"Are you going out with Jake?"

Nicole turned to him. "Excuse me?"

His face flushed. "I'm sorry. That's none of my business. I guess it's too much to hope you're free tomorrow night."

If he'd asked earlier, she would have been. "Afraid so."

She could do better than two-word answers and tried again. "I'll be at the shelter Saturday. We can talk about your proposal then."

"That wasn't— Never mind." He looked as though he were going to say something more when Boyd banged the gavel.

"Do you know what this is about?" Nicole asked as they climbed the steps.

"Hugh is resigning."

"So Jake was right." Her mind spun with the possibilities.

Peter frowned. "How did he know?"

"You'll have to ask him. Do you know who is going to be acting mayor?"

"He wants Boyd to take over until an election can be held. That's what we're doing tonight—appointing him acting mayor and setting an election date."

It surprised her that Hugh didn't want Peter to take his place. Unless…her hopes sank. The acting mayor would be someone not running for the office. Which meant that Peter must be planning to put his name forward.

No way could she beat him.

CHAPTER SEVEN

FROM THE BACK of the room, Jake doodled on a notepad as he listened to Boyd Anderson read the mayor's letter of resignation. So he'd been right. Now to convince Nicole she should run for the office. As mayor, she'd have more influence to help push the senior center through. If Peter decided to run and won, Jake's proposal would go nowhere. He brushed the worry aside. Nicole was highly electable, and with the right campaign manager...he turned his attention back to the meeting.

After Hugh spoke a few words on speakerphone, a motion was made to appoint Anderson acting mayor. Once it was adopted, a motion followed to set the date for a special election. In quick order, December 23 was decided on as the qualifying deadline for candidates with the election to be held on Tuesday, January 5. If a runoff were necessary, it would be held on the twenty-sixth.

Jake studied the council. Of the six members, three showed definite signs of interest in the election—Cal Sheridan, Peter and Nicole. Cal would not pose a problem for Nicole. He wasn't widely electable.

But Peter was and would be her most formidable opponent. Most likely, Peter had known all day that Hugh was going to resign and already had his intent-to-run statement ready to turn in. It wouldn't take him two days to get the required fifty signatures for his petition.

He jotted Nicole's strengths and weaknesses on his notepad. Stellar reputation, winsome, honest, smart. Then he smiled as he wrote his next thought. Able to handle tough questions. A woman who could put him in his place could field any question thrown at her.

He caught the words *Peter Elliott* and *proposal*, and Jake focused his attention on the council just in time to hear that the youth center would be taken under consideration with discussion tabled until the next meeting.

He stood as the meeting was adjourned and walked up to meet Nicole.

"You were right," she said.

"I'm always right. Ready to grab a pizza?" He wanted to escape before his cousin finished his conversation with the acting mayor.

Thursday night was slower at Venelli's than Jake expected, and he snagged a corner table.

"Do you always get what you want?"

"Always. But why do you ask?"

She swept her hand through the air. "A corner table away from other customers, for one, and I'm here against my better judgment, for two."

Jake laughed. "But you're having fun, right?" He tensed, not sure she'd say yes, then relaxed when her emerald eyes sparkled, and she nodded.

"Being with you is different, I'll say that. You're nothing like your cousin."

"I'll take that as a compliment. Now, let's talk about you running for mayor. And don't tell me you weren't thinking about it even before you knew Hugh Gordon was resigning."

"It had crossed my mind to run in the next election if Hugh didn't. I want to run it by my dad one last time, though. Besides, I want him and my mom to be the first ones to know."

A pang of disappointment surprised him. "My opinion isn't enough, huh?"

"In your dreams, Mr. O'Neil. But what makes you think I could win? I'll probably be running against Peter, and no telling who else."

He became serious. "I think my cousin will be your stiffest competition, but you can beat him."

"Why do you think that?"

"You're smart. Everyone likes you. You—"

"How do you know everyone likes me?"

His face grew warm. "I, ah, was, ah, having coffee with some friends—"

Her mouth gaped. "You asked them about me?"

"Uh…yeah, I did. You intrigue me. What I don't understand is why I haven't run into you before now."

"Your 'friends' didn't tell you that for some time I was in a serious relationship?"

The waitress saved him from having to answer when she appeared with water, then took out her pad to take their order. While Nicole made up her mind, he searched for an answer to her question. He'd learned all about her ex-boyfriend Stuart from his friends, how her ex strung her along for four years before Nicole caught him kissing his much younger secretary. But that happened two years ago. He couldn't believe she hadn't dated since then.

After the waitress left, Nicole clasped her hands on the table and questioned him with her raised eyebrows. "I'm waiting."

He ran his tongue over his lips. "I don't know the whole story, just enough to know this Stuart-guy was an idiot if he dated you for four years and let you get away. Have you really not gone out with anyone since then?"

She ran her thumb up and down the glass. When she looked up, her eyes were shiny. "Thank you. And yes, I've dated since then. Just haven't found anyone I care to go out with twice." She took a deep breath. "Do you really think I can get elected?"

"Yeah, I do. I could be your campaign manager, sort of."

"Why? Is it because you think Peter will run? The competition thing?"

The answer he gave would tip the balance one way or the other. "I'm not going to lie. That's probably part of it."

"You don't think Peter would make a good mayor?"

"I think you'd make a better one."

"You don't know me well enough to say that."

She was tough, and brutally honest. "One of the men I talked with today mentioned he'd been helping you develop a five-point plan for the city. That's how your name came up." It was only a little white lie. He'd gone to Judge Connors because the judge knew everyone in Cedar Grove, and if anyone could tell him anything about Nicole, he could.

Her eyes widened. "You're friends with Judge Connors?"

"Well, don't sound so surprised."

She shook her head. "You must be really good friends for him to tell you that."

"Not good enough for him to tell me what the *G* stands for in your name, evidently." He liked the way she blushed so easily. It helped him read her.

Nicole was different from the women he usually dated. She was very unaware of her effect on men, and he doubted she had a pretentious bone in her body. "I'll keep that little bit of mystery to myself," she said. "Did you ask anyone else about me?"

"No. And I wasn't gossiping with him. I had heard that Hugh was resigning, and I asked the judge who he thought would be a good candidate. Your name was the first one out of his mouth. How are you connected to him?"

A pleased smile graced her lips. "He's a friend of my dad's, and they've both been encouraging me to run in the next election. None of us thought it'd be so soon."

"I really would like to be your unofficial campaign manager."

A frown creased her brow. "I haven't gotten that far in my thoughts." She sipped from the water glass. "Do you think I need one? When I ran for the city council, I had posters and cards printed and just went door-to-door, asking for votes."

"You won't have time to go door-to-door this election, and it's the whole city voting. Ten thousand registered voters."

Nicole almost choked on the water, and when she got her breath, she leaned back in her chair. "It's a whole other ball game, isn't it?"

NICOLE SCARCELY TASTED the sourdough pizza. She wished she could stop focusing on the mayor's race —she had twenty days to qualify. Her mind was off and running again. It only took fifty signatures to get her name on the ballot, and she could practically get those from her friends and family.

What if the voters didn't choose her? Her heart thudded in her chest. Stuart hadn't chosen her. *No.* She ground her molars. This was not personal. It was about electing whoever was most qualified to run the city, and she believed with all her heart that she was the person for that job.

Some of the panic subsided, and she glanced up to find Jake studying her.

"I can practically see the wheels turning. So, are you going to run?"

"Officially, like I said, I want to talk to my dad first. But I do want to be mayor. I believe I can make Cedar Grove a better place to live."

"Good, and I want to help you." He reached

into his jacket pocket and withdrew his wallet. "Here's your first campaign contribution."

"No." She held up her hand. "I have the money to run."

He continued to write the check. "Do you realize who you'll be up against? Peter has more money than you do. If you want to get elected, the citizens of Cedar Grove need to see your name on billboards. You'll need flyers handed out. Radio and television time."

Blood drained from her face as he talked. She didn't have that kind of money. When she ran for city council, she'd spent maybe a thousand dollars. What Jake was talking about ran into much more. Panic gripped her stomach. She couldn't do this.

He tore out the check and handed it to her. *A thousand dollars*? Nicole tried to give it back. "That's too much."

Jake took it from her hands. "It's not too much, and tomorrow, as your campaign manager, I'll open an account and start raising money. And for the record, I expect no favors if you are elected."

She could only stare at him as hope inched its way up her spine. Maybe she could do it. She sucked in a deep breath and slowly exhaled. *She could do it.* "Okay. But if I pull out or don't even qualify, you get the money back."

"You won't do either of those things. Tomorrow night we'll have our first planning session over dinner instead of going to the movies. Unless this one counts," he said and winked at her.

Having Jake around so much would take getting used to. "Why don't I make you dinner at my apartment? It'd be easier than trying to talk in a restaurant."

"You can cook?"

"I'll manage to have something for you to eat." She wasn't about to tell him she usually burned water, and that when she didn't eat at her parents', her normal fare was frozen dinners. She'd get her mom to help, even though it would mean telling her that she and Jake were seeing each other. But not in a romantic sense. As if her mother would believe that.

"Sevenish?"

She nodded and gave him the address. Maybe her mother could bake something and bring it over rather than cook in her apartment's tiny kitchen.

Jake walked Nicole to her car. "Sure you don't want me to follow you?"

"I'm perfectly capable of driving by myself to my parents' house. Do it all the time."

He laughed. "I'm used to seeing my dates all the way home."

"But this isn't a date." It was the only way she could keep her perspective about Jake. He was too good-looking and too charming, and she could quickly lose her head, not to mention her heart. And that wasn't going to happen.

JAKE FOLLOWED UNTIL she pulled into her parents' drive, then tooted his horn and drove on. She'd called her dad from the parking lot of the pizza place, so her parents were expecting her. Excitement mounted as she pulled into the circle drive and parked in the warm glow of Christmas lights that decorated the yard and two-story house.

Maybe when she had her own house instead of an apartment, she'd go crazy with decorations like her mom. Maybe a house like this one that her dad had built early in his career. One floor would do for her, but she definitely wanted the wraparound porch.

She'd no sooner climbed out of her car than her mother appeared at the door. "Where have you been? The meeting was over an hour ago."

She should've known news would travel fast. "I had dinner with Jake afterward, remember?"

Her mom's eyes lit up. "How'd it go?"

Nicole didn't know whether to wait and ask

her mother later to make the Friday night dinner for her and Jake, or to get it over with now.

"It was business," she said. "Related to something I want to discuss with you and Dad, but first I need a favor. I asked him to dinner at my place tomorrow night."

"You what? Does he know you can't cook?" Amusement danced in her mother's eyes.

After Nicole put a pot of water on to boil and forgot about it, her mother gave up on teaching her how to cook. "Obviously he doesn't. I asked him, hoping you'd help me. Nothing fancy."

"Of course I'll help you. But you might want to think about taking cooking lessons from Barbara Louise's school downtown. They're not even that expensive. Just in case you get married one day."

Nicole laughed. "I will if that ever looks like a possibility. Or maybe I'll find a man who cooks. Where's Dad?"

"Waiting for you in the kitchen."

All her life, anything important was discussed at the kitchen table. She followed her mother through the swinging door and found her dad seated at the table, drinking a cup of coffee. On the table was a folder.

Her mom took down a mug. "Coffee or hot chocolate?"

"Hot chocolate."

"So Hugh resigned?" her dad said.

She nodded. "I...I think I want to run for his office."

A broad grin creased his face. "I thought you might."

"Are you sure, honey?" Concern laced her mom's voice. "It won't be as easy as the city council race."

"I know. Jake and I were talking about that."

Her dad tilted his head. "Jake, huh? Is there anything we should know about?"

"Come on, Dad. He's a friend, that's all. Well, maybe not all—he wants to be my campaign manager."

"What?" Her parents spoke at the same time.

"He already knew Hugh was going to resign and suggested I run for his office before the meeting started. Then at dinner, he wrote a check for a thousand dollars to start my campaign." She stopped to take a breath. "What do you think?"

Her dad took her hand. "I think he's right, and your mom and I want to help any way we can."

He pulled a sheet of paper from the folder. "I downloaded the petition you have to get signed—just in case you decided to run. Our names are the first ones on the list."

She gaped as excitement bubbled through her. "This is scary."

"I would never encourage you to do something I thought you couldn't do," her dad said. "You'll make the best mayor Cedar Grove ever had."

First she had to get elected.

CHAPTER EIGHT

BY ELEVEN O'CLOCK Friday morning, Peter had forty-nine signatures. He only needed one more, and he knew the one he wanted. At eleven twenty he parked in front of Montgomery and Sons Construction and got out with two cups of coffee and a Danish from Cups and More.

He didn't just want her signature, he wanted her support. And he wanted to warn her about Jake. If she was looking for a long-term relationship, his cousin wasn't the man she should be dating. Jake had said himself that he was like his father, and no woman would hold his interest for long.

Peter had returned to Cedar Grove in time to witness the tail end of Nicole's relationship with her ex, but he knew little of what had happened, only that Betty Atkins mentioned that she'd warned Nicole the ex was no good. And then he'd proven it by marrying his much younger secretary. Allie's image surfaced. Would he have listened if someone told him that Allie would never marry him? Probably not. Not that Allie had done anything wrong.

Peter had known all along she was in love with Matthew Jefferies. Evidently, some lessons had to be learned the hard way. It was a lesson he didn't want to repeat.

Nicole looked up when he came through the door.

"Nice bells," Peter said.

"Mom's idea. I don't know if I can take them all the way through Christmas." She stood and walked to the counter. "Can I help you with something?"

He placed the cups on the counter. "Since we didn't get to have coffee the other night, I thought I'd bring some by." He held up the white paper bag. "I have a Danish, as well."

She crossed her arms. "Did I fall through a rabbit hole this week or something?"

Peter tilted his head. "What do you mean?"

"Until this week, I don't think you've said ten words to me since high school, unless it had to do with the city council. And Jake didn't speak to me at all. But now whenever I turn around, one of you is here. What gives?"

"Stupidity?" Wow, where did that come from? He needed to be careful—he didn't want to give her the wrong idea.

"What?"

"I messed up big-time in high school not getting to know you. I don't even think I thanked you that time you slipped me your American History book when I forgot mine. If you hadn't, Mr. Crenshaw would have given me an F for the day—he was a bear about not bringing your book to class."

"You remember me doing that?"

"Yep. Something reminded me of it, and I realized I'd probably missed an opportunity for a good friendship."

She raised her eyebrows. "This has nothing to do with the project you want to get through the city council?"

"Actually it was when you supported me the other night that I was reminded of the history class. Although I do have an ulterior motive for dropping by today."

"Ah, the truth emerges." She took the top off one of the coffees and sipped it. "I'm nuking mine, want yours heated, as well?"

"Sure."

"Have a seat in the chair by my desk, and I'll be right back."

He took the white bag to the chair and sat down. Other than one stack of papers, Nicole's desk was tidy, unlike his office. Curiosity got the better of him, and he sat taller so he could see what she was working on.

The microwave dinged, and he jumped back, his heart hammering. He'd only gotten a peek, but it was enough to recognize a petition just like the one he had in his briefcase.

Nicole Montgomery was running for mayor.

His stomach sank. It would be awkward if he asked her to sign his petition, but he'd already alluded to wanting a favor. Besides, he didn't want her to know he'd been nosy.

"Your coffee, sir." She handed him one of the steaming cups and sat behind her desk. "Now, what was the ulterior motive that brought you here?"

Lie or tell the truth? Surely he could come up with some favor. No. That wasn't his way. He had no business snooping. "I was going to ask you to sign a petition to put my name on the ballot for mayor."

"What changed your mind?"

He nodded to the papers on her desk. "I see you're running, as well."

A smile tugged at her lips. "I don't see that as a problem. I'd be glad to sign your petition. I think you'd make a good mayor." She folded her arms across her chest. "But I'll make a better one."

"Do you think that would be legal? Signing my petition?"

"I don't see why not. If it would make you feel better, you can sign mine."

Nicole Montgomery was the most unusual woman he'd ever met. "Maybe we better not. I'd hate for either of our names to be taken off the ballot because of a technicality."

"Suit yourself. Jake probably wouldn't like it anyway," she said.

"Jake? That was another reason I stopped by. Be careful with my cousin. Don't trust him. He'll break your heart."

"Excuse me?" Her jaw shot forward.

"Jake has a history of breaking women's hearts. I wouldn't want to see you get hurt."

Her eyes narrowed. "*Not* that it's any of your business, but Jake is…is…"

Nicole clamped her mouth shut, and he could swear smoke came from her ears.

Finally she began again. "Jake is nothing but a friend. Actually, he's my campaign manager, and I don't think he would appreciate you making more of our relationship than it is."

"Campaign manager? When? How?"

She stood. "I think we've discussed this enough. In fact, now that you've raised this possible technicality, I'm not sure we should even be talking."

He'd really stuck his size elevens in his mouth this time, and he didn't see a way of getting them out. At least not with Nicole as angry as she was right now. Sometimes retreat was the only option.

He stood. "I didn't mean to upset you."

"Well, you did. I'm perfectly capable of looking out for myself. Thank you very much." She narrowed her eyes. "And I'm going to beat you in this election."

"We'll see." He stuffed his hands in his pocket. "I guess I'll go."

"That would be a good idea."

Peter left the Danish on her desk and walked out with his shoulders straight. He'd only been trying to help. He gripped the steering wheel as he drove away. So Jake was opposing him. He didn't know why that surprised him.

Did he need a campaign manager himself? No, but he did need an edge, a way to get his name and picture in the newspaper. At the light, he made a left turn and drove to the *Cedar Grove Gazette*. On the way he called Clint and asked him if they could meet as soon as possible.

NICOLE'S JAW ACHED from clenching it. She didn't know what Peter Elliott had more of— arrogance or money. The very idea, thinking she couldn't handle herself with his cousin.

She snatched up the white bag with the Danish and started to toss it into the trash. *Wait a minute.* Why should she let a perfectly delicious pastry go to waste because Peter brought it? She peeked in the bag, and her mouth watered. An apple bar. Her favorite. But much too large.

She looked up as the bells rang again. Her mother. "Oh, good." Nicole broke the pastry in half. "Would you like part of a Danish?"

"You're going to ruin your appetite." Joyce glanced at the empty bag sitting on the corner of Nicole's desk. "Who brought you a pastry from Cups and More?"

"The enemy," Nicole said, but at her mother's frown, she relented. "Peter Elliott. He came with the intention of getting my name on his petition."

"You told him no, of course."

"Actually, I offered to sign it if he'd sign mine, but he declined." She wasn't about to mention the other reason he stopped by. She bit into the Danish, and it was every bit as good as it looked.

"How many signatures do you have?"

"Ten—from customers and the brothers."

A victory smile spread across her mother's face. "Then we have more than enough signatures." Joyce pulled several sheets of paper from her oversize purse. "I have forty-five here, and your ten makes five more than you need. It's always good to have more than you need."

Nicole hid the grin trying to surface. If her mom were a man, she'd be the type to wear suspenders with a belt to make sure her pants didn't fall. "Thank you. I wonder if I should go ahead and file?"

"Why wouldn't you?" Joyce placed the signatures on Nicole's desk and broke off a piece of pastry.

"Oh, I don't know. It's only the first day, and Hugh only had surgery yesterday, and while I know he made it through fine, I don't want to appear too pushy…have you heard anything today?"

"Talked to Betty just before I came here. He was sitting on the side of the bed, eating. As far as filing, ask your dad…or Jake, but *I* don't think it'll look pushy." Joyce licked her fingers. "This is delicious," she said. "Have you decided what you want me to make for your dinner tonight?"

"I know Jake likes Italian, so how about spaghetti?"

"That will be easy. Can you pick up everything to make a salad?"

"That I can do," Nicole said as her cell rang. "It's Jake."

"Ask him about filing."

She took a sip of coffee to wash down the rest of the pastry. "Good morning."

"You sound bright and chipper."

"I am. I already have the required number of signatures on the petition." His voice sent an unexpected shiver through her. While she didn't appreciate Peter's comments, she might do well to heed them.

"That's great. Can you get away long enough to file the paperwork at the courthouse?"

"That answers the question of whether to file now or wait."

"Oh, definitely file now. Get your name out there, and let the voters get accustomed to thinking of you in that light."

"Peter will probably file today, too. He almost has his signatures."

"How do you know?"

"He came by here to get me to sign his petition."

"So he knows you're running?"

"And that you're my campaign manager."

Jake chuckled. "I'm sure he had a few choice words to say about that."

"A few." Not that she was going to repeat them. "What time are you coming for dinner?"

"Unfortunately, that's what I was calling about. I have a meeting in Memphis this afternoon, and it'll be late when I return. Can I have a rain check?"

"Uh, sure. Just let me know when."

"I will. Can we talk about it tomorrow?"

"I'll be at the shelter, helping get it ready for inspection."

"You're still doing that?"

"Why wouldn't I? I told Peter I'd be there earlier this week, and the fact that he and I are opposing each other in this race doesn't change anything."

"You have a strong code of ethics," he said.

"Don't you?"

Her question was met with silence. "Probably not as strong as yours." Regret sounded in his voice. "What time do you plan to go to the courthouse?"

She checked her watch. "When I close up in about thirty minutes."

"I'll see you there."

"You don't have to come. Won't that make you late for your meeting in Memphis?"

"It's not until five. Besides, I'm your campaign manager—I need to be there. You're not upset I'm not coming to dinner, are you?"

Nicole laughed into the phone. She didn't

know who had the bigger ego, Peter or Jake. "No. See you at the courthouse in a little while."

When Jake met her outside the circuit clerk's office, he had reporter Rebecca Caine with him, and Nicole shot him a questioning look.

"You're the first to qualify, and Becky here thought that was newsworthy."

Becky, huh? Nicole suspected the reporter's interest was probably due more to Jake's charm. No matter, the publicity would be good. She extended her hand. "Thanks for coming."

"No problem. I'm supposed to meet Peter Elliott here at two."

She exchanged glances with Jake. The twinkle in his eye told her they were thinking the same thing. Peter would not like that she got the jump on him. "Well, let's get it done," she said and pulled open the glass door to the circuit clerk's office.

Once she'd turned in her paperwork and the filing clerk told her the names would have to be verified, Rebecca interviewed Nicole on the courthouse steps. After the initial questions, the reporter asked, "What do you think you can do for Cedar Grove that our former mayor hasn't been able to accomplish?"

Talk about a loaded question. "First, I want to say that I think Hugh Gordon has done a fantastic job of running Cedar Grove. I totally supported his efforts to bring more industry to our town, and I want to expand on that."

Rebecca made notes on her pad. "One more question, and I'll let you go. "Do you think being a single woman will hurt your chances of getting elected?"

The questions didn't get any easier. "No more than if I were a single man."

"Good answer," Rebecca said. "And I totally agree. I can't say it in the paper, but I hope you win." She started to pack up her camera. "Oh, wait... I noticed you registered as G. Nicole Montgomery. Care to tell me what the *G* stands for?"

Nicole shot a dark look at Jake, and he raised his hands. "I had nothing to do with that question."

"Is it important?" Nicole asked. She didn't understand the preoccupation with her first name.

"Not really. I mainly was curious."

"It's a name that doesn't particularly fit me, so I never use it." She fumbled in her purse for change. "Jake, could you get me a soda from the machine?"

"Now?"

"Please. The machine is on the first floor."

He gave her a mischievous smile. "I'll leave

you two alone only if you agree to have lunch with me at Norma Jean's."

"Fine."

"Now I'm really curious," Rebecca said as Jake walked away. "Is there anything going on between you two?"

"No. You just have to know Jake."

"That I wouldn't mind," Rebecca said. "Now, what does the *G* stand for?"

"If I tell you, it stays with you, okay? Don't tell anyone, especially Jake."

The reporter pursed her lips but finally nodded.

"My mother loved ballet, and I'm named after the title character in *Giselle.*" She placed her hand on her hip. "Now, do I look like a Giselle?"

Rebecca looked her up and down. "Actually, you do."

"You're kidding."

"No, I'm not," she said. "It's a beautiful name."

"I agree that it's beautiful, but it suits someone like you. Tiny and delicate," Nicole said. "Not a five-foot-ten tomboy."

"Thank you, but I don't get it—there's nothing wrong with your looks. You're lovely."

Nicole shook her head. "Please do not mention this in the paper."

"No problem," Rebecca said. "But, you really should consider using it."

Nicole pressed her lips together. She'd use it the day she thought it fit.

CHAPTER NINE

NORMA JEAN'S WAS busy when Peter arrived, and he glanced around the dining area for Clint. Not seeing him, he looked for a table away from other customers. That's when he noticed Jake sitting with Nicole Montgomery. She'd probably already told his cousin what he'd said.

When Jake waved at him, ignoring them wasn't an option. He fixed a smile on his face and sauntered to their booth. "Afternoon, Jake. Nicole."

"Hello again, cuz. If I'd known you were coming, I would've saved you a place. Join us now, if you'd like."

"Sorry, I'm meeting someone." Jake was too friendly for Nicole to have spilled the beans about what he'd said about his cousin earlier at her office. His respect for her increased.

He turned to Nicole. "Is there any chance we can get together one day next week and discuss some of the projects and budget items for next year?" Money had been allocated for each department for the coming year, but Peter had been looking over the budget. He'd found a recurring invoice that expired in February, and noticed that money for it had been allocated for the whole year. A little over twenty-five thousand dollars.

He hoped the money had been allotted and it wasn't a clerical error.

"Sure. I plan to be at the shelter tomorrow."

He masked his surprise. Even though she'd said earlier this week she planned to help, he figured since they were opposing mayoralty candidates, she would cancel. "I never did know how you found out about the cleanup."

"Sarah and my mother are friends. And at least one of my brothers will be with me."

"Great. I look forward to seeing you. Are you coming, Jake?"

"If I get back from Memphis before midnight."

"Hot date, huh?"

Jake grimaced. "Business meeting."

"See you tomorrow, then," he said to Nicole before turning to scan the diner again. He didn't see Clint, but he did find an empty table across the room from Jake and Nicole. He wished he'd gotten Clint's cell phone number so he could text him. Then he saw the six-four former basketball college star coming his way.

"Sorry I'm late, but I got tied up at the bank." Clint sat across from him.

"I just appreciate you coming at all."

"It was a no-brainer. Gets old eating by yourself every day."

Peter unwrapped the knife and fork from the napkin. "How's Allie?"

Clint nodded slowly. "She's good. Enjoying marriage...and Memphis."

Even as painful as it'd been to lose Allie to Matthew Jefferies, he was glad she was happy. "Good."

The waitress approached. "What'll it be for you two?"

Peter turned and checked the menu board. "I'll take today's special."

"Country fried steak, salad and French fries. Drink?"

"Iced tea."

She turned to Clint, and he ordered the same thing. After she left, he leaned his elbows on the table. "What do you want to pick my brain about?"

That was one thing Peter had always liked about Clint. He didn't waste time. "I want to start a program similar to what you had in Memphis. A place where teenagers can gather and do things, play sports, have dances, be mentored by older teens and adults."

Clint's eyes lit up. "That sounds great. But it sounds like you have it all planned out. What do you need me for?"

"Three things. First, I need a volunteer director." The idea had been growing ever since he ran into Clint at the coffee shop.

"Whoa! That's a full-time job. You're not going to get anyone to volunteer for that, not even me."

"Hopefully, the volunteer part would be short-lived, and right now, you'd only have to give about ten hours a week. I need someone to help plan the project, and oversee and train other volunteers. I want to start it off with a New Year's Eve dance."

Clint didn't respond right away and seemed to be turning the idea over in his mind. He rubbed his jaw with his thumb. "I'd like to see something like you're talking about in Cedar Grove, but I'm not sure I have the time."

"Just think about it. Another thing I want you to think about is running for the city council."

"What?"

Peter laughed. "I wish you could see your face. Seriously, I believe there will be a vacancy after the mayoral race. I'm running, and so is Nicole Montgomery, and I wouldn't be surprised if Cal Sheridan didn't throw his hat in, as well. If one of us wins, there'll be a vacancy on the council, and I'd sure like to see you fill it."

The waitress brought their food, and they stopped talking until she left, then Clint said, "When you ask a favor, you don't ask for much."

"The city needs someone like you."

"That's a compliment, I suppose." He cut into his steak. "You said three things. I'm almost afraid to ask what the last one is."

"This one's easy. I'd like your vote."

"Got it."

"Great, now will you sign my petition to qualify? I need one more signature."

"No problem. I'll do it before I leave."

After they finished their meal and Clint had signed, Peter said, "I hope you'll seriously think about running for city council."

Clint would be an asset to the town, and he and his family carried a lot of weight in Cedar Grove. Maybe even enough to override any opposition to his youth center proposal.

"I will."

They shook hands and Peter tucked his petition into his briefcase. Now he had an appointment with the circuit clerk's office and Rebecca Caine.

SATURDAY MORNING NICOLE grabbed her work gloves and hurried from her apartment. Her brother Aaron's text said he was outside waiting. She wasn't sure helping Peter at the shelter was a good idea. She'd thought about backing out, but Aaron refused to let her. Sam, who was supposed to help their middle brother lay shingles, had canceled, saying Amy had contractions. It was too early for the baby, and Nicole hoped it was Braxton Hicks contractions. Either way, Aaron needed her.

"Good morning," she said and hopped in his truck. "Have you heard how Amy is?"

Her brother gave her his lopsided grin and handed her the newspaper. "Morning to you, too. Heard they sent her home, and you made the front page."

With a twinge of anxiety, she spread the paper on his dash. Oh, wow. Her photo and article took up the top half of the paper. Seeing it in black and white drove home that she was really running for the mayor's office.

CITY COUNCILWOMAN FIRST TO QUALIFY FOR MAYORAL POST

She scanned the article under the headline. No mention of her first name. But Rebecca had written about Nicole's landslide victory for her city council seat.

Farther down the page, a smaller photo of

Peter appeared, turning in his paperwork. She compared the two pictures. Dressed in a dark business suit, he looked like mayor material. She, on the other hand, was dressed too casually in black slacks and a red sweater. At least her hair was pulled back into a bun.

Jake should have warned her someone from the newspaper would be there. But at least she hadn't worn skinny jeans and an oversize sweater to work like she had earlier in the week. She would have to be more conscious of her attire. Image was everything in an election.

"I wish I'd worn a jacket," she said.

"That's a great photo," Aaron said. "Jacket or no jacket."

"You're my brother. You have to say that."

"Voters don't care what you wear."

"Maybe not for men, but with a woman, clothes and hair are talked about."

Too feminine and voters didn't see a serious candidate. Too businesslike and they viewed a female candidate as ruthless and uncaring. It was going to be hard to strike just the right balance. "All Peter has to do is look handsome," she muttered.

"What?"

"Nothing. Just commenting on what a pity it is to think an election could be won on personality and looks rather than qualifications." She had the qualifications, and a good plan for the city.

"I don't think voters are that shallow."

"You're probably right. That's just my insecurities showing up." She sighed. "Seriously, what do you think my chances of getting elected are?"

Aaron scratched his chin. "It won't be easy with Peter Elliott running against you, but I think you can beat him. He grew up here, but he didn't stay, and people might hold that against him. They might see it as him being interested in using the mayor's office as a stepping-stone to a higher political position."

"Do you think that?"

"It's crossed my mind. He doesn't seem the type to hang around a small town."

It had never occurred to Nicole to leave Cedar Grove, other than when she went away to college. She loved the town and the people in it. Maybe she should focus on that in her campaign.

"Why would anyone vote for me?"

"Because you're smart, you're a whiz with numbers and you love the town."

"Will people see that?"

"Yep." He squeezed her hand. "It'll be fine, you'll see. And thanks for helping out today."

Nicole hoped it would be fine. "How long do you think it'll take to repair the roof?"

"I drove by yesterday and looked at it. With only the two of us, probably until after lunch."

So much for getting in and getting out. Even though she'd been more than civil at lunch yesterday, she still smarted at Peter's assumption that she and Jake had something going. She smiled, remembering the surprise on his face when she told him she'd be here today.

It'd almost been worth giving up her Saturday.

CHAPTER TEN

PETER TURNED INTO the long drive to the children's shelter and steered his pickup around the potholes left by autumn rains. Maybe he could get the county supervisor to send a road grader the first of the week to do a little work. He parked beside the rambling ranch-style house that presently housed three toddlers, fifteen-year-old Tyler, and twins Logan and Lucas.

Cal Sheridan hadn't mentioned splitting the twins up again, but neither had he made any mention of Tyler.

Tyler. Peter had called the principal and talked him into letting the boy return to school Tuesday, and so far he'd stayed out of trouble. He blew out a breath, just glad there were no girls living at the shelter right now—Tyler's teenage hormones were enough to deal with.

But the occupants of the shelter were not his immediate problem. Getting the place ready for inspection Monday was the first step to insuring it stayed open.

Once that was done, Peter could concentrate on the youth center and the mayoral election. He'd already filed the paperwork with the state to form a nonprofit to run the center. And he'd started working on the 501(c)(3) application. Too bad he'd burned his bridges with Nicole. She had experience applying for the tax-exempt status.

But that would have to be for another day. He glanced up at the scattered clouds. It'd be helpful if the rain held off until they were finished, though at least it was still warm. He grabbed his work gloves from the seat and stepped out of his pickup. At the same time, the back door opened, and the twins bolted from the house in their shirtsleeves. Tyler trailed them, his face a picture of teenage indifference.

Sarah Redding brought up the rear. She glanced hard at Tyler, then looked at Peter and rolled her brown eyes. He didn't know what he'd do without Sarah. The shelter ran with the precision of the marching bands she was so fond of, but more important was the heart that beat inside her. It was big enough even for the angry teenager.

"Good morning," she called. "I have several people lined up to help."

He nodded. "Do you still have that list of what needs to be done?"

"The electrician you sent out yesterday got all the outlets and switches fixed, and me and Tyler and the twins painted the ceilings last night. That only leaves two rooms to paint and a couple of windows that won't open. The rest of the work is on the outside—shingles on the roof, replace a few of the boards at the back, the yard—it's all here."

She handed him a sheet of paper, and he glanced over it. A good day's work. Gravel crunched behind him, and he turned. Two vehicles inched toward the house and several more waited to turn in. He recognized the driver of the first car—Nicole's brother Aaron. He snapped his gaze to the passenger seat to see if Nicole was with him.

A warm sensation spread through his chest when he saw her. He hadn't run her off with his unsolicited advice. *Get a grip.* He didn't know what he was so happy about. The woman had beaten him to the courthouse yesterday and she'd become the headline instead of him. He needed to never forget she was his opponent, albeit a beautiful one, even in work clothes.

He waved as they climbed out of Aaron's truck, and Aaron waved back, but Nicole just nodded. He swallowed. She had a way of causing his stomach to knot. Cool, collected and well put together, she was back to her business mode with him. He'd enjoyed the easy camaraderie they'd shared earlier in the week.

Then he'd had to go and give her advice about Jake. She might be here, but she hadn't forgotten those comments or forgiven them. Looked as though today he would be dealing with the old, prickly Nicole—the one who had a particular fondness for picking his suggestions apart in the city council meetings.

Judging from her gloves and work boots, she'd come prepared to work. "I have shingles in my truck to take care of the roof," Aaron said as he approached.

"Good." Peter turned to Nicole. "You can take care of the yard."

She leveled her green eyes at him. "I'm sure someone else can do that. I'll help Aaron with the roof."

His eyes widened. "The roof?"

She gave him an odd smile. "I've been helping Dad put on shingles since I was ten. I can handle it." She slapped Aaron in the stomach with her gloves. "You ready to work?"

Without another word, she walked to the truck. When it was plain she intended to unload the ladder without waiting for her brother, he said, "Wait—"

"I wouldn't if I were you," Aaron said. "She won't take kindly to your help. We'll handle the roof, you take care of the rest."

Peter stared as Nicole carried the ladder to the house, leaned it against the side, and then scrambled up it as if it was the most natural thing in the world.

"You going to stand there all day, staring at the help?"

Jake? He turned around. "What are you doing here?"

"You need help, don't you? I can paint, and I'm pretty good with a hammer."

Eight thirty and the day was already full of surprises.

"Uh, sure. You want to be in charge of painting the shutters?"

"Sounds good." He scanned the parking area. "Figured you'd have the newspaper here this morning."

So that's why he was here. As Nicole's campaign manager, he was making sure she didn't miss an opportunity to get her name in the paper. "No reporter today—the shelter is off-limits." He surveyed the yard. "Hey, Tyler, come show Jake where the paint and brushes are and then help with the yard work."

The morning passed quickly. More people showed up, including Coach Dawson. Peter put him to work with Tyler on the yard, and the teenager doubled his efforts. After he'd finished, Tyler climbed up on the roof to help Nicole and Aaron.

Peter grabbed a couple of soft drinks and found Coach Dawson. "Thanks for coming. How'd it go with Tyler?"

The coach took the drink he held out. "Pretty good. He apologized again for the pepper incident."

"Good. He really wanted to try out for the basketball team, but he didn't transfer in time."

Dawson cocked his head. "He should have told me that. I figured he was just a smart-mouthed kid."

"He's had it pretty hard. Parents died in a car wreck, then his grandparents couldn't take care of him, and then they passed." Peter took a sip of his drink. "I noticed at the last game the team needed a three-point shooter. He might help you out there."

The coach shifted his gaze to the roof. "Is he any good?"

Peter nodded. "Beat me at HORSE."

Dawson laughed. "Yeah, but you're rusty. Anybody could beat you. But I tell you what… I'd like to see what he can do."

"Maybe after lunch when we're done." Peter

scanned the thickening clouds. "Or Monday if it starts raining."

Peter walked away, feeling pretty good. Tyler was a decent kid, and with a few breaks, he had a bright future ahead of him. Playing on the team might keep him out of trouble.

By noon the clouds hung low and heavy. A local deli delivered subs, and everyone except Aaron and Nicole took a break. Peter climbed up the ladder. "Lunch is here."

"It'll keep," Nicole replied. "Rain's on the way."

"Yeah," Aaron said. "We only have this section left to repair."

Peter noted the dark sky. It looked as though a downpour might start any minute, and if the roof leaked, it'd ruin the freshly painted ceilings. "Why don't I help you, and then we all can eat."

He ignored the skeptical look Nicole shot him and stepped up on the roof, wondering if he'd lost his mind. He wasn't crazy about heights. "Okay," he said, not looking down. "What do you want me to do?"

Nicole gave him a sideways glance. "See those curled shingles? They need to come up without damaging the ones next to them. Once they're up, pull the nails out and scrape off any tar you find. After that, slide the new shingle into the gap, lift the corners of the overlap—"

"You lost me at nails."

"Watch me," she said, then turned to her brother. "Aaron, hand me three of those shingles you have."

Step-by-step, she removed the old shingles and put the new ones in, finishing with rubber cement on the nails. She sat back on her feet. "Ready to try?"

A smile played around the corners of her mouth, and her green eyes twinkled. He'd much rather see her smile than the stony glare he'd gotten at her office. *Remember she's running for mayor.* He ignored the voice in his head. "Maybe if you show me one more time."

He watched as she repeated the process, and then she handed him a pry bar and a hammer and roofing nails. "You do that section, and I'll do the one beside it. We'll be done then."

He'd barely gotten the nails pried out when she finished her section. Instead of taking over his, she sat where she could watch him and took off her gloves. "Here, use these."

He slipped them on and scraped the old tar off the boards, then slid the new shingles in place. By the time he covered the nail heads with cement, he was feeling pretty good about himself. He looked up and caught her watching him, a question in her eyes. "What?"

Her gaze skittered away. "Nothing. Aaron went down five minutes ago, so that finishes the roof. Did you say there was food down there?"

"Yep." He stood and extended his hand. "Pull you up?"

She hesitated, then gripped his hand. "Sure."

Her skin was surprisingly soft after a morning of roofing. "Thanks for coming today. I'm sure you had any number of things you needed to do."

"I did actually cancel a hot date…"

He didn't understand why that disappointed him or why he'd never noticed the gold flecks in her green eyes. Too bad they were running for the same office. "…with an ironing board," she finished.

NICOLE RECLAIMED HER HAND, wishing she could take back the words. They sounded so…flirty.

He gave her an awkward grin. "Then I'm glad I saved you from a day at the ironing board. Maybe it'll make up for sticking my nose in your business the other day."

That was probably as close as she'd get to an apology from Peter Elliott. She'd do well to remember that he was her opponent, and even if he weren't, she was in no hurry to get her heart broken again.

It had been interesting watching his dogged attempt to replace the shingles. She imagined his experience with manual labor was limited, but she admired his determination to do it right. That shouldn't surprise her, given his attention to detail at the city council meetings.

He might even make a good mayor. She squared her shoulders. Time to end this conversation.

"I'll go down first." Nicole kept her balance as she walked to where the ladder leaned against the roof.

"Wait. Let me, and I'll hold the ladder."

Was he serious? One look at his face told her he was, and it was all she could do not to roll her eyes. "I'll be fine, but when I get down, I'll hold the ladder for *you*," she said.

Once they were both on the ground, Peter moved the ladder away from the house.

"Hey, what are you doing?" she asked.

"You did say you were through, right?" He adjusted it until the sections were even.

"Yeah, but I can get that—I don't need your help." She tried to take the ladder from him, but he wouldn't let go.

"I know that, but do you mind letting me take care of this?" He tugged at it again.

What part of "I don't need your help" did he not understand? She pulled the ladder toward her. "No, I'll put it back."

His jaw tightened. "I said—"

"Fine." She released her hold, and when she did, he lost his balance and fell backward on his rear.

Peter grimaced and grabbed his thigh.

Nicole scrambled to lift the ladder off of him. "Are you all right?"

He stood and rubbed his hip. "I'm okay. Nothing hurt but my dignity. If you'd just let me put it back on the truck for you—"

"Look, I grew up with three brothers, and I'm used to doing things like *this*." Nicole lifted the aluminum ladder and marched it to Aaron's truck. She turned around and brushed her hands. "Why, I can even change a flat tire." Not to mention govern a city.

He raised his hands. "I give up. I was only trying to do the gentlemanly thing. Helping you shouldn't be this hard."

I'm not helpless. She almost spoke the words, but the look of sincerity and confusion in his blue eyes stopped her. She just wasn't comfortable with anyone helping her, especially him. She sighed. "No, it shouldn't be that hard. Maybe we could start over."

He eyed the ladder on the truck and pointed. "Not if it includes that," he said.

"How about I let you get me a sandwich and a drink?"

"I can manage that." He folded his arms across his chest. "But are you sure that won't compromise your independence?"

"No problem."

Her brother was sitting at the picnic table, and she joined him. "Good job today."

Aaron popped the last of his sandwich in his mouth and nodded. "Interesting dynamics going on with you and Peter."

"Don't start."

"Just sayin', Miss Independence."

"Maybe I wouldn't be so independent if you three guys didn't make me do everything myself."

"If we hadn't, then you wouldn't be running for mayor, now would you?"

For half a minute Nicole had totally forgotten the election. She glanced over her shoulder. Peter was almost back.

He set their drinks on the table. "Ham or turkey?"

"Turkey." She grabbed a napkin and wrapped it around the canned drink. "What else needs to be finished today?"

He sat across from her and took out his list

and then surveyed the house and yard. "The roof was the last job. I think everything looks pretty good. I really appreciate your coming out today."

"Glad to help," Aaron said.

"Yes," Nicole agreed as she glanced around. Freshly painted shutters spruced up the house, and the yard crew had the grounds looking neat. Someone had even hung holly and cedar Christmas wreaths on the doors. She looked up at the roof. Aaron had done a good job matching the new shingles to the old. "It does look better."

Her brother's phone beeped, and he read the message. "I have to check on another job, but I'll drop back here and pick you up."

"No need for that," Peter said. "I'll take Nicole home."

Aaron grinned. "That would be great."

Nicole narrowed her eyes at her brother. Was he trying to throw her and Peter together? After the tussle with the ladder, turning him down would be awkward, and her brother knew it.

It would just have to be awkward.

"No," she said. "I'll wait for you to return."

After Aaron left, they ate in silence. Not a particularly comfortable silence. She tried to think of something to say.

"I wouldn't have bitten you," Peter said.

She looked up. "What?"

"I wouldn't have tried to bite you if I'd taken you home...or to give any unsolicited advice."

In spite of herself, she laughed, and just like that, the tension dissolved. "I didn't think you would. But with the election and all, people might get the wrong idea."

"I suppose. I'd really like to get to know you better, though."

"As in, know thy enemy?"

"Not at all. By the time this election is over, I hope we will be good friends, since we'll still be working together. I think it's a shame that we've been city council members two years, and all I know about you is what I remember from high school and that's not much." His blue eyes held her gaze. "Why is that?"

Maybe because the only person he'd had eyes for before and after high school was Allie Carson. He and Jake and Allie ran around with the popular kids in school. Nicole popped the lid on the drink. "We didn't travel in the same circles."

"Where did you go to college?"

"University of Tennessee. Basketball scholarship."

"I remember now. You led the girls' basketball team to the state championships."

"Where we won."

"So how did you get to be your father's financial officer?"

"You mean bookkeeper?" The job wasn't fancy enough for her to be called financial officer. She thought a minute. How did she explain her love for numbers? "I don't know. I just seem to have a knack for money and organization." That didn't seem to satisfy him, and she tried again. "Unlike people, numbers don't change. They're honest."

"And people aren't?"

"People always have a motive for what they do. Take you, for example. You've been extra nice to me this week, and that makes me ask why."

Instead of being offended, he laughed. "You certainly have a different way of looking at things."

She liked how his laughter went all the way to those blue eyes. "You're not going to disclose your motives?"

"What if I don't have any?"

"Everyone does. I bet I can guess yours. And it has nothing to do with the mayor's race."

Interest crossed his face. "Go for it."

She looked up toward the sky and tapped her finger against her lips. "It has something to do with the city council. You want my help on something, maybe on a proposal for a youth center."

"Wow, you're good," he said with a twinkle in his eyes. "Just remember, I want your help on everything I bring up in council."

The smile on his face faded as he looked past her.

Nicole turned around. "Jake! Did you get your business taken care of in Memphis?"

"Yep." Jake sat down beside her. "You don't mind if I join you, do you?"

Since he directed the question to Peter, she let him answer. She'd never seen two cousins so prickly with one another. Thinking back to the school days they were just talking about, she remembered how Peter had competed with Matthew Jefferies as well, so maybe the competition with his cousin was one-sided.

"You're already seated, so I guess not." Although his tone was light, there was an edge to the words.

"So you like how the shutters look?" Jake asked.

"You painted the shutters? I'm impressed. They look almost as good as your clothes." Nicole nodded at the white paint splattered on his shirt and pants. "I had no idea either of you knew how to get your hands dirty."

Jake grabbed his chest. "You wound me."

"You have no idea," Peter said. "When we were kids, Grandfather kept us busy in the summer repairing his rental houses."

"We did everything but roofing, and for free," Jake added. "But now I'm glad he did." He eyed Peter. "Do you remember that house with the basement?"

Peter groaned. "We had to climb into the crawl space and repair the water lines. I'll bet there wasn't eighteen inches between the floor and the ground."

So they did get along some of the time.

Jake leaned his forearms on the table. "I noticed your brother left. Need a ride home?"

"My brother is returning to give me a lift."

"Call him and tell him I'm taking you. You owe me a dinner anyway."

Nicole froze. She wasn't about to attempt a meal, especially with Jake present. She shook her head. "Afraid I'm the one who's taking a rain check tonight. I've been on a roof all morning, and I'm tired."

"Yeah, Jake, can't you see the lady's tired?"

She glanced at Peter. He had that same look he'd had yesterday when he warned her against Jake.

"Then I'll take you out," Jake said.

Her head was starting to ache with all the tension in the air. "No. I'm too tired. I'll wait for my brother, and then he'll take me home, where I will do absolutely nothing except read and chill for the rest of the day. Now let's talk about something else."

"Okay." Jake took her hand and flashed his winning smile. "I want to know how one Nicole Montgomery has stayed under my radar all these years. A problem I'm trying to rectify, by the way."

"Baloney. I told you I was tired. Way too tired for your foolishness, Jake." She removed her hand and nodded her head toward Peter. "He's already been down that route anyway."

"I wouldn't touch that subject again with a ten-foot pole," Peter said. "Although I will say that I find you quite refreshing, and I realize it was my loss that I didn't know you better."

By sheer willpower, she fought the urge to roll her eyes. Blarney she expected from Jake, not Peter. "Refreshing? No, I'm not refreshing. What I am is blunt, and I call things as I see them, and your attempts at flattery are no more believable than Jake's."

"Comparing me to Peter is more than I can take," Jake said. He checked his watch. "And if you're not going to let me take you home, I think I'll go home. I didn't get back from Memphis until two this morning."

"Hot date, huh?" Peter shot her an I-told-you-so look.

"I told you yesterday it was business."

But he didn't say what kind of business kept him there that long. And Nicole wasn't about to ask. Besides, she was tired of listening to the two of them. "Go ahead. Aaron should be back any minute."

Jake stood and winked at her. "I'll call you tomorrow, and we can discuss your campaign, okay?"

She nodded. After he drove away, she looked at Peter. "Do you two always go at each other like that?"

"Like what?"

He didn't even see it. "Like you both are competing for the same thing, even when there is no contest."

"There's always a contest," he said.

Nicole glanced up as raindrops the size of quarters pelted her head. The bottom of the sky looked as if it was about to drop out.

He grabbed her hand. "Come on, let's make a run for my truck—it's closer than the house. Then you can call your brother and tell him I'm taking you home."

She snatched the sandwiches neither of them had eaten and ran with him, barely making it inside the truck before the deluge.

CHAPTER ELEVEN

PETER CRANKED HIS truck and flipped the defroster on, then the windshield wipers. He glanced toward Nicole, who stared straight ahead. Today hadn't gone as badly as yesterday, but he'd still acted like a spoiled kid, arguing with her about the ladder and then with Jake.

He didn't understand what got into him when he was around her. But she confused him. Like right now. He'd finally identified the light fragrance that filled the cab, but someone as independent as Nicole should not smell like baby shampoo.

"That was close," he said.

"We never would have made the shelter. I did manage to grab the sandwiches and the drinks. Would you like yours?"

"I think I might know a place with better ambience than my pickup." He'd never liked eating in a vehicle.

"Really?"

"You've heard a lot about it this week."

She shot him a questioning look.

"The building where I want to have the dance, and later, if the city council agrees, the youth center."

"And you think the atmosphere will be better there?"

"Probably not, but at least you'll be able to check it out. Or we can ditch these sandwiches and get something at Norma Jean's and *then* go see the building. Unless you really are too tired."

"Right now I'm hungrier than I am tired and craving one of Norma Jean's burgers. Let's go there and make a decision about anything else after we eat."

By the time they got to the diner it was after two, and they pretty well had the place to themselves. Nicole ordered Norma Jean's specialty—a blue cheese burger topped with Monterey Jack and sweet potato fries.

"With extra onions," she said. "And coffee, no cream, then a Coke when you bring the burger."

The waitress turned to Peter. "Coffee with cream and I'll have the same, with extra onions, as well."

"What, no hot date tonight?" Nicole asked when the waitress left.

"Nope, unless this counts."

She opened her mouth and closed it as a flush crept into her cheeks.

Finally he'd said something she didn't have an answer for. "Do you come here often?"

Nicole shrugged. "Probably a couple of times a week. But other than yesterday when you were with Clint, I don't remember seeing you here."

"That was the first time I've been here in a while. It hasn't changed," he said as the waitress brought their coffees.

"I hope it never does." She took a sip of her coffee. "What did you mean when you said I was 'refreshing'?"

"It wasn't an insult. And, I wasn't trying to flatter you." He emptied the small creamer into his cup and stirred the coffee. "You don't tiptoe around anything, for one."

"I guess that's what makes me so *refreshing*. It's probably also why I rarely date." She shook her head. "I think I intimidate men."

"You think? You're the youngest city council member Cedar Grove has ever had, former all-state basketball star and probably the best forward to come out of Cedar Grove High, not to mention you went to UT on a basketball scholarship *and* an academic one. And you can lay shingles. Yeah, I think most men would be intimidated by you."

She pressed her lips together in a slight smile. "How about you?"

"Nope." He took a sip of his coffee. "Well, maybe a little, but I think I could take you in a game of HORSE."

"In your dreams. You just got through saying how good I was."

Nicole was probably as rusty as he was, and he stood a better chance of winning with her than with Tyler. "Did you forget I was all-state, too?"

"That wouldn't matter. I'd still win."

"I'll take you on one day, but right now we have a couple of burgers to eat." The waitress set their plates down and moved on to the next booth. He lifted the top of his bun and stared at the meat patty and two thick slices of onions.

"Want one?" He forked a slice and laid it on the side of his plate.

"I figured you'd wimp out."

"A couple of hours from now you'll wish you'd done the same thing." He squeezed mustard over his burger and spread it with his knife. "Have you given much thought to your campaign?"

She took a bite of her burger and nodded. "It's all I've thought about since I qualified."

"Me, too. I thought once the qualifying period ends and we know how many candidates there will be, we could set up a town hall meeting, but at the high school auditorium to accommodate the crowd."

Nicole knit her brows together. "My thoughts exactly. I even mentioned it to Jake. The twenty-eighth would be a good date—after Christmas but before New Year's."

He took out his phone and checked the calendar. "With the election on January 5 that should work."

"Do you realize it's just a month away?"

He swallowed. "One of us will probably be mayor." The thought made his blood race.

The two of them ate in silence for the next few minutes. He looked up as she cleared her throat. "When is the shelter inspection?" she asked.

"Monday, but there shouldn't be a problem after all the work everyone has done." He slapped his forehead. "I don't think I thanked you or Aaron for helping out today."

"Yeah you did, and we don't need any thanks. It's a good place, and we need to keep it open."

"So you think it's been a good thing for Cedar Grove?"

"Well, sure. Actually, I'll be helping out there now."

That was a surprise. "How?"

"Tyler and I talked this morning—he's a

good kid, but he's having a little trouble with math, so I offered to tutor him." She looked thoughtful. "You were responsible for getting the shelter here, weren't you?"

Peter nodded. "I was working in DC for our local congressman and pulled a few strings."

"You have a good director in Sarah."

"I know. He dragged his last fry through the ketchup. "I want the youth center to be the same kind of safe place. I've asked Clint Carson to help run it. If you're through eating, I'd like to show you the building."

"I'd like to see it." She slid out of the booth as he stood. "How about the tax exempt application. Where do you stand on it?"

"I've looked over all twenty-six pages and have just about decided to hire a lawyer to fill it out."

"Chicken."

"I won't have time to complete it now that I'm running for office, and I only have ninety days to get this youth center approved."

"What do you mean?"

He suppressed a groan. That was the last thing he meant to say. "Do me a favor and forget I said that."

PETER LOOKED AS if he'd sucked on a lemon. "Forget you said it? Why?"

"Right now I can't explain." He quickly changed the subject. "So, are you ready to leave?"

"Sure," Nicole said.

They walked to his truck and he opened the door for her. Once he was behind the wheel, she thought he'd give her some kind of an answer, but he pulled out of the parking lot without saying anything. Which made her even more curious. She turned to look at him. "Do you and Jake have some sort of contest going?"

He paled. Bingo.

"Could you just drop it?"

"All right, already." But letting it go was easier said than done. His secretiveness sent her mind on a bender, worrying the question like a bird with a mirror. "If your proposal is approved, how will you fund the center?"

"Same way as Jake. Grants and private foundations." He turned his blinker on and turned into the city park.

"I didn't realize the building was this close to the park," she said.

"The land butts against it."

"You should have made that clear in your proposal. Having access to the ball fields and tennis courts would be a plus."

"I did. Have you not read the proposal?"

"I scanned it, but I haven't had time to really look at it. A lot happened this week."

"Then you haven't read Jake's, either?"

She looked uncomfortable. "I did read his proposal before Hugh's heart attack and resignation threw everything upside down. Have you heard how he's doing?"

"I went by there last night, and he was walking down the hall."

"Good." They parked in front of a large brick building with wide double doors and windows on the front. "Is it two stories?"

He nodded. "The front half is, and there's an elevator. The back is all open and that's where I want to put the gym. And have the dance. Come on and I'll show you."

When they climbed out of the truck he pointed to the vacant property bordering the park. "Over there is where I'd like to build additional athletic fields. Maybe even put in a skateboard park."

"Skateboard park?" Alarm bells went off in her head. "Do you know what the liability for something like that will be? You'll never get that through the city council."

He frowned. "We'll be insured."

"Have you forgotten who you're dealing with? Cal Sheridan and George Bivens will never sanction a skateboard park. Even with insurance, if someone sued the center, the city would be sued as well."

"I didn't include it in the proposal you have, but the park can be added later if I get council approval. Come on inside and I'll show you where the gymnasium will be."

Someone had already renovated part of the building, partitioning rooms in about a third of the huge building.

"This area will be for activity rooms and office space." He swept his hand toward the partitioned space, then they walked down a hall to a large room.

"Here, I want to put in some gymnastic equipment."

Another hallway opened up to a huge room with steel arch supports for a ceiling. "This will be the gymnasium with a basketball court and dressing rooms. Eventually, I'd like to put in portable bleachers."

He spread his hands. "Now that I have the permit, I want to start decorating for the New Year's Eve dance."

Peter's blue eyes lit up as he spoke, and Nicole couldn't keep from catching his excitement. She scanned the space. A lot of work had to be done. "You plan to hold a party here in twenty-seven days?"

He nodded. "I don't want another accident

like last year because kids around here don't have any place to go. Like I said at the meeting, those two teens are still recovering. One's in a wheelchair and the other is still in therapy."

She understood where he was coming from. "But the country club always has a dance."

"Not all the kids can afford the country club. I want a dance everyone can attend. I want a rocking DJ and plenty of atmosphere without alcohol. And that's just the beginning."

"I like it," she said. "But twenty-seven days…?"

"I know it sounds impossible, but we can do it. Lighting is already in place. It just needs cleaning up and decorating. Will you help?"

When he looked at her like that, it was impossible to say no. She nodded. "But we're going to need more people."

"Not a problem."

Nicole turned as the metal doors scraped open and footsteps clattered in the empty building.

"Anyone here?"

She recognized Jake's voice and glanced at Peter. From his hard-set jaw, he wasn't happy his cousin had shown up. "We're back here," she called.

"I saw your truck and decided to stop." He

looked pointedly at Nicole. "I didn't know you were here."

She felt like a choice piece of meat being eyed by two bulldogs. While she didn't feel the need to explain why she was with Peter after refusing to let Jake take her home, she did. "We almost got caught in the rain, and Peter brought me to see the building."

Jake looked over the cavernous room. "This will make a great place for a walking track and to exercise, maybe even have a few dance classes."

"If you get city council approval," Peter said.

Nicole was curious. "You both have good ideas. Why don't you work together?"

"Can't. Mr. Micromanager here would drive me crazy," Jake said.

She stared at them, pieces of the puzzle falling into place. Ninety days. Two proposals. It *was* a contest between the two men. Scratch that. Between two boys. She pressed her fingers to her temple. "You two give me a headache. I'm ready to go home."

"I'll take you," Jake said.

"Nicole came with me, I'll take her home."

She fished her phone out of her pocket and speed-dialed her brother. "Aaron will take me."

Then she spoke into the phone. "I'm at the park. Would you come pick me up?"

"Look," Peter said when she'd hung up. "I apologize."

"Me, too," Jake added.

She held up her hand. "Right now I don't want to hear it. I just want to go home and relax. Good day, gentlemen."

JAKE FLINCHED AS the front door slammed shut. "Methinks the lady is not too happy with us."

"Really?"

He grinned for an answer. He would drop by her apartment later, after Nicole had time to cool off. He and Peter had acted like schoolboys, and he wished there was a way they could work together. But that would mean compromise, and their grandfather's contests had never been set up to teach them give and take. It was always winner-takes-all. But maybe there could be a little trade-off.

He turned to Peter. "Tell you what," he said. "I'll help with the cleanup since my group will be using the building New Year's Eve, too."

"That's generous of you." His cousin still had his arms crossed. "What's your interest in Nicole?"

"What?"

"You heard me. I know you, and she's not your type. Back off."

"We don't have that kind of relationship. I'm simply her campaign manager." Not that he hadn't toyed with the idea of another kind of relationship.

"That's not what I see. She's vulnerable after her ex broke up with her Christmas two years ago, and you're really turning on the charm."

"You're not jealous, are you?"

"No."

The *no* came a little too fast. Whether he knew it or not, Peter was very much interested in Nicole, and not because they were running against each other in the election.

But his cousin was right about one thing. Nicole wasn't the type Jake usually went after. He tended to prefer women like Bobbi. More sophisticated, worldly even. She was the reason he'd been in Memphis last night. Women who weren't looking for a wedding ring and the white house with a fence and sandbox. But Peter's sudden interest made Nicole all the more intriguing.

Jake scanned the huge room. "Show me what you plan to do in here."

Peter's eyes narrowed, but he pointed to the far side of the room. "I plan to use that area for dressing rooms and storage and make the center the basketball court. I—"

"That's the wrong place for dressing rooms. They need to be here." Jake indicated the front of the building next to the partitions.

"This is why we can't work together. If you put the dressing rooms there, it would be impossible to close them off, and you'd be running kids out of there every fifteen minutes."

"But you have plumbing right here. It'd save on cost."

"You don't have to run plumbing to the back. We'll start it there and tap into the water and sewer lines on that side."

He wasn't ready to agree with Peter, but he'd wait until another time to bring it up. "Saw your photo in the paper this morning. Are you running your own campaign?"

"Yeah." Peter sounded disgruntled. "And I figure you'll last about two weeks on Nicole's. Either you'll quit or she'll fire you. She's too independent for you."

Jake rocked back on his feet. "She has good ideas that I'm going to channel in the right direction. And I'll last to the end."

"Want to bet?"

"Name your limit."

Peter stared at him, then shook his head.

"Nah, if I do that, you'd find a way to hang in there. I'm out of here."

Jake slapped him on the back. "Gotta give you credit for having brains, cuz."

As they walked to the front, he gave Peter a sideways glance. "You want my tax exempt application to go by?"

"Sure."

"I'll drop it by your house later. Or I could get my lawyer to fill it out for you."

"You'd do that?"

"Sure, that way the contest will be fairer, and I won't feel bad when I win."

"In your dreams."

Outside, the rain had stopped, and he scanned the area to make sure Nicole wasn't still waiting for her brother. When he didn't see her, he slid under the steering wheel of his Lexus and waved goodbye to Peter. Sometimes Jake wished he and Peter weren't so different and oddly so much alike. Like Peter, Jake was an only child, and his cousin was the closest thing he had to a brother. Cain and Able, Peter would probably say.

He pointed his car toward home, but soon found himself turning in the direction of the gated condos where Nicole lived. When he pulled up to the gate, there was no guard, only a keypad. She'd failed to give him the code when she invited him for dinner. With no one behind him, he punched in her cell number on his phone and waited. And waited. He was ready to cancel the call when she picked up.

"Hello?"

She sounded out of breath.

"Are you okay?" he asked.

"Jake?"

"Yes. I'm at the gate and can't get in because I don't have the code."

"What part of 'I don't want to see you anymore today' don't you get?"

"I thought you were talking to Peter."

She groaned. "Jake O'Neil, back your car up and turn around and go home. I was napping, and in one minute, I'll be back napping. Got it?"

A horn sounded behind him. "Uh, I'm afraid you'll have to give me the code. Someone is behind me, and I can't back up."

"Three-six-four-five. Once you get in, then you can turn around and leave."

"I really do have campaign issues to discuss with you."

"Oh, all right." She sounded resigned. "I'm at 610."

"I know, you gave me the address earlier this week."

He whistled as he drove through the gate and found her condo. It was on a corner lot with a nice view of the lake. Still whistling, he parked and grabbed the folder that he'd been working on. He really did have things to talk over with her.

She opened the door before he could ring the bell.

"Coming in?" she asked.

"After all the trouble I went to, you bet."

She twisted her hair up in a ponytail as he followed her in to the combination den and kitchen. But he didn't see one Christmas decoration.

"My great room," she said. "It's where I spend most of my time."

"Nice."

"Now, what did you want to discuss?"

"I thought we'd plan speaking engagements and decide which neighborhoods you want to go door-to-door. You won't have time to canvas all of them."

"I know. I want to set up a town hall meeting and use the high school auditorium."

"Good idea. City hall would be too small to accommodate all the people who'll come. Now, about posters and door hangers. I've found a place where we can get them printed fairly cheap, and I thought we'd hire a few high school students to distribute them."

"I like that. How about speaking engagements?"

He shook his head. "It's Christmas, and no one is going to take the time to come out to hear you or Peter speak. I think we need to run an ad in the newspaper and get you on TV."

"How much will that cost?"

"The newspaper ad—not too expensive. The editor has agreed to do a feature article on you. And the TV spot is free. I have you lined up to be on the morning program that airs out of Springfield. They have a broad viewership in Cedar Grove."

"You've been busy."

"Don't sound so surprised." He didn't know why people thought he was a lightweight. He glanced around the room again. "Where are your Christmas decorations?"

Her green eyes darkened. "My mother has enough for both of us."

Something Peter said rang in the back of his mind. Something about her ex-boyfriend. Oh, yeah… Stuart broke up with her at Christmas. "My mother is the same way."

Tonight he'd find out where his mother

bought the pink poinsettias sitting on her mantel, and tomorrow Nicole would at least have one something Christmassy.

CHAPTER TWELVE

TYLER RUBBED THE side of his face. "Miss Nicole, I'll never get this. I hate geometry. Why do I need it?"

"To teach you how to reason and how to solve problems," Nicole said. At least that's what her teachers had always told her when she'd complained.

"Well, it's killing me," he grumbled.

"It won't kill you, and my mom always says what doesn't kill you will make you stronger."

She shifted in her chair in the kitchen at the shelter. They'd been working since Tyler got off the school bus, and after a week of tutoring him, she'd discovered that while he was a quick learner, he was a visual learner as well and needed examples.

"I sure am glad you're here," Sarah said. "I barely passed math in high school. Now, English, that was my subject." She placed a sandwich and cookies in front of Tyler, then poured him a glass of milk. "Would you like something to eat or drink, Nicole?"

"Not today. If I keep eating your cookies like I did last week, I won't be able to get into my clothes."

"Honey, you could eat a whole plateful and not have to worry about gaining weight. Unlike me." Sarah patted her ample hips.

Nicole laughed, then turned her attention back to the problem Tyler was working on. She picked up the knife beside his plate and handed it to him. "Let's use your sandwich to figure this out. Think about the information you're given, and then cut your sandwich in the correct shape for the triangle. You already know one angle is forty-six degrees and that two sides are equal. What else do you know?"

"That it's an isosceles triangle. And that means the other two angles are equal." He cut a triangle and pointed to the top where he'd cut a narrow angle. "This is the forty-six-degree angle. And forty-six from one hundred eighty divided by two is..." He figured on his paper. "Sixty-seven."

"Explain how you knew which was the forty-six-degree angle."

"Because all of the angles equal 180, and that's the smallest angle because the other two are sixty-seven degrees. Yes!" He pumped his fist.

"Very good." She loved it when the lightbulb

flickered on in a teenager's mind. "You see why it's so important to learn the formulas?"

He nodded, then turned as the back door opened. A smile spread across the boy's face when Peter came inside.

"How's it going, Tyler?"

"Pretty good, for a Monday."

Peter shifted his gaze to Nicole with a question in his eyes.

"He's a quick learner," she said.

"Good. Can I borrow him for a bit?" Peter said, his face deadpan. "Coach Dawson is here, and he'd like to see Tyler shoot a few baskets before it gets dark."

Beside her, Tyler gasped. It must be a big deal, and she shot a questioning look at Peter, who was now grinning from ear to ear.

"I told the coach when he was here helping repair the shelter that Tyler beat me at HORSE, and he didn't believe me. I want Tyler to show him and Cal Sheridan what he can do."

The teenager jumped up from the chair. "Really? Is the coach really here?"

"He is. Cal, too. Grab your coat, son, and come on."

Nicole followed them outside, pulling her jacket close against the December air. The sun was low in the sky, and it would soon be much colder. She walked to the picnic table where Cal sat. "Afternoon," she said.

He nodded. "Looks like the three of us are going to go against each other in the mayor's race."

"You qualified?"

"This morning."

"Good, and normally, I'd think either you or Peter would make a good mayor, but not so much anymore," she said with a smile.

The corners of his eyes crinkled. "Change that up a little, and I'd agree. I heard there are a couple more people who are going to qualify."

He turned to watch Tyler, and she took the opportunity to study Cedar Grove's truant officer. Cal was in his mid-fifties, and she figured he'd use his age and experience as part of his platform. He was also good at his job. Cedar Grove had a low rate of truancy.

And he was a decent man. After raising two boys, he and his wife were foster parents to a sweetheart of a little girl. "How's Emily?"

He shifted his glance to her. "We're finally seeing her come out of the addiction. She's not crying all the time like she did at first. Even smiles sometimes. And she's walking."

"What you two have done with her is amazing."

His eyes softened. "She's special."

"I think Tyler is pretty special, too," she said, but he seemed not to hear her. Nicole's attention was drawn back to the coach as he bounced the ball a couple of times.

Dawson smoothed his hands over the basketball. "Peter says you're even better with a basketball than you are with a pepper shaker."

Tyler ducked his head and shrugged. "I beat him. He *said* he used to be an all-star."

Dawson laughed and bounced the ball over to the boy. "Well, let's see what you've got."

Tyler dribbled a few steps, then lifted his hands and let the basketball fly. It swooshed through the rim. Peter retrieved it and shot it back to him. Bouncing it again, Tyler backed up and made another hoop. A few minutes later he was shooting from twenty feet away.

Coach Dawson snagged the ball. "You're pretty good. Can you come out to practice, starting tomorrow? I'm not saying you'll play much at first, but I'd like you to be on the team."

"Yes, sir!" Then he looked at Peter. "I can, can't I?"

"I don't see why not, but you'll have to keep your grades up." He turned to the coach. "Does the school run a bus that late?"

Cal walked close to the edge of the driveway. "I'll see to it that he gets home."

Nicole's heart warmed, but her reaction was tame judging from the gleam in Peter's eyes. He looked as though he was about to burst or pump his fist in the air like Tyler had when he *got* the geometry problem.

"Thanks, Cal. I appreciate it," Peter said.

Tyler stuck out his hand. "Yes, sir, Mr. Sheridan, thank you very much."

"No problem," he said and checked his watch. "I better get home."

The coach checked his watch, as well. "And I better get back to the school. I left my assistant working with the other boys."

"You two go on in," Peter said and walked with the two men to their vehicles.

"Congratulations." Nicole draped her arm over Tyler's shoulder as they walked toward the back door.

"You'll still help me with my math, won't you? There's a big test just before we get out for Christmas, and I have to pass it, or I probably won't be able to stay on the team."

"You'll pass it. Just keep learning those formulas. We'll figure out a time that won't interfere with your practice."

THE AFTERNOON HAD gone better than Peter had dared to dream. He'd been worried after Dawson hadn't shown up last week that he wouldn't make an appearance today at all. And then for him to bring Cal with him and have Cal offer to get Tyler home—it was more than Peter ever expected.

He took the porch steps two at a time and pushed open the back door. Nicole and Tyler were once again working on his math, and they both looked up when he came in.

"We're almost done for today," Nicole said.

"Finish up—I need to talk to Sarah, anyway." He found her in the toddlers' room, rocking a little boy. He checked to see if the child was asleep, and then gently lifted him from Sarah's arms and laid him in the crib. The toddler would be leaving later in the week with a family who wanted to eventually adopt him.

Warmth radiated through his chest. Placing a child with the right family was the best part of his job. He sighed and turned, surprised to see Nicole talking quietly to Sarah outside the door.

"What's going on?" he said as he joined them, shutting the door behind him. The baby monitor would let them know when the child woke up.

"I just found out Tyler's birthday is Friday," Nicole said.

"I plan to bake him a strawberry cake," Sarah added.

Peter frowned. He didn't usually forget a birthday, but with the cleanup and mayor's race, everything was upside down. "We'll have to have a party Friday afternoon. Can you come?" he asked Nicole.

"I'll be here. And if you could take Tyler to get his driver's license, you'd have one happy boy on your hands."

"He doesn't have a car."

"I don't think that matters, and he has his learner's permit. It's more of a rite of passage," she said. "That's why I know Friday is his birthday—he was wondering if anyone would take him to the Department of Motor Vehicles."

Peter mentally went over his schedule for Friday, and he didn't remember anything that would keep him from taking the boy. Helping Tyler get his license was a great idea. So many things were out of the boy's control, and having his license would give him a measure of self-sufficiency. He realized Nicole was waiting for a response.

"I'll see what I can do." Her shoulders drooped. "I'll make sure he goes."

She gave him a winning smile. "Good."

The look on Tyler's face when they told him

was worth finding the time to take him for his test. Peter left the shelter humming. Maybe he could even find a decent car he could leave at the shelter for Tyler to drive. Or a small pickup. Yeah…boys liked pickups.

CHAPTER THIRTEEN

TUESDAY AFTERNOON JAKE clicked on the computer screen and images of the high school and other points of interest in Cedar Grove appeared as Nicole narrated the voice-over.

"You have a good voice," Jake said.

"I don't know…"

"No, it's very natural, and you don't sound stilted at all." Most people didn't like hearing their own voice recorded.

"What time did you say Rebecca would be here?"

He checked his watch. "In fifteen minutes. Or not," he said as the bells on the door jingled, and the newspaper reporter entered the construction company's office.

"You're early," Jake said.

"Is it a problem?" Rebecca asked.

"Of course not. We were just looking at Nicole's first political ad. Would you like to see it?"

Rebecca nodded, and he clicked on the thirty-second commercial.

"That's really good," Rebecca said. "It has a nice, homey feel to it."

"That's what we were hoping for," Nicole said.

Rebecca took out her tablet. "Are you ready to get started?"

He gave Nicole a reassuring smile. "Sure."

"First question. Why do you want to be mayor?"

"Because I love Cedar Grove. I want to see the city grow, and under my five-point plan, I believe it will."

"Can you elaborate on your plan?"

Judging from the interest in Rebecca's voice, Nicole had immediately captured the reporter's attention with her passion for the city. It came through every time Nicole spoke, whether in the ad or canvassing door-to-door. Her passion was the one thing that would set her apart from Peter—who cared, but it wasn't quite the same—or Cal, or whoever else ran.

"It's very simple. I want to focus on increasing job opportunities by bringing in new companies so we can keep our young people here," Nicole said. "I want to implement a scholarship program targeting the average student. There are plenty of scholarships for the students who excel, but very little for students who have a C average, but who show initiative. I'd like to see a separate scholarship program based on volunteerism, creativity and entrepreneurship, rather than simply academic grades."

Nicole waited for Rebecca to finish typing before continuing. "The other parts of my plan focus on infrastructure improvements because our streets are in terrible shape, and I'd like to initiate a program for getting derelict properties and buildings either cleaned up or torn down.

"And last of all, while our crime rate is low, I've heard rumors of gang members from Jackson infiltrating our community. I want to ensure our police officers have training to deal with this and also provide our youth with alternatives to gangs."

Rebecca glanced up from her pad. "So you agree with Peter Elliott that Cedar Grove needs a youth center, rather than one for seniors?"

"I hope we can find the money for both," Nicole replied.

"But if you had to choose, which one will you vote for?"

"I can't answer that until all the information is in."

Nicole surprised Jake at how adept she was in fielding questions. He'd worried that she might be too honest.

Rebecca nodded. "Moving on, you indicated

you wanted to bring new companies into Cedar Grove. Do you think Mayor Gordon missed opportunities to bring growth to our area?"

Jake held his breath. The wrong answer here could lose votes.

"I think Mayor Gordon faced different circumstances than the incoming mayor will face. During his entire tenure, we've been in a recession. Companies were reluctant to relocate. But with the improvement in the economy, that will change, and with our low taxes and other incentives, like good schools and the proximity to larger cities, Cedar Grove will stand a much better chance of snagging some of those companies."

Perfect answer. He released the breath he'd been holding.

"Do you think you might be too nice to be mayor?" Rebecca asked.

A smile tugged at Nicole's lips. "Being nice doesn't cost anything, and it doesn't mean I'm a pushover. Ask my brothers. I have the backbone to do whatever it takes to get a job done."

Twenty minutes later, the reporter put her tablet away. "I think I have enough information for my story."

"Thanks for interviewing me."

"My pleasure. You're the first woman to run

for the job, and just between the three of us, I bet you'll be our first woman mayor."

"Have you interviewed any of the other candidates?" Nicole asked.

"You're the third. Two more qualified today, and I have them to interview. This is the fifteenth, so that should be all unless someone else qualifies. And I will say, yours has been the best interview. What does your schedule look like for the rest of the week?"

"City hall meeting tonight, then knocking on doors, speaking at the Civitans, that sort of thing."

"She's cooking dinner for me one night," Jake said. When she eyed him sharply, he held up his hands. "You gave me a rain check, remember? And I'm using it."

He turned to Rebecca. "Brains, beauty and she can cook."

A stricken look crossed Nicole's face when Rebecca took her tablet from her purse. "Don't put that in the paper."

"Why not?" the reporter asked.

"B-because…" She sighed. "I can't cook. I can't even boil water."

Jake laughed. "Then who was going to cook dinner for me?"

"My mother?" she said, wincing.

Rebecca slipped the tablet back into her purse. "I think I'll leave on that note."

Nicole turned to him after the reporter had gone. "Sorry, I didn't mean to deceive you."

"What if I drop by one night and give you a cooking lesson?"

"*You* can cook?"

"Don't sound so surprised. How about tonight?"

"City council meeting tonight."

"Friday night, then?

She hesitated. "I can't. It's Tyler's birthday party. You know, the boy at the shelter. He's turning sixteen."

Saturday night was out—he was attending a gala in Memphis. "Thursday?"

"Okay, but I'm warning you, it's a lost cause. Even my mother says so."

"We'll see."

PETER DIALED NICOLE'S NUMBER, hoping she would be free to meet with him before tonight's city hall meeting.

"Hello, Peter."

"Hello to you, too. How's the campaign coming?"

"Good, and yours?"

"Same here." He hated small talk, and so did she from the tone of her voice.

"I was calling to see if we could get together an hour before the meeting tonight. I'd like to go over something I found in the budget."

"I'd planned to knock on a few doors, but I can skip that. The planning room?"

"Perfect."

He arrived at city hall ten minutes early, and Nicole was already there, her attention focused on a spreadsheet in front of her. The numbers she loved. He took a minute to watch as she moved a pencil down each line, then rested it against her lips. Full, red lips.

Desire to test the softness of those lips stirred in his heart, surprising him. *No.* Not only were they rivals, but he couldn't bear the thought of giving his heart to someone again and having it handed right back to him in pieces.

Besides, he'd seen how Jake looked at Nicole. If Peter showed any interest at all in her, Jake would go after her. With the campaign and his grandfather's contest, he couldn't and shouldn't consider her in a romantic way.

Nicole looked up, her green eyes luminous. She blinked, focusing. "I didn't hear you come up."

He entered the room. "I just got here and you were so engrossed in those numbers, I hated to disturb you."

"Yeah, well, you know how I am," she said and stacked the papers. "But I may have found some money."

"The Evans invoices?"

She startled. "How did you know?"

"I saw last week where the note would be paid off in January, but that the amount still showed up each month in the budget."

"It comes to a little over twenty-five thousand dollars," she said, sounding pleased.

He raised his eyebrows. "Enough for one of the projects."

"Yep. I've been looking to see if there were any other accounting mistakes similar to it so we could fund both proposals."

"Find any?"

"Only that one, but I'll keep looking. And I want to go over my figures again before I tell the other council members. Just to make sure the money really is there."

"I appreciate your help. Care to see a movie after the meeting? I understand there's a great comedy playing."

"Not trying to influence my vote, are you?"

"Sure. Lobbyists do it all the time."

"How do you think it would look for us to be seen together? Two of the candidates running for mayor going to the movies together?"

"I really don't care, do you?"

She grinned. "Nope."

"Good, it's settled. Meet me at Venelli's first?" he asked as footsteps sounded on the stairs.

She nodded.

Once the work session adjourned for the open meeting, the city council moved to the larger room. Jake arrived just as the city clerk banged her gavel and gave a report on the mayor, who was rapidly recovering. Then the meeting progressed through all the department reports until finally it was time for Peter to recuse himself and take his place at the podium facing the other members.

"I hope you've had time to look over the proposal for the youth center," he said. "I believe it will benefit the city. A center of this type will be a plus in luring businesses to our area."

Cal raised his hand and Boyd recognized him. "We have one center, why do we need another one?"

Peter tamped down his irritation. "Because the one we have accepts kids up to the age of sixteen. After that..." Peter lifted his hands and shrugged.

"How many teens are you talking about?" Boyd asked.

"I have a hundred signatures from parents

supporting the center. These parents have older teens who would appreciate such a facility."

Cal leaned forward. "Will you have enough staff to handle that many teenagers?"

"Yes. Clint Carson will volunteer his time initially, and I have at least ten other adults who have agreed to help. Eventually, I plan to hire a full-time staff. And I want to buy a van that can be used to pick up kids who don't have a way to get to the center."

After fielding a few more questions, Peter ended his presentation and returned to his seat on the podium. He was anxious to see what Jake had come up with.

His cousin took his place in front of the council and thanked them for allowing him to speak. Then he said, "The youth center is a worthwhile project, and I wish the city had funding for both it and a senior center. But since we don't, I want to explain why the funds should go to the senior center."

He turned and acknowledged the group of older adults in the back of the room. Peter had not seen them come in, and he did a quick count. Twenty-five.

"This is half of the group who have signed up to attend the center," Jake said. "They have poured their lives into this community, and providing a place for seniors to gather is small repayment."

Jake laid out his plans, and then, like Peter, he answered questions from the council. Once he finished, the council voted unanimously to defer consideration of both projects until after the first of the year.

Once the meeting adjourned, Peter looked for Nicole. She and Jake stood at the back of the building with the group of senior citizens. Not sure he wanted to be confronted about his youth center proposal, he thought about slipping out the side door. *No.* He'd never run from anything before, and he wasn't starting now. Peter squared his shoulders. He needed their vote in the election, and besides, at some point he would encounter them in town. Might as well get it over with.

Peter walked to the back of the room and stood quietly next to the seniors, giving Nicole time to finish speaking with them.

"Peter Elliott, we want to talk to you." Millie stood in front of the group, her arms folded.

He winced. His grandfather's housekeeper knew all of his weaknesses. "Promise not to take my head off?"

"Not if you can give us a good reason for opposing this."

"I'm not opposed to it. We just don't have the money."

"But you have the money for the kids' place."

He turned, recognizing the speaker. Estelle Jones. He'd been terrified of her most of his childhood. Standing as tall as Peter and outweighing him by fifty pounds, she was a formidable woman.

"Estelle, we have gang members infiltrating our schools and places where the kids hang out. Like the parking lot of the grocery store. They need somewhere of their own, a place to meet besides parking lots, where there will be less chance for them to get into trouble."

"I understand that, but why can't we have both?"

"Because we don't have the money this year." Or next. The problem was, he'd like to support both. If he won the contest, could he use some of the money to fund a senior center? He'd have to ask the lawyer. "I wish I could tell you we'll have the money for both next year—"

"Next year, it'll be something else to take it," she sniffed.

Millie looked from Jake and Nicole to Peter. "Seems to me like you three could put your heads together and come up with something."

Jake put his arm around the housekeeper.

"Millie, honey, I wish there was a way, but until we find it, I'm going to do all I can to get the city council to accept my proposal. And having Nicole come talk to your group is the first thing on my list. How about tomorrow afternoon?" He glanced at Nicole. "Is that a good time for you?"

Nicole blinked and the surprise in her eyes vanished. "Tomorrow afternoon is perfect."

Peter felt at a disadvantage. "How about me? Can I come?"

Millie turned to him with a frown. "Why?"

Why indeed. But he didn't like anyone being upset with him, especially people old enough to be his grandparents. And he still needed their vote. "So I can lay out my position so you'll know where I'm coming from."

The two women reluctantly agreed and three o'clock was set for a meeting at city hall.

"They will eat you up and spit you out," Jake said as the seniors dispersed.

"Me?" Nicole asked.

"No, me," Peter said.

Jake slapped him on the back. "Yep, you." He turned to Nicole. "Want to grab dinner?"

"I'm taking her to Venelli's and the movies." Peter couldn't help gloating a little.

"You two need a chaperone, so I'll come along."

"Is this going to be a repeat of Saturday?" Nicole asked. She looked from one to the other. "I think I'll just go home, and let you two go to dinner and the movies by yourselves."

Peter stared at her retreating back. *What happened?* He turned to Jake. "Why did you do that?"

"I didn't want her going out with you."

Peter glared at him. "Are you making a play for Nicole? Because if you are, and you're not serious about her, I'll—"

"You'll what? You aren't interested in her— you haven't been interested in anyone since Allie Carson married Matthew Jefferies, but you keep asking her out. You've told *me* not to hurt Nicole. How about you?"

Peter started to argue the point and stopped. He was as bad as Jake.

CHAPTER FOURTEEN

NICOLE PULLED HER bedspread back and folded it, placing it on the hope chest her dad had given her two days after his birthday. Not really a hope chest—just a cedar chest. However, she didn't know when she'd ever been as flattered as she had been lately with two men paying attention to her.

Not that she took either of them seriously, and as long as she remembered that, she wouldn't get hurt. Being a numbers person made it easier for her to analyze the situation and keep everything in perspective.

And in this situation Jake and Peter were competing for a prize, and neither of them liked losing. They were interested in her only because she was tied into the prize—both men wanted her to vote for their project.

Keep that in mind, Nicole, and you'll be okay. You know you can't trust either one of them with your heart.

Still, it wouldn't hurt to daydream about what it'd be like to have someone like Jake or

Peter really interested in her. What if both of them wanted to date her? Not to get her vote, but because they thought she was pretty...or interesting. Which one would she choose?

She banged her toe against the bed, shooting pain up her leg. Hopping on the other foot, she grabbed her throbbing toe. That's what she got for even thinking someone like Jake or Peter would be interested in her. She wasn't curvaceous like the women she saw Jake with, and she was not the kind of woman Peter would be interested in, either.

Why not? Because she was nothing like the petite woman he'd dated previously, that's why not. Allie was cute and the kind of woman men wanted to protect. Nicole was too independent for the likes of Peter Elliott.

She shook her head, dispelling her fantasies. Right now her primary objective was getting elected mayor. She had to remember that she was trying to win this race over Peter. All the more reason he wouldn't be interested in her.

She'd better be planning her strategy for how she was going to beat him. She did have one advantage over Peter. His attention was divided between the youth project and his run for mayor, while hers was focused 100 percent on the campaign. Like tomorrow afternoon. If he'd been thinking straight, he wouldn't have horned in on her meeting with Millie and her senior citizens group. There was no way he could come out ahead. Jake was right. Those older folks would eat Peter alive.

Still rubbing her toe, Nicole climbed into bed with a notebook. She had to craft a better response to keep the same thing from happening to her if that article appeared in the paper tomorrow. She'd all but endorsed Peter's plan for the youth center.

THE NEXT AFTERNOON, Nicole climbed the city hall steps, feeling the flutter of hundreds of butterflies in her stomach. She hoped she would be able to come up with a fair answer when she was asked if she intended to vote for the senior center. And she would be asked. She'd looked at both proposals and checked with the chief of police about the rumors of gang activity in Cedar Grove.

While it wasn't a problem yet, two youths from Jackson with gang ties had been arrested last week. There was definitely a need for youth programs in the town. Armed with this information, she hoped to get the seniors to see the need for a youth center.

Millie met her outside the boardroom. "Is Peter with you?"

Nicole shook her head. "I haven't heard from him, but I figure he'll be here soon."

The older woman looked thoughtful. "Do you think us old folk are being selfish in wanting our own center?"

Nicole shook her head. "Not at all. I truly believe we need it, but we also need his youth center."

Footsteps hurried up the stairs and she turned. "And here's Peter now."

"Good afternoon, Millie. Are all of your people here?"

"Inside waiting on you two. I didn't say this last night, but they aren't here just for the senior center. We're expecting both of you to tell us why you should be mayor."

Nicole had come prepared to do just that. And from the pamphlets in Peter's hands, so had he.

He nodded. "Give us a minute, if you don't mind."

Millie nodded. "Take your time. I'll go see if there are any tea cakes left."

After Millie disappeared through the doorway, he turned to Nicole. "Sorry about last night. I really did want to go to the movies with you."

"That's all right. I'd had a busy day anyway, and I was ready to unwind."

He nodded toward the closed door. "Do you think we'll come out alive?"

She laughed. "That question has crossed my mind. Are you ready to face the music?"

He opened the door. "Might as well."

Peter grabbed a couple of the tea cakes and sat beside Nicole. Meanwhile, Millie introduced them, and Nicole almost laughed when his grandfather's housekeeper asked him to speak first. He gulped down what was left of his tea cake and stood. No one could doubt his sincerity as he explained how the parents of the two teens injured in that car accident had come to him and asked for his help in providing a place where Cedar Grove's young people could meet. "A youth center isn't going to keep kids off the road to Jackson," Gunner said.

"That's right," Estelle agreed.

"Not all of them, but at least they would have a choice." Peter looked each of the seniors in the eye. "I've spent time with those kids who were in the wreck, and I keep thinking—if only there'd been a dance or…anything they could have gone to in Cedar Grove. And not just on New Year's Eve. Have you seen the empty beer bottles in the grocery store parking lot on Sunday mornings? We need a place for the older kids to hang out, a place where they can get direction and have something to do besides drink alcohol."

Silence followed as he sat down.

"What's your thoughts on this, Nicole?" Millie said.

She stood. "I agree with Peter that we need a place for youth to meet, but I'd like to add another component." She took a stack of papers from her black bag and handed them out. "These are statistics from other cities the size of Cedar Grove. The cities that provided a supervised center for their youth had overall lower crime rates, particularly in the thirteen-to-eighteen age group. Taxes also remained lower. And more businesses were willing to locate to these cities."

Peter had one of the sheets and was looking it over.

"You know the city has been struggling financially, and we simply don't have the funds for both projects. I want to tell you now that the youth center will probably get my vote."

The room was quiet.

Nicole sat and now Gunner stood. "Thanks for being honest, Nicole, and since you're both here, what are some of the other ideas you're running on?"

Excitement coursed through her veins as she laid out her five-point plan for the city. She finished up by mentioning how it all tied together to bring more industry and tourists to Cedar Grove. "This city is rich with history. History we could use to draw tourists here. I'd like to see something like Vicksburg has—a tour of several of the old homes that have been restored. Some of them are over a hundred years old. And maybe a reenactment of how the city was founded. Something like that could bring in tourists from all over the country."

When she sat down again, she noticed Peter looking at her strangely, and then Millie asked him a question.

"Do you have any long-range plans for Cedar Grove?"

"Definitely," he said. "I don't have it as well thought out as Nicole, but I think we are missing an opportunity by not playing up our strengths."

Discussion continued for thirty more minutes, and then Millie said, "We want to thank you both for coming. I wish we'd thought and asked some of the other candidates to be here, as well. Maybe we can do this again. Would you two come back?"

"Actually, we're having a town hall meeting at the high school auditorium on the twenty-eighth," Nicole said. "I hope you'll all attend."

"And," Peter said, "on the thirtieth, I'd like

to invite you to help decorate the building on Washington Street for your New Year's Eve party and for the teen dance later that night. You, too, Nicole."

"I'll be there," she said.

Later, after everyone had left except for the two of them, Nicole leaned against the doorway.

"That went much better than I thought it would," she said.

"Thanks to you."

She noticed he had that strange look in his eyes again. "You did fine."

"But you were really prepared," he said.

She should be. Judge Connors had been mentoring her ever since she'd expressed an interest in being mayor. "I've had help putting the five-point plan together."

A twinge of doubt flashed through her mind. It was obvious Peter didn't really have a plan. He wouldn't steal hers, would he?

Maybe she shouldn't have revealed her plan until the town hall meeting.

PETER GRABBED ONE of the tea cakes Millie had left behind. "Want one?" he asked.

Nicole shook her head. "Too close to dinnertime. Be careful you don't get the frosting on your hands again."

"Too late." He wiped the icing off with a napkin. "I'm surprised Millie brought these. She knows they're my favorite."

"That means she's not angry with you, at least."

"Yeah. I wonder if she'd make Tyler some for his birthday." He popped the last of the cookie in his mouth. "Are you coming Friday?"

Nicole's eyes lit up. "I wouldn't miss it. Do you know how his first practice session went?"

"Very good. The other team members made him feel welcome. I think he was worried about that."

"Great." She picked up her briefcase. "Dad hung around this afternoon, but I better get back to the office and let him go home."

"I have work to do as well, but I'm curious. Where did you get the statistics you used earlier?" Peter still couldn't believe how prepared Nicole had been for the meeting…or how unprepared he'd been. It was evident she'd been thinking about running for mayor for a while now.

She lifted a shoulder in a half shrug. "The internet, a few phone calls. Like I said, I've been working on this plan for a while."

"Well, I'll see you Friday."

After she left, Peter walked to the washroom

to rinse his hands. He glanced at himself in the mirror. He loved those cookies, but he'd never mastered eating them without getting his hands sticky.

Peter dried his hands and checked to make sure he didn't have crumbs or frosting on his face. It had been known to happen. He paused and stared at his reflection.

Nicole would make a better mayor.

The thought had been nagging at the back of his mind for a while now. He'd never considered running for mayor until Betty Atkins approached him. He'd sort of gotten caught up in the excitement of it all, but maybe he should have thought it through better.

What if his running cost the city a really good mayor? Unofficial polls showed Peter was the front-runner, with Nicole trailing him by ten points. Of the other candidates, only Cal Sheridan polled out of single digits.

It was too late to do anything about it. He wasn't a quitter. In fact, he planned to win. And he had twelve days to put together his own five-point plan to present at the town hall meeting.

THREE O'CLOCK FRIDAY, Peter tucked away the outline he'd been working on for how he would run the city once he was elected and drove to the school to pick up Tyler.

"Have you studied the driver's manual?"

"Yes, sir! I know it frontward and backward."

"Okay. Just remember to keep both hands on the wheel when you take the driving test. I know someone who failed it because he kept one hand propped on the window the whole time."

"Good point."

"Are you nervous?"

Tyler shook his head. "Not much. Not nearly as nervous as I was Wednesday when I went to basketball practice."

"It went well, though. Just like this will." Peter parked in front of the DMV station. "How's it going with Mr. Sheridan?"

"I don't think he likes me."

"Really? Do you know what the problem is?"

"His granddaughter. He made it plain he doesn't want me hanging out with Lori. Maybe he thinks I'm not good enough for her."

Peter's heart sank. He'd hoped if Tyler and Cal spent time together, he'd come around.

"Do you know why he doesn't like me?"

"I don't think it's just you. I'm pretty sure

he wouldn't like any young guy being around Lori. Just don't give him any ammunition."

"I won't."

An hour later, Peter escorted a bursting-at-the seams sixteen-year-old back to his car. "Congratulations." He tossed him his keys. "Why don't you drive us to the shelter?"

Just when he thought Tyler's grin couldn't get any bigger, it did. "Yes, sir!"

"And maybe when this election is over and I have a little free time, you and I will look for a pickup for the shelter."

"A pickup?" Tentative hope sounded in his voice.

"Yeah. There'll be limbs and stuff to haul off this spring…and maybe you can drive occasionally."

"Yes, sir!"

When they pulled into the shelter driveway, Peter noticed Nicole had arrived.

"Why is Miss Nicole here?" Tyler asked. "I didn't think we were going to work on math today."

Good. He hadn't found out about the party. "I don't know. Let's go in and see."

When they entered through the back door, streamers hung from the ceiling and a cake sat on the kitchen counter beside several festive packages. Tyler turned to him, his brows knit together in a frown.

Suddenly, people jumped out from their hiding places.

"Surprise! Happy birthday!"

Tyler beamed. "I didn't think anybody remembered. Nobody said anything this morning."

"We didn't forget," Logan said.

"And you better not forget our birthday," Lucas added.

Nicole hugged him. "Don't pay any attention to Lucas. Happy birthday, Tyler."

"Time to blow out the candles," Sarah said.

Logan nudged him. "And make a wish."

Peter caught Nicole's eye and winked as the boy closed his eyes briefly before blowing out the candles.

"You got them all!" the twins yelled together.

Soon everyone was enjoying Sarah's strawberry cake as Tyler opened his presents. The back door opened and Peter blinked as Cal stepped inside.

"Hope I'm not too late to join the party."

"No, come on in," Peter said.

The older man approached Tyler and held out his hand. "Happy birthday, Tyler. I don't think I've been fair to you, so could we start over?"

"Yes, sir, Mr. Sheridan. I'd like that."

Nicole beamed at Cal. "I'm so glad you made it to the party."

Peter shook hands with Cal as well. He still had hopes that Cal would take Tyler in. "Glad to see you here. Are you ready for the town hall meeting after Christmas?"

"I am. Are you?" Cal said.

He nodded. "So is Nicole."

Cal shrugged. "Voters won't take her seriously. She's too young and not experienced enough."

Peter glanced to see where Nicole was. Evidently she'd left the room. "She's the same age I am."

"Enough said," Cal said with a laugh. "Seriously, though, it's one thing for a man to be inexperienced. A woman going into a race already has one strike against her."

"You really believe that?" Peter said.

"I didn't say it was fair, and I didn't say she wasn't capable of doing the job. But she's running against you and me, and it's going to be an uphill battle for her. I figure the runoff will be between the two of us, if for no other reason than name recognition."

"You may be right," Peter said, but he hoped

not. Nicole deserved to be in the runoff election. Actually, she deserved to be mayor if preparation and vision, not to mention experience, counted. A little later, Peter went in search of Nicole and found her washing dishes.

"What are you doing in the kitchen?"

"Tidying up before I leave. I don't have one present bought and next week is Christmas. Thought I'd run over to the mall and pick up a few gifts."

"Mind if I tag along? I'm in the same boat."

She pointed to him, then to herself, surprised. "*You* want to go shopping with me? I didn't think men liked to shop."

"I don't, normally, but it's Christmas. What do you say?"

"What you're really saying is you have female gifts to buy, and you don't have a clue what to get."

She was good. "Busted."

Nicole's green eyes twinkled. "Since you were so honest, how can I turn you down? My car or your truck?"

"My truck. I'll tell Sarah we're leaving."

"Do you want to start with your gifts or mine?" Nicole asked. She could not believe she was on her way shopping with Peter.

"Do you have a list?"

"On my phone." She clicked on the note app. "I have to buy for four men, four women and five children."

"I have to buy for my mother and a few small gifts for the secretaries in my office." He looked up. "Oh, wait. I want to buy gifts for the kids at the shelter. And Sarah."

"Me, too. Do we want to get toys for the children?"

Indecision crossed his face. "All of their names were on the Angel Tree at city hall and have been adopted by families. They'll probably get lots of toys. Why don't we stick to clothes, and maybe one toy?"

"Let's get those first."

Nicole didn't remember when she'd had more fun selecting presents. She laughed when Peter didn't stick to their plan and piled more toys in their basket.

"Oh, look, here's a yo-yo," he said. "I know the twins would each love one." He found a demonstrator and put the string on his finger. For the next few minutes, he dazzled her with his expertise. He made the yo-yo spin, and then walked it across the floor. "This is rock-the-baby," he said and made a triangle for the yo-yo to spin in.

"Are you sure you're getting this for the twins?"

"I might get one for me, too. Then we can have tournaments."

"Don't you do anything without competing?" she asked as they pushed their buggy toward the checkout.

He shook his head. "My grandfather thought competition made us grow."

"Us?"

"Me and Jake."

At the checkout she removed the gifts for her nieces and nephews, and then they divided the cost of the presents for the children at the shelter. It was the best money she'd spent in a long time. It was also the most fun she'd ever had shopping.

They strolled past a food court as they took the packages to the truck. "Why don't we grab a sandwich? My cake and ice cream is long gone," he said.

She agreed and found them a table while he chose something for them to eat. "Pimento cheese?" he said when he sat down. "Or roast beef?"

"Pimento cheese." Nicole stuck a straw in the drink he'd bought. She was thirsty and almost drained it before she unwrapped her sandwich. "Why was competition so important to your grandfather?" she asked and took the top off the drink. "Wait before you answer—I want to get a refill."

When she arrived back at their table, it warmed her heart that Peter had waited for her instead of starting on his sandwich. He wasn't like anyone she'd ever dated. Not that this was a date, technically. But it was nice.

Be careful. Stuart was nice in the beginning, too.

Peter didn't answer her question until she was seated.

"Grandfather said iron sharpens iron."

She understood that. "But didn't he realize what all that competition did to your relationship with Jake?"

"Unfortunately, I don't think he meant for that to happen. Or for us to be so intent on winning."

"Winning isn't the most important thing. It's how—"

"You play the game. I'm sorry. I just don't believe that. It's all about winning. Period. Ask any coach. If you don't win, you're fired."

"I don't believe winning is the most important thing."

"Name the loser of last year's big football game."

"I don't know who won, much less who lost."

"Okay. What about movies?"

She nodded.

"Tell me one person, or even one movie, that was runner-up for one of the big awards recently."

Nicole racked her brain. She remembered who'd won, but couldn't recall a single loser. She made a face at him. "So you want to be remembered?"

"No. I want to win. I *am* working on making sure I win in an honorable way." He slipped something from his pocket. "I didn't always. Not until my grandfather gave me this watch after I beat Jake at some competition in high school. A race, I think. It wasn't the first time I'd sabotaged Jake in order to win. Grandfather never mentioned what I did. Just said whenever I looked at the watch, he wanted me to remember winning wasn't everything. That if you won by cheating, you didn't really win at all."

She took the watch he handed her, and smoothed her thumb over the gold case. Turning it over, she found the initials P.J.E. and the date 1923.

"My great-grandfather's initials."

"It's something to treasure."

"And I do. It's a good reminder that people are always watching, and I need to set a positive example."

She handed it back to him, and he flipped it open. "It's almost eight. If we're going to do any more shopping, we need to get a move on. By the way, who is going to wrap all these presents?"

She hadn't given wrapping a thought. "You?"

He shook his head. "They'd never get done, but I'll help. Why don't you take them home with you, and I'll come over one evening and we'll divide and conquer."

"Sounds like a plan." She finished her sandwich. "Did you buy your mother's gift?"

"Afraid not. You?"

"Me, neither. I really didn't see anything in here I want to get her."

"We still have another hour. I saw a jewelry store when we first came into the mall. We could have a look there after we put these packages away."

There was something magical about the night as they walked to his truck. Until now, she'd been more comfortable around Jake because he was like one of her brothers, always teasing, keeping her off guard. And Peter, well, she certainly hadn't thought of him as her brother, and any time they veered away from talking about the mayor's race or city council business, or even Tyler, her words stuck in her throat.

Maybe her thoughts of him had veered into more of a brotherly relationship. She glanced up, right into his blue eyes, and her heart fluttered. No, she definitely didn't think of Peter as a brother.

She yanked her gaze away. Her heart was still reeling after being trampled by her last boyfriend, and she refused to go there. *Keep it light.* "I should have brought my car," she said as they loaded the presents into his truck. "Now we'll have to transfer these again."

"I'll follow you home after I drop you off at your car."

No way. At this moment she wanted nothing more than to escape his presence and get her heart calmed down. "That would be too much trouble."

He bumped her with his shoulder. "Not as much as moving this toy store again."

He had a point, and if she protested too much it might make him wonder why. "Okay, but I think I've had enough shopping for one night."

"But what about our mothers' other gifts?"

"We've still got a week to find something. There's plenty of time for more shopping."

"If you say so."

The ride back to the shelter was quiet, the magic gone, and her tongue seemed stuck to the roof of her mouth. She was glad to escape to her own vehicle.

"This has been fun," Peter said a short while later as he followed her inside her apartment. "Let me know when you want to do it again."

"Oh, I'll probably just pick up something here and there." She set her packages in a corner of the living room and Peter followed suit.

"Did I do something wrong?"

She glanced at him, and tried to ignore the way his questioning blue eyes made her stomach flip-flop. It wasn't his fault she found him appealing. "No. I'm just tired."

That, and it was hard to view him as an adversary when his presence made her body do funny things.

He glanced around her apartment. "Where's your tree?"

"I don't have one. Just the poinsettia." That Jake brought over last night when he gave her a cooking lesson. But no need to tell him that.

"Everyone should have a tree."

"My parents have one that brushes the ceiling. It's been up since the day after Thanksgiving. That's enough for me."

He didn't seem convinced, but nodded. "Well, I guess I better go. This was fun. Oh, wait. What night do you want to wrap these presents?"

She'd forgotten all about that. "You don't have to come back. I'll wrap them."

"Don't count me out just yet. And I will help you wrap them. Just name the day."

She closed the door after him and leaned against it.

Rats.

Double rats.

CHAPTER FIFTEEN

CHRISTMAS EVE THE stately magnolias welcomed Peter as he pulled into his grandfather's drive. With a sigh, he corrected himself. His aunt's drive. His aunt's house. He hoped she never sold it.

He didn't know how many times he'd heard the story about how his great-grandfather had taken twelve thousand dollars out of the bank in 1929 and used six thousand of it to start Elliott Manufacturing. The other six thousand he used to build and furnish the house for his new bride. That same year the banks failed.

His great-grandfather had passed his business savvy to his son, who grew the furniture company to its present day success. Peter's father had been well on his way to taking over when he died too young. Only time would tell if Jake possessed that same business acumen. Probably, given how hard he was working to retain leadership of the company.

It wasn't that Peter didn't have the skills to run the business. He did, but for him to take over the furniture company would be all wrong. He didn't love it the way his cousin did. Peter had spent more than a few hours trying to figure out how to win the contest and yet not accept the reins of the company. He'd reviewed the terms of the contest and had seen nothing that said he *had* to accept managing Elliott Manufacturing.

Since gaining that control seemed to be Jake's driving force in getting the senior center approved, perhaps Peter could offer him a deal. If Jake would withdraw his proposal, Peter would sign over leadership of the company.

He parked in front of the door and walked to the stoop, looking forward to laying out his proposal to Jake. Unfortunately, his good mood crashed when Millie opened the door, her lips pursed tightly.

"Merry Christmas, Millie," he said and pecked her on the cheek.

"Humph," she grunted.

He guessed his stance on the senior center still had her riled up. He balanced his aunt's gift with one <u>hand</u> and took two envelopes from inside his coat pocket. He'd made the mistake of combining Millie's and Gunner's Christmas presents once in the past. The very distant past. "Where's Gunner?" he asked.

"In the kitchen. Your aunt and cousin are in the den."

"I'll join them after I see Gunner." He handed her the envelope with her name on it. "I hope you enjoy this."

"Thank you," she said stiffly.

He followed her to the kitchen. Finally he could stand it no longer. "Just what's the problem, Millie?"

She turned around, her hazel eyes blazing. "I can't believe you are going forward with opposing the senior center after we met last week."

He took a step back. And swallowed. "I'm not against the senior center. I—I—"

"Don't give me that. I see what you're doing. And I know your grandfather wanted to start a senior center. He discussed it with me and Gunner."

"You know about the contest?"

"I don't know anything about any contest. I just know he wanted that center."

"He also wanted a youth center. He talked to *me* about that."

"I don't understand why we can't have both."

He pressed his lips together. If one more person said that... "Not enough money, Millie. That's why. And only one building."

"There are other buildings."

"Not free, and not centrally located like that one. Not to mention ready to go except for changing rooms and setting up the basketball court."

"Seems to me," she sniffed, "smart as you two boys are, you could figure out something."

"We're working on it." It did seem something could be done, but when he'd looked over the terms of the contest, searching for a way to have both centers, he'd found no loopholes. It was an all-or-nothing proposition. He pushed the kitchen door open, and found Gunner making a pot of coffee.

"Merry Christmas," Peter said and handed him his gift.

"Thank you, young man." He pocketed the envelope. "I heard Millie giving you the dickens. Sorry about that, but she is right. There ought to be a way to have both centers."

"You figure it out and let me in on the secret," Peter said. He wished he could tell him about the will and Grandfather's crazy contest.

"Well, you and Jake keep thinking on it, and maybe something will come to you."

That would mean him and Jake working together. Something they hadn't done since their teenage years when they were repairing their grandfather's rental houses.

He left Gunner making coffee and walked to the den.

"Merry Christmas," he said to his aunt and handed her the fancy-wrapped box.

"Thank you, and a merry Christmas to you, too, Peter," Amelia said. "I'm so glad you could join us. I just wish your mother could be here."

"Me, too, but with Grandmother just getting out of the hospital today, we decided I'd drive to Georgia Christmas Day for an overnight stay." He turned and spoke to Jake, who had taken over his grandfather's recliner. "Thanks for setting Millie on me."

Jake grinned. "Merry Christmas. No present for me?"

Peter kept his face straight as he took another envelope from inside his coat and handed it to his cousin. It had taken him a while to find exactly what he wanted.

Jake opened the envelope and stared at the gift certificate for an online manners class. Peter had also included a donation to a charity he knew his cousin supported.

"You beat me this year," Jake said and handed him a similar envelope.

Peter stared at the card inside. He wasn't too sure he'd outdone Jake. The card was for an online book. *A Hundred Ways to Catch the Girl.* Immediately his mind went to Nicole. There was also a donation to a charity he supported.

"I don't know," Peter said. "I might actually be able to use this."

Millie appeared at the door. "Brunch is ready."

As usual, Millie had outdone herself. The scent of her gingerbread waffles made his mouth water. And no one made hollandaise sauce like his grandfather's housekeeper. The only thing missing was his grandfather. But as he looked around the table, he felt his presence. It would always be in this house.

"Millie, that was delicious," Amelia said as the older woman refilled their coffee cups.

"Thank you," Millie sniffed. "Doesn't seem right without Mr. Richard."

"I know."

After they finished their coffee, Amelia stood. "Gentlemen, I have a couple of errands to run." She turned to Peter. "I'm so glad you could join us, and be sure to tell your mother I asked about her."

"I will." He pushed his chair up under the table. "Jake, do you have a minute? I'd like to talk to you about this contest."

"Let's go into the den."

Once they were settled in their usual spots,

Peter said, "I have a proposition. If you'll withdraw the senior center proposal, I'll sign the company over to you."

"Are you offering a compromise?"

"You know I don't compromise where you're concerned. I'm trying to buy you out."

Jake steepled his fingers and tapped them against his chin. He looked up. "As enticing as your proposal is, I have to decline. I want to win this last contest of Grandfather's, and I want to build that senior center because he wanted it. I think it has a good chance of getting the support of the council."

"Once I'm mayor, I'll get you that center."

"What makes you think you'll be mayor? Nicole is going to win."

Peter shook his head. "Not in a million years. I've had polls conducted. I'm going to win. They all say so."

"That would be a pity. Nicole has great ideas for running Cedar Grove, and I think once the voters hear her ideas at the town hall meeting, she'll be ahead in your polls. Besides, Grandfather intended for us to play this out according to his rules. If we did what you're suggesting, it would be cheating."

"No, it wouldn't. It would be a smart business move on your part." He rammed his hand in his pocket, seeking the smooth metal of his grandfather's watch. Even as he'd said the words, Peter knew Jake was right. The watch weighed heavy in his hand. "Forget I suggested it. We'll play it out, and I'll win."

"In your dreams. Speaking of dreams, have you seen Nicole today?"

"No. Have you?"

"Before I came to Mother's. She's going to her parents' for dinner early this afternoon. Not sure what she's doing tonight." He glanced down at his nails. "Oh, yeah, she said something about wrapping presents for the kids at the shelter."

Peter suppressed a groan. He'd totally forgotten that the gifts needed wrapping. "I wanted to help her."

"She mentioned that. Said you must have forgotten, and she didn't seem at all sorry about it."

"I'm surprised you didn't offer to help her."

"I may be going to Memphis."

"She turned you down, huh?"

Jake's face was three shades of red. "Not exactly. And she certainly didn't turn down my offer to give her a cooking lesson. Like I said, I'm thinking about going to see a girl I met a couple of months ago."

Fire ignited in Peter's chest. *Jake went to see Nicole last night?* Not in a thousand years would he let Jake see that bothered him. "Are you ever going to settle down?"

"Not in the foreseeable future, although Nicole has tempted me to change my ways." Jake's eyes narrowed. "But, that's a strange question coming from you, considering your dating status. I don't see you finding someone and settling down."

"Don't toy with her emotions," Peter said. "If you're not serious, leave her alone."

"Nicole and I are just friends...and I'm her campaign manager. Although working with her in that tiny kitchen was fun. Might even do it again."

Pain throbbed in Peter's jaw, and he forced himself to release the grip on his molars. "You've never had a platonic relationship with a woman in your life. I'm warning you—don't lead her on. She deserves better than you."

"I think it's up to the lady to decide."

"WHERE'S DAD?" NICOLE ASKED her mother as she entered the kitchen. She smiled at Sam and Amy, saving a special one for little Grace. Her other two brothers and their families should arrive soon. Every other year, the siblings came together on Christmas Eve for an afternoon meal before making the rounds to the other grandparents...except for Nicole, who would remain behind to help her mother straighten up.

"I sent him to the grocery after pickle relish."

For the potato salad. Her mom followed her into the living room, where Nicole placed her gifts under the tree. They wouldn't open them until tomorrow, probably after a very late breakfast when the whole clan would gather once again.

Her mom had encouraged each of her brothers to establish their own Christmas morning traditions, but no one had wanted to give up the family's Christmas Day brunch. So she moved it closer to noon. That way the children had time to enjoy playing with the gifts Santa brought, and Nicole had a bit of extra quality time with her parents.

"Oh, what pretty presents," her mom said as Nicole emptied the canvas bag.

"I love wrapping once I get started. It's the getting started that's hard." She dreaded tackling the presents for the shelter kids. Well, not really. She'd put it off because she really hadn't had time. It'd been all she could do to get back to the mall and buy the rest of the gifts for her family.

She'd avoided Peter since their shopping trip, but she hadn't been able to get him out of her mind. No matter how many times she told herself it was futile and that he only saw her as a friend—if that—or that she wasn't ready, her heart tripped her up, racing at the very thought of him.

Her mom moved one of the prettier gifts to the front of the tree. "How is the campaign coming?"

Nicole admired the tree one last time, then turned and followed her mom back to the kitchen. "I don't know. Everyone I ask says they'll vote for me, but who knows? By the way, thanks for staying at the office this week so I could go door-to-door. Do you think we should consider hiring someone to help in the office?"

"Might not be a bad idea. We'll have to any-way, once you're elected."

Nicole grinned. "Want me to help set the table or peel potatoes?" she asked as they rejoined her brother and his family in the kitchen. Peeling the potatoes was her job, and there was little danger of Nicole ruining them. Besides, she knew better than to ask if she could help with anything else.

"The potatoes, please. By the way, did you check into those cooking classes I told you about?"

"Not yet. Although I'll have you know I can

now make steamed shrimp and corn on the cob."

"What are you talking about?"

"Jake came over and gave me a cooking lesson."

Her mom put her hands on her hips. "And you're just now telling me?"

"It wasn't a biggie. He felt sorry for me after I confessed I couldn't boil water."

"You're not quite that bad. I blame myself for you not knowing how to cook, but I never could track you down to teach you. You were always traipsing off with your brothers."

"She was always a pest," Sam said.

"Sam," Amy said from across the table. "That's no way to talk about your sister."

"How much longer?" Nicole asked. Her sister-in-law looked as if she was ready to give birth any day now.

"Three weeks and two days."

Nicole laughed and took Grace from Sam's lap. She nudged him with her knee. "You were all I had to play with. In case you never noticed, there weren't any little girls around for me to be friends with, except at school. And I was too much of a tomboy for them."

She'd certainly not been the most popular girl in class. She squeezed Grace. "You are the sweetest little angel. You're not going to be a tomboy, are you?"

"I want to be wike you," Grace said.

"No," Nicole said. "You are going to be a ballerina."

"Wike dis?" Her niece wiggled down and gracefully pirouetted for them.

"Very good," Joyce said.

Thank goodness her mother finally had a dainty little girl, Nicole thought. The back door opened and Aaron and his brood thundered into the kitchen.

"Boys, calm down," Aaron yelled.

Asher stopped in midstride, and Zane crashed into him. Two seconds later they were wrestling on the floor.

His wife, Debbie, grabbed Asher while Aaron grabbed the other one. "Did you boys forget Santa comes tonight?" he warned.

Immediately the squabble ended. "We were just playing," Zane said.

"Yeah." Asher looped his arm over his brother's shoulder. "Where's Davy?"

"Chris called, and they're on their way, so Davy should be here soon," her dad said from the hallway door. "Room for one more at the table? I found this fellow at the grocery buying a frozen dinner for his supper tonight. I convinced him to leave it and join us."

Her dad was the worst to bring stray people home for holiday meals. But he just couldn't stand to think someone didn't have family to connect with on special days. Nicole turned to see who his victim was this time. She swallowed the gasp that tried to escape her lips.

Peter. Looking as though he didn't quite know if he should be there. "Mr. Montgomery wouldn't take no for an answer, but I had brunch just a short while ago, so I won't eat much."

Her mom recovered faster than Nicole. "Nonsense, Peter, I'm glad you agreed to join us, although it may be a little noisy for you."

"It sounded pretty good to me," he said. "When I was a kid, our dinners were awfully quiet and boring. Is there anything I can do to help?"

"Can you peel potatoes?" Aaron asked.

"Uh, yeah."

"Good. Take the knife away from Nicole before she cuts herself."

Nicole waved the paring knife at her brother. "I'll have you know it's been six months since I sliced my finger."

Peter shed his coat and rolled up his sleeves. "Let's make sure you don't break your record today," he said and took the knife away from her.

Nicole tried to take it back and her mother

held up her hand. "If anyone wants to help, how about taking the children outside since it's warm. You big boys can play basketball or toss horseshoes, anything. Just get out of my kitchen until dinner is ready."

"Works for me," Sam said and kissed his wife on the cheek before taking Grace's hand.

Grace stopped at the door. "You coming, Aunt G?"

Nicole glanced at the potatoes on the counter and started to shake her head, not sure if her nerves could take having Peter here. Her energetic family would wear him out.

"Put the potatoes here, and I'll peel them," Amy said, patting the table. "It'll give me something to do."

By the time Nicole joined the others, they had gathered in the backyard near the basketball hoop their dad had put up years ago. All four Montgomery siblings had played the game through college. She and Sam had gone to school on basketball scholarships, and Sam now coached the Cedar Grove junior high team. Aaron and Chris had opted to join their dad building houses.

It wasn't unusual for family gatherings to end up in the backyard in a competitive game or one-on-one. In the past few years, another court had been made for the grandchildren, and the three boys were playing their version of one-on-one—when Grace would give them the ball.

"Play nice," Nicole said. "Teach her how to shoot." Maybe she should stay there and supervise the kids.

"We're waiting, Nic," Aaron yelled.

"Coming." With a glance at the overcast sky, she trudged over to the other court and took the ball Aaron handed her. It wasn't supposed to rain today, just turn cold. She was glad. It would seem more like Christmas. "So, what are we playing?"

"You call it," Sam said.

She eyed the four men, remembering how Peter said he could beat her at HORSE. It was tempting to show him otherwise. But it *was* Christmas. "We don't have a lot of time, and we don't want to get all hot and sweaty. How about three-pointers?"

When they agreed, she bounced the ball twice and made a clean shot twenty feet from the goal. The surprise on Peter's face was all she needed to make two more in quick succession. Then she handed the ball to him. "Your turn."

"No, let one of your brothers shoot."

"Afraid you can't hit the rim?" she said with a wicked grin.

"No."

"Then shoot."

He bounced the ball a few times and then sank it through the hoop. He gave her a triumphant look and quickly scored another goal.

"Let's have a shoot-out with you two," Chris said.

Nicole glared at him. Her brother was doing his version of matchmaking. "No, I don't think—"

"Afraid I'll beat you?"

She stared at him and narrowed her eyes. "Somebody flip a coin and see who goes first."

"No need," Peter said and passed her the ball. "I'll let Nicole go first."

"Your funeral." She turned to her brothers. "House rules?"

"House rules," Sam repeated.

"What are you talking about?" Peter asked.

"Layups count for two points, shots from the free-throw line count for three and from the edge of the pad they're four-pointers. You can retrieve the ball, or steal it, or try and block her. First one who gets to fourteen, wins."

"Can I say where she has to make the first shot from?"

Sam questioned her with raised eyebrows.

"As long as it's on the concrete pad."

"From the edge," Peter said.

Thirty feet, ten more from where she'd already shot. He wasn't cutting her any slack. "No blocking on this one, and if I miss, that's where you'll have to shoot from."

CHAPTER SIXTEEN

PETER EYED THE distance from the edge of the concrete pad to the rim. Too late to take back his challenge. "I can make it."

"In your dreams."

He believed her. Nicole did not intend to let him win, nor would he want her to. No, he wanted to beat her fair and square. She deserved nothing less. Now, if he could just get his mind off how beautiful she looked today with her black hair out of the usual ponytail and curling around her face. Her green eyes glowed with the challenge. And those lips.

The ball swishing through the net as she made the first shot brought him back to earth. He moved into place as she bounced the ball. She was going to try a layup. Nicole feinted to the left, but he didn't move and was ready when she tried to go around him on the right, stealing the ball. He made two quick layups, putting him one point ahead of her, but she made the retrieval and bounced the ball slowly, moving out to the free-throw line.

"Hey," Aaron said. "Mom said come get washed up for dinner."

"Y'all go ahead," Nicole said. "I want to finish this game."

"We can quit," Peter said.

"Not with you ahead. By the time I beat you, the bathrooms will be clear." She arced the ball to the rim, where it circled and hesitated before bouncing out.

He grabbed it. "Now we'll see who's better," he crowed, and dribbled the ball to the edge of the court. She would be expecting him to shoot for three points, but he figured two quick layups would be better. He whirled and raced to the hoop, but she was quicker than he expected. She planted herself right in front of him, and with his slick soles, he couldn't stop himself and crashed into her. She hit the ground hard.

"I'm sorry!" He knelt beside her, his heart thundering in his chest. Her eyes were closed and her face was white. He must have knocked her out. What was he thinking?

Her eyelids fluttered open, and her green eyes zeroed in on him. A rush shot through him like a thunderbolt, tying his thoughts up in knots. Her full lips curved into the barest smile.

"You play for keeps, don't you," she said, huskily.

Relief coursed through him. "Looks that way." Like a caged bird, his heart fluttered against his chest, and it had nothing to do with the adrenaline rush from their collision. He extended his hand. "Help you up?"

He thought she was going to say no, but then she took his hand, sending a shiver up his arm. He pulled her up, and she swayed. "Maybe you better sit back down."

Nicole took a deep breath, then another one and shook her head. "I think I'm okay. We better go in, or they might send a search party to find us."

They walked slowly to the house. "Are you sure you're okay?"

"I'm fine. Nothing hurt but my dignity, and I do want a rematch. I would've beaten you if—"

"No way would you have beaten me." He wasn't sure he wanted to give her the chance to try again. He liked winning, and he wasn't sure he would have outshot her if they had continued—she was too much of a distraction for him to keep his mind in the game. "Let's confine our battles to the political arena."

"I'm going to beat you there, too."

"Remember, don't count me out," he said as he opened the back door for her.

Dinner was unlike any holiday meal he'd ever experienced. He hadn't been joking when he'd said his family celebrations were boring. Not true here. Laughter and warmth filled the dining room. He'd always hated being an only child, and this family drove home why.

After dessert, the men gathered in the living room where a huge Christmas tree dominated the room. No wonder Nicole said she didn't need a tree. Thankfully, the conversation steered clear of the election and eventually made its way to sports and then to Cedar Grove's basketball teams.

"The varsity team should make it to the state finals," Sam said. "Especially since Coach Dawson said he'd picked up a good three-point shooter you told him about."

Peter nodded. "I'm glad that worked out. Tyler is a good kid, but he needs purpose, and I think the basketball team will be it. How is the junior high team doing?"

"Good. I have my eye on those twins at the shelter for next year," Sam said.

Logan and Lucas had shot up in the past year, and would be going into junior high next year. "They'll make good players. I just wish I could find a family for them."

"I'll keep my eyes open," Daniel Montgomery said.

Peter nodded. If anyone knew all the people in Cedar Grove, it was Nicole's dad. A little later, Peter thanked him for the invitation to share their Christmas Eve dinner and then looked for his wife. Peter found her in the kitchen with Nicole.

"Mrs. Montgomery, I want to thank you for making me feel so welcome," he said. "When Mr. Montgomery found me in the grocery, I was dreading the long afternoon and evening alone."

"I enjoyed having you here. And call me Joyce. You make me feel old, calling me Mrs. Montgomery."

"I will." He turned to Nicole. "Have you wrapped the presents for the kids at the shelter?"

"Uh, not yet."

"I'll help you. What time?"

"You really don't have to. It's actually easier for me to do it by myself."

He shrugged, not quite understanding why she didn't want his help. He thought they'd had a good time picking the presents out. "Okay... well, I'll see you at the shelter in the morning."

"Walk out with him, Nicole," Joyce said.

He didn't miss the look she shot her mother,

but she dried her hands and walked to the front door with him.

"That is one beautiful tree," he said when they entered the living room. "But I still don't understand why you don't have one."

Her gaze went to the blue spruce. "There's nothing lonelier than hanging ornaments by yourself."

So, the only reason she didn't have a tree was because she didn't want to decorate it by herself.

"Do *you* have a tree?"

He thought of the small artificial one in the corner of his den that required no decorations. "Sure."

"Oh. And you don't find it lonely putting it up by yourself? Oh, wait. You probably had someone to help." Her face turned a lovely shade of pink.

"Actually, I did it all by myself." No need to tell her he just took it out of the box and plugged it in. The fiber optics and color wheel in the base provided the rest. "Would you like me to swing by and help you with the presents for the shelter in the morning?"

"No," she said quickly. "I'll meet you there. Eight o'clock?"

"Eight is fine."

He walked to his pickup, trying to remember where he'd seen those blue spruce Christmas trees in town. *On the corner of Main and Fifth.* He checked his watch. Three o'clock. He hoped they were still set up there.

When Peter got to the corner, the trees were gone. He could always go to the grocery store where he'd seen a few Christmas trees just this morning. He frowned, remembering how dried-out they'd been. His cell phone rang, and he checked the ID. Jake? He rarely called him. "Hello?" he answered.

"Hey, cuz. Drove by your house, but you weren't there."

"No, I had a late lunch with friends."

"After Millie's brunch?"

"That was hours ago. What do you need?"

"Nothing, just wanted to let you know that after you left, I gave your proposition some thought, and I ran it past grandfather's attorney."

That Corbett worked on Christmas Eve didn't surprise him. The surprise was that Jake asked him about the proposition. "And?"

"Corbett said no, it wasn't possible. One of us has to win."

Peter's stomach sank. He'd hoped for a way out of the contest. "Well, we tried. Say, you don't know where I could find a Christmas tree, do you?"

"A Christmas tree? For Nicole?"

"What makes you think it's for Nicole?"

"Well, you have a tree, I have a tree, and she's the only person I know of who doesn't have one."

"Never mind who it's for. Do you know where I can find one?"

"Yep."

Peter waited. He huffed. "Where?"

"It'll be on top of my car in an hour."

"What?"

"I had the same idea you did. It just didn't seem right that she didn't have one."

"Oh." How did Jake know she didn't have a tree, unless he'd been to her house? He tried to ignore the dart of jealousy that stung him. "Would you consider selling it?"

"No, but I might match you for it. Meet me at my house in an hour and a half. It'll take me that long to drive to the tree farm and return home."

"Where are you?"

"On my way to the Christmas tree farm."

"Pull over and wait for me. I'll go with you, and we'll take my truck."

Jake had not made it out of town yet and had done as Peter had asked, meeting him at the welcome center on the highway. After they argued for five minutes over which vehicle to take, Peter said, "It only makes sense to go in my truck. That way we don't have to tie the tree down. I can't believe you would take a chance on scratching that new Lexus."

"I have a tarp. But you're right. Let's take your truck."

By the time they reached the farm, cold air had filtered in from the north. Nicole was right. The cold did make it seem more like Christmas. Or maybe it was buying the tree. "I'm surprised you're not on your way to Memphis," Peter said as they climbed out of his truck.

"I may go tomorrow."

"Still seeing Bobbi?"

Jake didn't answer, instead he scanned the area, and when a man on a four-wheeler inched toward them with a small tree on his trailer, Jake waved him down. "Where do we find someone to help us?"

The man adjusted his red cap and smiled. "That'd be me. And you're in luck if you're in a hurry. The folks that wanted this tree decided on a larger one." The corner of his mouth turned down. "After I cut it down."

Peter stepped closer to the trailer, and the farmer stood it up. It wasn't tall enough to brush Nicole's ceiling, but he didn't think she'd want one that big anyway. He glanced at Jake. "What do you think?"

"I like it."

"How much?" Peter asked.

The farmer named a price that sounded fair, and Peter paid him. They loaded the tree in his truck bed and were soon headed back to town. "How do we decide which one of us gives it to her?" he asked.

Jake drummed his fingers on the armrest. "We can flip for it."

Peter didn't like that. Fifty-fifty was not good odds when it came to Jake. "I can't just talk you into letting me have it?"

"Maybe."

"What do you mean?"

"Tell me why I should give it to you. Are you interested in Nicole?"

"No. Not the way you mean. She's just a friend who doesn't have a Christmas tree."

"Then why should it matter to you who gives it to her?"

Why was it so hard for him to admit to Jake he *was* interested in Nicole? An image of him arriving at her door and her surprise when he gave her the tree and then the two of them decorating it flashed in his mind, and he knew why.

Because then he'd have to admit to himself his feelings for Nicole were much stronger than friendship.

"Do you have a better way to decide who gets credit for the tree?" Jake asked, eyeing his cousin.

Peter frowned. "No. I don't have any change. Do you have a quarter?"

"I think I do." He fished a quarter from his pocket and flipped it in the air. "I call tails."

"But you flipped—"

Jake sighed. "It's heads. You want to go two out of three?"

A grin spread across his cousin's face. "No."

Peter had it bad, whether he knew it or not. "Do you have any ornaments?"

The grin faded. "I…was going to buy some on the way to her apartment."

"I think you'll be hard-pressed to find a store open around here this late on Christmas Eve." Jake shook his head. "You're so out of practice when it comes to women, you're pathetic. There's a box in my car."

"Can I have them?"

"Flip you for them."

"Aw, come on. If you win I might as well let you go with me to deliver the tree."

"That's a thought." Jake's phone alerted him to a text, and he checked to see who it was. Bobbi, wanting to know if he was coming to Memphis tonight. "Let me take care of this."

He started to type "no," uncertain if he

wanted to make the long drive, then hesitated. Did he really want to spend Christmas Eve by himself? His plan had been to drop by Nicole's with a tree until Peter had come into the picture. He'd sounded so desperate for a tree, and there'd been something else in his voice when he denied being interested in Nicole. Something that told Jake his cousin was falling in love with her.

Too bad he wasn't ready to settle down himself, Jake thought. But, he figured Peter was, even if he didn't know it. Either way, Jake didn't want to hurt Nicole.

His phone beeped again. Bobbi. Party at Camilla's—ten tonight. Want to go?

He deleted the "no" and texted that he'd see her in a couple of hours. Then he looked up. "That box of ornaments? You can have them."

NICOLE LET HERSELF into her apartment and closed the door. By now her niece and nephews were getting ready for bed, or maybe already dreaming of the toys that would be under their Christmas tree in the morning. One day...

Sighing, she hung her jacket in the closet. At least it was getting colder, although there was little chance for snow. Their part of Mississippi rarely got snow, and if she stopped to count the white Christmases she could remember, it would only take one hand.

She glanced around the room. The shelter presents still had to be wrapped. Maybe if she put on carols and set Jake's beautiful poinsettia in the middle of the room, her mulligrubs would go away. Now she wished she'd let Peter come and help.

Just as she pulled the wrapping paper out of the closet and piled it in the middle of the floor, her doorbell rang. When she looked through the peephole, she caught her breath. *Peter?*

She restrained herself from flinging open the door and dragging him inside. Instead, she opened it and casually asked, "How did you get past the gate?"

He blew on his hands. "It's cold out here. Jake gave me the code. Can I come in and bring this with me?"

"Where did you get that?" She stared at the tree she hadn't noticed until now. She moved to let him in.

"The Christmas tree farm. Where do you want it?"

Nicole glanced around the room. "The corner. It'll look good in the corner. Do you have a stand for it?"

"And ornaments."

"I... I don't know what to say. Yes, I do. Why?"

"Because I saw the way you looked at the tree at your folks' house. We'll decorate it together."

She'd hoped he hadn't paid any attention to her comment about hanging ornaments. Tears stung her eyes. This was about the nicest thing anyone had ever done for her. "You said you have ornaments, too?"

He nodded. "Let me get them. They're still in the truck."

Time passed quickly as they strung lights and started on the ornaments. "These are beautiful. Where did you find them?"

"Uh... Jake provided that part. I'm not sure where they came from."

"Jake?"

"Yeah. He helped me get the tree, too."

That was almost as strange as Peter showing up at her house. And given the vibes Nicole had picked up on, she couldn't lay the reason for his attention solely on wanting her vote for his project. *But what about when you win the election?* Because she *was* going to be the next mayor. How would he feel then?

Peter Elliott lived and breathed to win. When he didn't, resentment and anger would kill any feelings he had for her.

But there was no reason for her not to enjoy his company now. Once the last ornament was hung and the last present for the children at the shelter was wrapped, her apartment looked and smelled like Christmas. She and Peter had talked, and she'd told him about her family's traditional Christmas Day brunch at her parents'.

He'd told her he was going to Georgia to see his mother and grandmother, and that his grandmother wasn't doing well at all. Once or twice their gazes had locked, and she imagined what it would be like for him to kiss her.

Now, the two of them sat on her couch, watching the colored lights twinkle as they drank hot chocolate. His nearness kept her on edge.

"I like your apartment," Peter said. "It's… eclectic."

"Then, eclectic is what you get from yard sales."

"Well, you have a real flair for putting yard sale items together."

They laughed, and then she asked, "Why do you want to be mayor, Peter?"

He was quiet for a minute. "Hugh asked me to run. Before that I hadn't given it a thought. How about you?"

She used her spoon to dip out the tiny marshmallows. "I love Cedar Grove, and I want to see the town grow." She hesitated. "Are you nervous about the vote?"

He shook his head. "No…well, probably a little. By the way, the pollster I hired indicates you and I are the front-runners."

"Really?"

"You sound surprised."

Nicole was. "I have this irrational fear that no one will vote for me. Dad says I'm being silly."

"Why? You handily won your council race."

"I know. That's what he keeps reminding me. It's just…"

Memories of not being popular clicked through her mind like PowerPoint slides and stalled on the one of her sitting alone at the kitchen table on her tenth birthday.

"The only birthday party I ever had, no one came. Except my brothers, and they had to." She could still see poor Sam trying to make her laugh.

"That's hard to believe," Peter said. "Did the people you invited say why they didn't come?"

"Snotty, snobby Rachel Beaumont. That's why."

"I see." He tipped his cup and sipped his hot chocolate.

Nicole could tell he didn't *see* at all. "Rachel

decided to have a skating party the afternoon of mine," she explained. "And it wasn't even her birthday. What kid in their right mind is going to pass up a skating party? Heck, I probably would have gone if she'd asked me." She sighed. "And then there was senior prom. No one asked me, and I had to go with my brother Chris. Do you want me to go on?"

"You went to senior prom with Chris? Wasn't he already in college?"

"Yes. I found out later Daddy bribed him. But *you* wouldn't have noticed. You and Matt Jefferies were trying to kill yourselves over Allie Carson."

"Ah. Right. I think I took Allie, and Matt horned in."

She hated the yearning in his voice. "How did we get on this stroll down memory lane?"

"Something about the election."

"Oh, yeah. Well, I want you to know that if you get more votes than I do, I won't like it, but I won't call you Snotty Snobby Peter Elliott."

He laughed. "That's decent of you. Whatever happened to Rachel, anyway? And by the way, I don't think I went to her skating party."

"She married some bank president in Atlanta." Nicole never did know why Rachel hadn't liked her. "More hot chocolate? There's still some in the pot."

When he nodded, she put marshmallows in the bottom of the cup and poured the hot cocoa over them. A month ago, she wouldn't have believed she would be sitting in her apartment, drinking cocoa with Peter on Christmas Eve. Or that he had brought her a tree and helped her decorate it.

"Thank you," she said.

"What for?"

"The tree. For thinking about me."

"I enjoyed doing it, and I'll help you take it down." He turned so that she was looking straight into his intense blue eyes. "It's been one of the best Christmas Eves I can ever remember. And we still have tomorrow morning at the shelter to look forward to."

She gasped. "What time is it?"

He checked his watch, while she glanced at the wall clock.

"Midnight?"

They spoke at the same time, then looked at each other and laughed.

"I better go," Peter said.

"Yeah, eight o'clock will come around pretty early now."

"Why don't I pick you up?"

"That would be nice." She walked him to the door, her step light.

"Thanks for the hot chocolate."

"No, thank you for the tree."

Their gazes collided, and desire welled up from deep inside her. His lips looked so kissable. She moistened her own and closed her eyes. He leaned toward her, but then the next thing she felt was him stepping back.

"What are you doing New Year's Eve?"

"Nothing," she said, hating how breathy her voice sounded. Was he actually asking her for a date?

"Come to the youth dance with me. Help me chaperone."

Youth dance? All evening she'd been imagining all sorts of romantic things between them, and now he was asking her to the youth center dance as a chaperone? The hopes she hadn't even known she held deflated like a snagged balloon. "That's a week away. I'll let you know."

"Oh, okay."

At least he had the decency to sound let down. She shut the door firmly behind him and marched to the couch. Never again would she set herself up to be disappointed.

CHAPTER SEVENTEEN

PETER HELD THE box behind his back when Nicole opened the door. He hoped she liked what he'd bought her. "Merry Christmas," he said.

Her smile reached all the way to her eyes. "Merry Christmas to you, too. What are you hiding?"

"Can't get anything over on you, can I?" He presented her with the package. "It's nothing big."

"It's wrapped beautifully," she said, touching the silver bow. "Yours is under the tree, and not wrapped as nicely as this."

"Which one?" he asked, surveying the presents they'd placed there last night. He didn't notice that any new ones had been added.

"This one." She reached for a small package wrapped in gold foil perched on a bough and handed it to him.

"You go first," he said.

She shook her head. "Ladies go last. I want to see if you like it."

He unwrapped the foil paper and opened

the small box. A gold key ring lay nestled on black velvet, and attached to it was a silver basketball.

"To remind you to practice," she said.

"It's beautiful."

"I didn't know what to get someone who has everything."

"It's perfect. Now open yours."

She slowly untied the bow and folded the ribbon neatly, then without tearing the embossed paper, she slid the box out and lifted the lid. "Oh, Peter, this is too much." She took the pale green sweater from the box. "It's cashmere."

"I thought it would look good with your eyes."

"Let me try it on."

When she came out of her bedroom, he caught his breath. Just as he'd thought. The sweater made her emerald eyes even greener. And the color set off her creamy skin. He found himself focusing on her lips, and the urge to take her in his arms and kiss her almost knocked him down.

For the past eight hours, he'd berated himself for not doing just that last night. He should have kissed her at the door. But he was afraid of rushing things with her.

"Thank you," she said. "I'll treasure it."

He checked his watch. "We better go."

"I decided to take my car so you won't have to bring me home. That way you can get on the road to Georgia earlier."

Two hours later, Peter scanned the living room at the shelter and caught Nicole's gaze. The floor was a sea of wrapping paper and from the glint in her eyes, he knew she was feeling what he was. Their presents had been a hit.

Two-year-old Ella clutched the doll they'd picked out, and the twins focused intently on getting the yo-yos to spin. Getting two had been a good idea. They'd even surprised Sarah with a World's Greatest Cook apron. But probably Tyler was the proudest of his NBA sweatshirt.

The back doorbell rang, and Peter went to see who was there. It was Clint, and he had people with him. "Come in," he said as he gestured for Clint to step inside. He looked past his friend to see Clint's parents, Mr. and Mrs. Carson, trailing him. And Allie. She was as beautiful as ever. Her blue eyes gleamed. He'd have to admit that marriage agreed with her.

"Matthew's parking the car. We wanted to see Logan and Lucas, and ask if we could take them back to Memphis for the rest of the week."

He had the power to approve or deny the request. "Of course they can go with you. How long are you staying in Cedar Grove?"

"Until tomorrow."

"Come by the office in the morning, and we'll do the paperwork." Allie had history with the twins, had been their guardian ad litem temporarily and often took them to her home when she lived in Cedar Grove.

Matthew knocked on the back door, and Peter let him in. "Good to see you."

"You, too, man. I hear you're running for mayor. I imagine you're stomping the competition."

"I hope so. Of course, one of the people I'm running against is in the next room."

"Is Nicole here?" Allie sounded delighted.

The two men followed her as she hurried to the living room. The twins mobbed her and Matt. It was the most excited he'd seen Logan and Lucas in months, and it did his heart good.

A few minutes later, Peter grabbed a cup of Sarah's strong coffee and leaned against the door, watching the interaction in the room. They'd given up on a regular breakfast, and Sarah handed out snacks for the children, adults, too, if they wanted them. Allie and Matt admired the gifts the twins received from the Angel Tree Project, then the ones he and Nicole had picked out.

He glanced at Nicole, reading a story to little Ella, then back to Allie. So different, yet so alike. Allie looked up into Matt's eyes, and her love for him was so very obvious. A person would think they were newlyweds.

With a start, Peter realized that after the initial shock of seeing Allie, his heart wasn't going crazy like it had in the past when he was around her. Looking at them, he smiled. It was clear Allie was happy. And that was what he'd wanted for her all along. It just hadn't been with him. And he was okay with that now. He would always love Allie—that was a given—but not in the same way he had before she married Matt.

NICOLE LOOKED UP from the book Ella held in her small hands. Peter was staring at Allie, and it was obvious he was still very much in love with her. *Don't be stupid, Peter.* She needed to tell herself the same thing. Peter Elliott had been in love with Allie since grade school, and her marriage hadn't changed the way he felt toward her.

It was Stuart all over again, with a slightly different twist. Her ex-boyfriend had left her for a younger and prettier woman, while Peter was hung up on an old love. But the outcome was the same.

Allie broke away from Matt and the twins and approached her. "It's so good to see you," she said and sat on the floor beside Nicole and Ella. "What are you two reading?"

"*Cinderella*," Ella said.

Allie smiled. "I love that story."

"Me, too," Nicole said as Ella climbed from her lap.

"I play wif my dolly now."

"Okay, honey." Nicole turned to Allie. "She's leaving us after the first of the year. Her mother died when she was born and the courts finally gave up on locating the dad. Peter found a couple who want to adopt her."

"That's a happy ending to a sad beginning. Peter has such a heart for this place."

Nicole was beginning to realize just how much.

"I hear you're running against him for mayor," Allie said.

"And it's an uphill battle. He doesn't know how to lose."

Allie laughed out loud. "You know him pretty well. He's not going to be happy when you beat him."

"Thanks for the encouragement, but I'm not sure that'll happen."

"I do. We have the *Cedar Grove Gazette* mailed to us in Memphis, and I've been reading about you. You're the only candidate who seems to have a clear platform. Even Peter hasn't said how he's going to run the city."

"He'll probably have to next week at the town hall meeting," Nicole said.

Allie grew quiet beside her. Nicole had always liked her and had understood why Peter and Matthew both were enamored of her. Petite, blonde and blue-eyed, not to mention kind and giving. Men just naturally gravitated to her.

"Are you and Peter dating?"

"Oh, no." Nicole rushed the words.

"But you're here with him on Christmas Day."

"We're not spending the day together. I'm going to my parents' soon, and I think he's going to see his mother and grandmother in Georgia."

Allie sighed. "I was hoping you two were dating."

"What?" Surely she didn't hear that right.

"You'd be perfect for him." Allie grinned at her. "You would challenge him and keep him on his toes."

That would be all fine and dandy, if Peter wasn't still in love with the woman sitting beside her. Poor girl didn't even realize the efing?" she asked me to leave."

on him. Nicole checked her watch.

nd wished her a merry

looked for Peter.

"I didn't pass the big test. he math com-
spot on the floor. "But my teacher said since
I've been trying so hard, she'll let me retake it
when we go back to school after New Year's.
Coach will kill me if I don't pass."

"I'll help you study for it before school starts
again. Is everything else okay?"

Peter laughed. "I'd say so. Lori Sheridan
has told him she'll go to the dance with him
New Year's Eve. I'm letting him borrow my
truck to pick her up in the afternoon so she
can help us decorate the building. Millie said
the senior adults would be finished with their
party by two."

"That's great." The New Year's Eve party
Peter wanted her to help chaperone.

"Why don't you help us decorate, Ms. Montgomery?"

"Yeah," Peter echoed. "And with your help,
maybe I can even get Nicole to go to the party
with me." He winked at Tyler.

If he thought he could pressure her into accepting an invitation to chaperone on New

Year's Eve by asking ....

had another thoug.... giving in. "I'll think

Come on, tell ....

said, his e....

"Oh....

ab....ray!" Tyler and Peter high-fived.

"I haven't said yes."

"You haven't said no, either," Peter said. "At least say you'll help decorate."

"Oh, all right. I'll help decorate."

"She'll go to the dance with you, too," Tyler stage-whispered, and then walked back into the great room.

"Humph." If she had a knockout dress, she might go. That was a thought. One better left alone. She glanced up and Peter was looking at her in a way that made her heart lurch. She skittered her gaze away. "I came to say merry Christmas before I leave for my family's brunch."

Peter checked his watch. "And I need to get going to my grandmother's."

Nicole took a chance and glanced back at him. "Well, merry Christmas."

He took her hands. "Thanks for making this the best Christmas in a long time."

Her legs turned to water. *Remember that he's in love with Allie.* That gave her the strength she needed. "I've enjoyed it, too. The shop-ping, the tree and today." She pulled her hands away. "See you at the town hall meeting?"

His eyes darkened, as if maybe he'd thought she would say something else.

"Yeah, I'll see you then." Then he smiled brightly. "And again for the party."

She nodded. The thought of a knockout dress popped in her mind again. Maybe she'd say something to her mother... "Yes, the party."

CHAPTER EIGHTEEN

MONDAY EVENING PETER stood in the wings of the high school auditorium, adrenaline pumping through his body. It looked like half of Cedar Grove had turned out for the town hall meeting.

He adjusted the cuffs on his white shirt and smoothed the jacket of the navy suit he'd worn. He almost felt overdressed with Cal Sheridan wearing a tweed sports coat and another candidate in shirtsleeves. Nicole looked nice. Beautiful, actually. And aloof, though.

He didn't know what had happened to the two of them. They'd seemed to be getting closer, then suddenly she was avoiding him. He hadn't seen her since Christmas Day. With a start, he realized he really missed being around her.

Evidently, Jake had spent time with Nicole, probably giving her another cooking lesson. He stood beside her, holding one of her hands and probably giving some last-minute advice.

Then he gave her a hug and walked off the stage to take a seat in the front row.

If Jake broke her heart…

Betty Atkins motioned for the candidates to take their places on the stage, and they filed out. Each of them had a podium to stand behind, thank goodness. Nothing was more uncomfortable than not knowing what to do with your hands. A few minutes was taken up with the candidates greeting each other. Nicole's hand was freezing.

"You'll do fine," he whispered in her ear.

She looked startled, then threw him a grateful smile.

Each of them was given five minutes to tell the voters how they planned to run the mayor's office, and it was requested that the applause be held until the last candidate spoke. While public speaking had never been a problem for him, as the evening started, it was plain that most of the candidates were not comfortable on the stage.

He stepped up to the microphone. "First of all, I want to thank everyone for coming out. If this is any indication of voter turnout, we'll have a lot of votes to count."

From there he launched into his plan to run the city much like Mayor Gordon had done. People didn't like change, and Gordon had been popular with the voters. Peter finished up with his youth center proposal and talked for a minute about how Cedar Grove would grow only if the young people remained in town.

The next two candidates were still polling in the single digits, and Peter didn't think they posed a problem for him. Their plans sounded similar to his. While Cal Sheridan's speech offered a few more details than the last two, it was more of the same.

Nicole stepped closer to her microphone and smiled. "Good evening. First, I want to wish you all a merry Christmas and a happy New Year and to thank you for taking the time to come tonight. Then I want to say thank you to the gentlemen up here with me for taking the challenge." She glanced at the men and nodded.

"While I think Hugh Gordon has been a great mayor, times have changed since he was first elected, and we need to move forward with getting new businesses to relocate to Cedar Grove. To attract those new companies, we must make our city more appealing. Like repairing our streets. I don't know about you, but I'm tired of dodging potholes."

Spontaneous applause broke out, and Nicole held up her hand. "Let's hold your applause until I'm finished, and then we can acknowledge everyone up here. Besides, you might not like everything I say. We need to find funding for things like Peter Elliott's youth center and Jake O'Neil's senior center for our older adults. We have to make sure crime remains low, and that means better funding for our police department.

"I've traveled the state, examining other cities and what's worked for them to bring in more revenue. Cedar Grove is rich in history, and we need to capitalize on this history by drawing tourists with a museum and a tour of our beautiful old homes. But all of this means more resources, including money." Nicole let herself scan the room.

"If elected, I hope to get most of the funding from grants and the state, but I won't promise not to come to you with a request to float a bond or raise the sales tax. You'll have to decide if you want to stagnate with potholes and a higher crime rate and no place for your seniors or youth to gather, or be part of a growing, vibrant city. Thank you for listening."

Dead silence filled the air. Then in the front row, Millie stood up and clapped. More people joined until there was a standing ovation. For a minute when Nicole mentioned taxes, Peter thought her race was over. But, she was the only one of them with the guts to say what needed to be done. He wanted to applaud himself.

There was a fifteen-minute break while the audience wrote out their questions for Betty to read. When they reconvened, the first question was for Nicole.

"Are you planning on raising taxes?"

Peter had known that question was coming.

Nicole smiled and shook her head. "I hope not, but like I said, I won't promise. I've been doing some research and have found several matching grants from the federal government as well as the state. However, I have looked at asking the state legislature to raise the sales tax in Cedar Grove a half penny for two years to fund repairing the roads. I believe that's the fairest tax."

As the evening wore on, all of the candidates were asked various questions, but it was Nicole who had the ready answers. Peter had to admit she'd done her homework on what Cedar Grove needed to grow. He'd also have to admit she was better qualified to run the town. The results on January 5 would determine if the voters agreed with him.

After the meeting ended, he started toward Nicole at the same time Jake appeared. Peter plowed ahead. "Great job," he said.

"Great job, nothing." Jake smiled, joining them. "She was fantastic."

"I don't know." Nicole shook her head. "I think I lost voters tonight."

"No way," Jake argued. "As soon as they hit one of the thousands of potholes between here and their houses, they'll agree you are 100 percent right."

Peter stepped back as Nicole's family mobbed the stage. Daniel Montgomery turned to him and stuck out his hand. "Good job, my boy," the older man said.

Peter shook his hand. "Thank you, sir. Nicole did extremely well, too."

"I know."

It was evident he wouldn't get another opportunity to speak to her, so Peter decided to leave. Cal Sheridan bumped into him as they both headed for the stairs. "Good job, Cal," he said.

"Thanks. You, too. But Nicole outdid both of us. I didn't realize she was so smart. If I'm lucky enough to win the election, she will definitely be on my advisory board."

"I feel the same way." He didn't think Cal had to worry about that possibility.

And he might not, either.

JAKE STEPPED OUT of the way as Nicole's family crowded around her, but he kept his eye on his cousin as he walked off the stage. He would give his two-headed quarter to know what Peter's thoughts were. Jake had observed him during the meeting, and Peter's expression had gone from casually confident to thoughtful. And now Millie had him pigeonholed.

Millie noticed Jake watching and motioned him to join them.

"I had an idea," she said. "We finished decorating for our party this afternoon, and I think some of the decorations will work for the kids' dance. Several of us want to stay after the party and help finish setting up for their dance."

"Good idea." He swallowed a chuckle. Millie was smart. She knew once Peter connected with the seniors, he'd end up wanting to help them. Wouldn't do any good, though. The contest didn't allow for compromise. Not that he or Peter would. Winning was the name of the game with the two of them.

"You are coming to the party, right?" Millie asked. "And then stay for the dance? Peter has agreed to come."

Peter laughed. "I'm sure Jake has plans for New Year's Eve in Memphis. You'll be lucky to get him to your party."

His cousin was wrong. He didn't have plans. Not after breaking it off with Bobbi the day after Christmas. Once he realized she had expected a ring for Christmas, it wasn't fair to lead her on. He just wasn't ready to settle down.

Out of the corner of his eye, he caught a glimpse of Nicole, a smile on her full lips, and turned to watch her. "Is Nicole going to the dance?" he asked.

"I've asked her to go with me," Peter said.

Jake ignored his cousin's stern tone. "Maybe she'll help us decorate that afternoon."

"Stay away from her, Jake."

He locked gazes with Peter. "Is that a challenge?"

"No, it's a warning."

"Boys!" Millie blurted. "You two haven't changed since diapers. Always competing. Wanting what the other wants. If either one of you hurts that girl because of your silly games, you will have to answer to me."

Jake hugged her. "Aw, Millie, I'm sure Nicole Montgomery can take care of herself. See you two later."

He bounded up the steps and hurried to her side. "We need to go over your campaign."

She nodded. "Mind if we go to Venelli's? I can use a few carbs after tonight."

"Absolutely."

Once they arrived at the restaurant, he chose

a table in the corner with low lighting. "Glass of wine?"

When she agreed, he ordered a Pinot Grigio along with their pizza. After it arrived, he held his glass up and she lifted hers. "To a successful campaign."

"Yes."

She had shed the red blazer she'd worn during the meeting, and for some reason, Jake couldn't take his eyes off Nicole tonight.

"Have I ruined my chances by mentioning the T word?" Nicole asked.

Business. He sipped his wine. "I don't think so. People in town are sick and tired of the potholes, and everyone wants new businesses to come here. They know if we don't spruce things up, the companies won't give us a second look."

"I hope that's how they'll look at it."

She glanced around the room. "If I'm elected, this is a good place to bring prospective CEOs."

He agreed. One thing Cedar Grove had going for it was the mom-and-pop businesses like Venelli's. People drove a hundred miles to eat there. And Venelli's wasn't the only draw. From antiques stores to the historical old homes, Cedar Grove was rich in history. They had a volunteer symphony, and they had an art gallery that drew people from New York even.

"Tourism could be a great source of revenue with the right promotion."

"I know. I've tried to get the city council to allocate money for advertisements in different travel magazines, but Hugh just didn't agree with me."

"Hugh should have retired five years ago," Jake said.

"You said it, not me."

"Well, when you're elected, it's going to be a whole new world."

She sighed and a dreamy look crossed her face. "But not too fast. People don't like change, even when it's good for them."

He laughed. "Especially when it's good for them."

The waiter appeared with their pizza and Jake ordered another glass of wine. They ate in silence, except for an occasional groan.

"Oh," Nicole said as she finished her last slice. "This was so good."

Jake placed his hand over hers, resting his thumb on her wrist. "You know what else would be good? What are you doing New Year's Eve?"

She stilled, and he felt her pulse speed up before she withdrew her hand.

"I…ah, I'm going to chaperone Peter's youth dance."

"What a strange coincidence. So am I." At least, he was now. Interesting that she didn't mention going with Peter.

She blinked. "You?"

"Don't sound so surprised. I'll be at the building anyway with Millie and her group. Have you heard what they're calling themselves? Young at Heart. They're going to help decorate for the dance."

"I like that name. That's what they are, young at heart. And I'm glad they're helping."

He caught her gaze and held it. "Go with me to the dance instead of Peter."

His heart sank as her expression changed and those lips disappeared into a thin line. If he could catch his words...

"I never said Peter asked me." She leaned back and folded her arms across her chest. "That's what this is all about—asking me out, the wine, hand-holding. You and Peter have gotten it into your heads that I'm some sort of competition, a prize, if you will." She stood and tossed her napkin on the table. "Well, I'm not. You'll have to excuse me, I'm going home."

"You can't. I brought you."

"My car is parked at the school. It's only a five-minute walk. Although maybe by the time I reach it, I'll be far enough away that you won't hear me scream." She grabbed her jacket and started to storm off.

He blew out a breath. *Way to go, Jake.*

NICOLE STOPPED AND eyed Jake. "By the way, you're fired as my campaign manager."

Then she turned on her heel and marched out of the restaurant. By the time she reached her car, she'd cooled down. Slightly. One thing she knew. Life was a lot calmer before Peter and Jake came into it. She now felt as if she was on some kind of an emotional roller coaster.

A vehicle pulled into the school parking lot and stopped behind her car. Jake got out. "Go away," she said. Her breath created white streams of vapor, and she shivered, just realizing she was all but frozen.

"Not until I apologize," he said.

"You can apologize a hundred times, and it won't change anything."

"At least, let me try."

"Well, hurry. I'm cold."

He slipped his arm around her shoulders. "You're not leaving until I say this."

She waited.

He took her hands and rubbed them between his. "First, I want to say I'm sorry. Some of what you said was right. Peter likes you.

Maybe even more than I like you, and that did make you more…desirable. I even tried to make him jealous by flirting with you in front of him."

She stared at him, unable to break his gaze. Something was different about Jake. His eyes reflected the regret she heard in his voice.

"But that's not why I asked you to go to the dance with me. Oh, maybe at first, but not now." He twisted his mouth in a wry grin. "You make me want to be a better person. Nobody's ever done that before. Except maybe my grandfather. Otherwise I wouldn't be standing here, freezing to death, asking for you to forgive me. Will you?"

Her lips twitched. "Well… I don't want to be responsible for your death, so yes, I forgive you."

A grin split his face. "Good."

He drew her into his arms, but she pushed away from him. "I don't forgive you that much."

He threw back his head and laughed. "G. Nicole Montgomery, you're different."

"So I've been told."

"Will you go to the dance with me?"

"No. Peter asked me first. But I'm not going with him, either. I'm taking myself."

"Will you dance with me?"

"If I dance. Not sure I'll do anything other than stand on the sidelines and keep things under control."

"Okay." He tilted his head and stared at her for a minute, the moonlight catching the twinkle in his eye. "So what *does* the *G* stand for?"

"That, my good man, is for me to know and you to never find out. And now it's time for this girl to go home. Tomorrow is a workday."

She opened her car door and slipped behind the wheel. He knocked on her window and she rolled it down.

"Am I still your campaign manager?"

She hesitated. Did she really want to be around Jake that much? He did have some good ideas. Finally she nodded. "Yes, you're still my manager."

He pumped his fist in the air. "See you tomorrow. Sweet dreams."

She shook her head and backed out of the parking space.

Life might have been calmer before Jake and Peter, but not nearly as interesting.

CHAPTER NINETEEN

AFTER THE SENIORS' PARTY on New Year's Eve, Peter sipped the cup of hot cider one of the older ladies handed him and glanced around the room for Nicole. He wanted to ask what time he could pick her up. Not that she'd ever agreed to come with him tonight.

She had disappeared half an hour ago with Millie. His gaze caught Bud Wilkins showing Tyler how to tie a bowknot in a rope they were stringing across the entrance.

"Son, when you're trying to tie it, just remember the end of the string is the rabbit and this here post is the tree. The rabbit comes out of the hole and goes around back of the tree and then jumps back into the hole."

Bud looped the rope around the post and ran the end behind, then threaded it through the hole created and pulled. "And that's how you make a bowknot."

"Wow. Thanks, Mr. Bud. That's cool." Tyler glanced up at Peter. "Did you know he's been all over the world?"

"Yeah, I think I did. Where's Lori?"

"She's helping Mrs. Millie make the swags. I'll go check on her."

"Nice young man," Bud said when Tyler was out of hearing range.

"He is, isn't he?"

"You know," the older man said. "I'd like to volunteer at the youth center, if we get one."

Peter had been amazed at how well the teens and seniors had gotten along. It was almost as if both were hungry for something the other had. He turned to Bud, the seed of an idea sprouting. "That would be great. Maybe teach the kids some of the things life has taught you?"

Bud's chest puffed out. "I'd love to do that. Kinda be like the grandkids I never had."

Peter had read somewhere about centers that utilized senior adults to connect with teenagers.

"I like young folks," Bud said. "And I'm glad you came and brought a few of them with you."

Peter was, too. He'd arrived early enough to make the rounds at the get-together, coming away with the feeling from each of the seniors that today was something special.

He hated that his grandfather put him in this position of having to choose one good thing over another. If only they could find… But that meant compromising with Jake. Peter had never done that, except for last week when he'd offered a deal, sort of. It'd always been a win or lose situation with them. And now, both had too much pride to give in, especially since Nicole was in the picture.

But even if they compromised, they needed the building and the money from the contest. While both he and Jake could afford to donate some funds to the programs, neither could give enough to sustain them.

Still, it wouldn't hurt to look at the other room where he'd meant to put a smaller basketball court. He turned to go check it out and stopped in his tracks. Lori Sheridan straddled one of the ceiling beams, her legs dangling like the streamers she had attached to the beams.

"Lori!" He kept his voice as low as he could to keep from startling her. If she fell, she'd more than likely break her neck.

She peered down at him. "Oh, hi, Mr. E. Don't they look great?" She looked over her shoulder. "Toss me another one, Tyler."

His heart almost stopped when he realized she wasn't alone. From three rafters over, Tyler pitched her a roll of crepe paper. "That's enough streamers. You two get down here. Now."

"Just a sec," Lori said. "Let me tie this one on."

Lori was just as stubborn as her grandfather, and if Cal came into the building now, he would probably... Peter didn't want to think what he might do. "Come on, you two, get down!"

He looked for the ladder, but there wasn't one. How did they— Surely not with the rope he saw hanging from the ceiling. His eyes widened as Lori walked the cross piece to the rope, then rappelled down. His heart didn't slow until Tyler was also safely on the floor.

Peter pointed at the ceiling. "Don't ever do that again. Tyler, you should have known better."

"Aw, Mr. E.," Lori said. "That was a piece of cake. And it wasn't his idea. It was mine. I thought the streamers would be real pretty hanging from up there."

He rubbed his forehead. Cal didn't need to be worried about Tyler getting Lori in trouble. "How did you get the rope up there?"

"We tossed it, and then Tyler tied it in a bowknot." She turned to him. "Isn't that what you called it?"

He stared at the rope, trying to figure out how he was going to get it down. Maybe he could find a ladder. "From now on, find something on the ground that you can do, okay?"

They assured him they would, but he waited

until they were hanging crepe swags around the walls before he left. And then he had to think a minute before he remembered what he'd planned to do next. Right. Go look at the other room.

His ears picked up the strains of a waltz. Was it coming from the smaller gym? He glanced in. Empty. With the music guiding him, he walked down the hallway, searching for the source.

Peter stopped dead in his tracks in front of a room he planned to make into an office and stared through the window. Nicole stood with her back to him and her arm linked in Millie's, her ponytail swaying to the music. In her rolled up jeans and shirt tied at the waist, she looked like a teenager.

What are they doing? The music stopped, and he stepped back to make sure neither of them saw him. The music started again and Millie took the lead, moving in a circle, taking a step with each beat. Was she teaching Nicole to dance?

The music came to an end and from their actions, so had the lesson. He quickly eased into one of the other rooms. So maybe that was why Nicole had hesitated to come to the dance with him. She didn't know how to dance.

He grinned. He didn't know why that bit

of information touched him so, unless it was because *finally* he could do something she couldn't. Nicole was so talented. She could do anything…except dance. That would just have to be his little secret. And Millie's.

He remembered why he was in this part of the building and walked to the room he originally came to inspect. Although it was a good size, it might not be large enough for the basketball court he envisioned. He stepped it off, measuring the space. It'd have to be a small court, but it would work just fine for the seniors. Put tables in and leave room for dancing.

Peter shook his head. Jake would never go for a compromise that would jeopardize his chance of becoming CEO of Elliott Manufacturing. That's where Jake was now. He'd called earlier and said he'd be getting to the party late, if at all, because of a problem with one of the machines.

The door to the room opened, and he turned. Millie and Nicole.

"I thought I heard someone in here," Millie said.

"I was looking to see what to do with this space."

"This is such a nice old building," Nicole said. "It's big enough to do most anything with."

Millie nodded her agreement. "I'll meet you two in the gym. I better get back and see what kind of mess Gunner has made."

It looked as though Nicole was leaving with her. "Wait," he said. "I want to ask you something about this room."

She shot him a quizzical glance, but waited until after Millie was out of hearing range. "What do you want to know?" she asked.

"What time do you want me to pick you up tonight?"

A smile played around her lips. "That's not about this room, and I didn't say I was coming with you."

"Didn't say you weren't."

She ducked her head. "No, I guess I didn't. Why don't I just meet you here?"

"Because it's New Year's Eve. Please, come with me."

"Peter," she began.

"I'm not taking no for an answer."

"Why?"

"Why do I want you to come with me?"

"Yes. Is it because Jake wants me to come with him?"

"No!" He narrowed his eyes. "I didn't know Jake…when did he ask you?"

"Monday night."

"See—I asked you Christmas Day." He frowned. "I figured Jake would go to Memphis."

She shook her head as if to clear it. "You confuse me."

"Will you go with me?"

She held up her hands. "Yes. Just…yes, I'll go."

"Good." Satisfaction welled in his chest. "I'll pick you up at six, and then we'll get Tyler and Lori."

"What did you want to ask me about this room?"

This room? "Oh, never mind. It's getting late. We'll discuss it later." He needed to talk to Jake first.

NICOLE SCANNED THE dance floor one last time. The room looked amazing. Streamers dangled from the ceiling and there were silver swags on the bandstand and the walls. She'd dressed the tables with white vinyl tablecloths and poinsettias. Around the flowers, she'd spelled out Happy New Year in glitter, then sprinkled gold and silver stars around. The kids would have a great time tonight. Adults, too.

She didn't know why she had just agreed to let Peter pick her up tonight, but once again, her mouth seemed to have a mind of its own.

She needed to remember she was only going to the dance to chaperone.

Yeah, she thought as she opened her car door, that's why she had Millie give her a dance lesson. Not that they'd probably even play a waltz. But then, maybe they would. Carl West, one of Millie's friends, had agreed to act as DJ. That had been one of his jobs before he'd retired. He said he still had friends in the business and could get a variety of music, so maybe he'd slip in a waltz or two for fun. He was already busy setting up his equipment when she left.

It amazed her how well the teens and senior adults had connected. A few minutes later, she parked in front of her apartment, and the fresh scent of the Christmas tree greeted her at the door. She would never go another year without a tree. She almost stumbled over the box that contained the ornaments Jake had sent, and she picked it up, intent on putting it in her closet. She'd meant to do it earlier. She checked to make sure it was empty. Nicole frowned. She didn't remember putting anything in the box, but something white lay in the bottom, a letter maybe? There were several sheets, and after glancing at them, she realized the documents were an affidavit. Did Jake need these papers tonight? She scanned the first few paragraphs and stopped halfway down the page.

This belonged to Jake, and it was evident the papers were private. But she'd read enough to know it had to do with the building she'd just left. She laid the papers on the island and walked to the refrigerator for a drink of water.

So, she'd guessed right when she thought there was a contest going on between the cousins. But from what little she read, she was even more confused. She reached for the affidavit, then drew her hand back. It was none of her business.

But, as a member of the city council, if what was in the papers shed light on the two centers the council planned to vote on...

Once again Nicole reached for the affidavit, and her cell phone rang.

She froze. Maybe that was a sign she wasn't supposed to read it. She checked the caller ID on her phone. Her mother. *Her conscience.* "Hello," she answered.

"What are you wearing tonight?"

"A pale green sheath I found at The Band Box." The store was an expensive boutique and Nicole rarely shopped there. She wandered back to the island and picked up the papers.

"Good. I was worried you wouldn't even

look for a new dress. Do you have earrings and a necklace?"

"I meant to ask you for your emerald set." She knew what her mother wanted. Joyce Montgomery was itching to come over and help her dress. Nicole understood it in a way. There hadn't been many opportunities when she was a teenager, except for her senior prom when her brother Chris was her date. Without thinking, she unfolded the affidavit. "Would you like to bring the earrings and necklace over?"

"Be there in ten minutes. Go ahead and put your hair up."

"Give me twenty. I have to shower first." Smiling, Nicole hung up. Her mother's excitement was contagious. She glanced at the papers in her hand. *Put them down. Whatever is in them is none of your business.* Maybe just a quick peek. She scanned the first page, her mouth dropping open at the half-million-dollar figure. All either of them had to do was get the city council to approve the project and agree to kick in twenty-five thousand dollars.

Anger burned in her chest. What a formula for creating lifelong resentment between Peter and Jake. Why didn't their grandfather just split the money to create the two centers? Two hundred and fifty thousand dollars was more than enough to get them started.

She folded the affidavit and placed it in the box, wishing she'd never found it. It wasn't as if she could do anything with the information. Or was there? If there were some way to fund both projects, she'd do it.

Nicole glanced at the wall clock and caught her breath. Her mother would be there in fifteen minutes. After a shower, she sat at her dressing table in her bathrobe, staring at the paltry amount of makeup she owned. She rarely wore anything other than a tinted moisturizer and maybe a dab of powder. Perhaps she could use the time to do her hair, and leave her makeup to her mom.

Using her brush, she swept her hair up on top of her head and clasped it in place with a long pin. That just looked messy, and she jerked the pin out. Next she wrapped it in a bun at the nape of her neck. Too matronly. The doorbell rang, and she went to let her mother in.

"I didn't mean up like that," Joyce said as she bustled in. "But I am glad you haven't put your makeup on."

She held up what looked like a brand-new cosmetic bag. "I picked this up the other day. Would you like me to apply your makeup? I bought it all in your shades. And maybe do something different with your hair?"

Her mother's makeup was always perfect and understated. Nicole nodded and sat in the chair her mother directed her to.

"For the light," Joyce said.

Nicole sat still as foundation went on, then closed her eyes for eye shadow. "I'll put the lipstick on," she said.

"Be sure and outline your lips with the pencil, first," Joyce said as she brushed Nicole's hair.

As her mother pulled and twisted, Nicole fidgeted. "I'm not sure this dance is worth going through all this."

"It will be worth it, now hush and be still."

After what seemed like an hour, Joyce said, "There. Put these earrings on, and after you get your dress on, you can see how you like everything."

Nicole stared at the jewelry. Her mother's diamond and emerald earrings? She'd only asked for the plain emerald ones. Once she had them in her ears, she slipped into the sheath and walked to the mirror. She touched the elegant upswept do, hardly recognizing herself. Her mother's face glowed.

The doorbell chimed, and she gasped. It couldn't be six o'clock already. She checked her watch. Peter was fifteen minutes early. What man *ever* came early? "I don't want Peter to find you here. He'll think I can't even get ready for a party myself."

"I'll wait in the kitchen and leave after you two."

Nicole nodded and shooed her out of the living room, and then she took a deep breath and opened the door. The look on Peter's face was worth every ounce of effort she'd gone through. It was evident he liked what he saw, and a thousand watts of joy shot through her.

"You're early."

"No, I'm on time."

"But my watch says—" She glanced at it. The hands hadn't moved. "It's stopped. Come on in, and I'll get my purse. It's in the kitchen."

When she grabbed her purse, she gave her mother a wide grin and a thumbs-up.

Her mom hugged her. "You look beautiful. Have fun."

Tears stung Nicole's eyes. Not trusting herself to say anything, she nodded and slipped back into the living room. "Is it getting colder?"

"You'll need a wrap."

She grabbed her emerald cape, and he helped wrap it around her, then held out his arm. "I don't think I've ever seen you look quite so different."

She hooked her arm in his. "Good different or bad different?"

"Definitely good."

"So, I don't usually fall into the definitely good category?" For a second the expression of panic on his face reminded her of a trapped rabbit, and she laughed. "I was teasing."

But she knew what he meant. For some reason, she felt different tonight. *Maybe this is how Cinderella felt.*

CHAPTER TWENTY

A LITTLE BEFORE SIX, Jake parked his Lexus next to the Washington Street building. He hadn't made it to Millie's party or to help decorate, which he hated in part because that meant he'd missed seeing Nicole. And Peter hadn't. He was pretty certain his cousin made every effort to score points with her.

Whistling, he let himself into the building. If the streamers and balloons down the hallway were any indication, everyone had done a great job. The door opened behind him and he turned around. Millie and Gunner, dressed to the nines.

"I didn't know you were coming," he said.

"We are chaperones, remember," Millie said.

Gunner tugged at his tie. "Can I take this thing off yet?"

Jake laughed while Millie informed him he could not. "Great job on the hallway," he said.

"If you think this is good, come on and see the dance floor," Millie said.

Jake followed her down the hall and stopped just inside the door. Streamers and balloons were everywhere. Someone had painted silver slippers on the swags around the stage and the walls. He followed the streamers up to the ceiling. "How did you get those up there?"

Gunner chuckled. "Better not ask."

Jake laughed with him and said, "That's probably good advice." He touched a tablecloth. Vinyl. Looked like damask and very festive with gold and silver stars and Happy New Year written in gold glitter.

Jake glanced around, wondering when Nicole would show up. "Millie," he said. "Do you know what the *G* stands for in Nicole's name?"

"*G*? What *G*?"

Evidently not. "Do you know Joyce Montgomery?"

"We play Bunco together."

"Do me a favor and ask her what the initial stands for."

"Why do you want to know?"

"Because Nicole won't tell me."

"Jake." Millie crossed her arms in front of her. "You know your cousin is interested in Nicole. And I think the feeling is mutual."

"So?"

She put a hand on his arm. "Are you *really*

interested in her? Or is it because you don't want Peter to go out with her?"

He shrugged. "I'm interested."

"With your charm, you could probably make her head spin." Millie patted his arm. "Just make sure it's for the right reasons. Nicole is too special to be trifled with."

He held Millie's gaze. "I'm not going to trifle with her. I promise you that."

"See to it that you don't."

The front door opened again, and they turned to see who it was. Jake caught his breath. Nicole, looking like a vision in a long green dress that fit her exquisitely. Green was definitely her color. He strode toward her, but Peter appeared behind her, followed by two teenagers.

Wait. Nicole was supposed to be coming by herself. How could he get her alone if she was with Peter? He stopped and spoke to the teenagers as they rushed past him to get to the ballroom. When Nicole reached him, he half bowed to her. "You are looking spectacular tonight, Miss Montgomery."

She grinned. "You don't look half-bad yourself, Mr. O'Neil."

He nodded to Peter. "I see you lucked out."

"What do you mean?" his cousin said.

"I thought Nicole was coming by herself."

"You aren't the only one who can turn on the charm," Peter replied.

Carl West squeezed in the front door, his arms filled with boxes.

Jake jumped to help him.

"Thanks. I thought I could handle them all," Carl said.

Jake, along with Peter, helped him carry the CDs to the stand. Soon the building was rocking with music and teenagers. Even some of the adults were dancing to the beat. Jake had to hand it to Peter. The dance was a success. Except he hadn't seen Nicole on the dance floor yet.

Near midnight, he stopped by the bandstand and spoke to Carl, then wandered over to where she stood. "Would you care to dance?"

She pointed to where the teenagers were swaying to the beat and waving their arms about. "To that? Don't know how."

"Aw, come on."

She shook her head.

Carl West's voice came over the speakers. "Boys and girls, this song is for our chaperones, so if you want to see how to dance, watch the old folks."

Jake raised an eyebrow as a slow song started playing. "How about this one?"

"It's perfect," Peter said from behind him. "Perfect for me and Nicole, that is."

She gave him an apologetic smile. "I haven't danced with Peter, yet."

"Next one is mine," Jake said.

Or maybe not, he thought as he observed the expression on his cousin's face as he swung Nicole out onto the dance floor. Jake had been right Christmas Eve—Peter had it bad.

NICOLE'S MOVEMENTS WERE STIFF, and she kept looking down at her feet. Peter stopped and gently lifted her chin. "Watch my eyes, and let the music and me guide you."

She started to shake her head.

"Try it. Just relax in my arms. I won't step on your toes."

"I might step on yours," she muttered.

"No, you won't." He pulled her closer. "Feel the music?"

She nodded. With his hand on her waist, he guided her around the dance floor, and gradually she loosened up in his arms. She was so beautiful. The feeling in his chest almost hurt. The music ended way too soon. "Another dance?"

A new song started, hip-hop, and she said, "I absolutely don't know how to dance to that."

"Don't feel bad. Neither do I. Would you like to get some fresh air?"

"I would."

He checked with Millie to let her know he was stepping out for a minute, then escorted Nicole outside. "Want to walk to the park?"

She glanced down at her heels.

"I take it that is a 'no.' We'll stay here on the landing."

She pulled her wrap closer.

"Are you cold?"

"Not much."

Overhead a full moon filled the sky with silvery light. Nicole stood beside him, their shoulders almost touching. He couldn't identify the light fragrance she wore, only that it made him want to hold her in his arms.

Strains of music filtered outside. "They're playing another slow song," he said. Then he bowed. "May I have this dance? There's plenty of room here."

"You didn't get enough of me stepping on your toes the first time?"

"You only did it once." He held out his hand and she took it. This time she wasn't as nervous and soon relaxed. He drew her closer and swung her around. When the music ended, he looked into her emerald eyes.

"You are beautiful," he said, his voice husky.

Her perfume tantalized him, making him dizzy. He glanced at her full lips and desire to cover them with his welled up in his chest. Nicole closed her eyes, her lashes thick and long against her porcelain skin. He stroked her cheek, and she leaned toward him. Gently, Peter cupped her face and bent to brush his lips against hers.

She gave a small moan and slipped her hands behind his neck, pulling him closer.

He captured her mouth, tasting the sweetness of her lips. Church bells pealed as fireworks exploded in the sky above the park, and he kissed her again before releasing her. "Happy New Year."

"Happy New Year to you," she said before he once more covered her lips with his.

When they broke apart, Nicole leaned her head on his shoulder, and he smiled, contented. "I guess we better go in. They may have torn the building down."

Everything was still standing when they reached the ballroom. The floor was covered in confetti and music boomed through the speakers. Peter scanned the room for Tyler and didn't see him or Cal Sheridan's granddaughter.

"Have you seen Tyler or Lori?" he asked Millie over the music.

"No. Not for a while now."

His stomach sank. His pickup. He didn't remember seeing it in the parking lot. He'd let Tyler drive after he picked him up, and now he felt his empty pockets for his keys.

Gone. The truck was gone. He couldn't believe the boy would take his pickup without asking. He returned to the dance, looking for Tyler's friends. Maybe they knew something.

Nicole had one of the basketball players cornered, and she turned as he approached. "He said they ducked out of the dance thirty minutes ago."

"Do you know where they went?" Peter asked. "We've looked everywhere."

The boy shrugged. "Did you check the park near the swings?"

"He wouldn't need my truck for that."

The boy's eyes widened. "He took your pickup? That's just plain stupid."

"Tell me about it," Peter muttered as he went looking for Jake. He needed wheels to search for the boy. His cell phone rang. Lori Sheridan's name showed up on caller ID. "Hello!"

"Mr. Elliott?"

Not Lori. "Tyler? Where are you?"

"The ER."

"What happened?"

"Uh…"

He heard a deep sigh over the phone. "Tyler, what's wrong?"

"You see, we…me and Lori, we just wanted to cool off. So, uh, we—"

"Just tell me why you're at the ER."

"Lori broke her arm."

Peter's stomach flipped.

"She wouldn't let me tell you. So I drove her to the emergency room. Would you call her mom? She won't tell the nurse who she is 'cause she doesn't want the hospital to contact her parents. Said it'd scare them to death, but I thought maybe if you called, it wouldn't be so bad."

"I'll be right there." He searched his memory. "I don't have her mom's number. Text it to me."

"Okay, but hurry. The doctors won't do anything until they talk to her parents. Her arm is hurting real bad."

He disconnected.

"Are they all right?"

"For now." When he got through with Tyler, he might not be. "Lori broke her arm, and they're at the ER."

"How?"

"No clue. Would you find Jake for me? Tyler

took my truck, and I don't have a way to the hospital." His phone alerted him to a text. It was her parents' number and he dialed it. "Mrs. Sheridan?" he said when a woman answered.

"Yes?"

"This is Peter Elliott, and I'm afraid there's been a little accident. Lori is at the ER with a broken arm."

A gasp sounded on the other end of the line. "What happened? Why didn't she call me?"

"I don't know. I'm on my way to the hospital, but they won't treat her until they have your permission."

"I'll call on my way. I'll see you there."

He disconnected and glanced around for Nicole. She'd found Jake, and Peter hurried toward them. "Can you give me a ride to the hospital?"

"Of course."

"I'm coming with you," Nicole said.

The ride to the hospital was quiet until Peter broke the silence. "I don't understand why those two didn't let me know Lori had broken her arm."

"Is that the girl who hung the streamers from the rafters?" Jake asked.

"You heard about that?"

"Yeah, Gunner told me. But a girl who

climbed those heights would want to have her broken arm fixed before anyone found out."

Jake was probably right. "That doesn't explain why Tyler went along with her."

Nicole said, "Actually, it's probably what I would've done when I was sixteen."

Peter stared out the window. Tonight was supposed to seal the vote for the youth center. Now he'd be lucky if Cal and the other council members didn't run him out of town on a rail.

Cal Sheridan was hurrying toward the ER doors when they pulled into the parking lot. His daughter-in-law must have called him.

Jake, Nicole and Peter followed Cal into the ER.

"I'm so sorry this happened," Peter said when he reached the family.

The older man crossed his arms. "Why didn't you know *when* it happened?"

Maybe because Peter was kissing Nicole? "They didn't tell me. I didn't know they'd left the dance."

"Where were the chaperones?" Cal demanded.

Peter didn't blame him for being angry. "They got past them somehow. I'll be investigating. I'll also be checking into what type of training our volunteers need."

"May be too little, too late."

The nurse directed Cal and his daughter-in-law into the treatment rooms.

"We'll talk about this later," Cal said and followed Lori's mother through the doors.

Peter scanned the room for Tyler and saw him sitting with Jake and Nicole. He marched over to them.

"I'm sorry, Mr. Elliott. I…" The boy's shoulders slumped. "I should've come and told you."

"Yes, you should have. What happened?"

"We'd been dancing, and Lori said she was hot. The park was close by, and we just kinda walked over there. And then she wanted to climb the slide, only her foot slipped, and she fell on her arm. I didn't think it was broken, and she said they could wrap it here, and maybe no one would ever know. And I apologized to Mr. Sheridan. He wasn't very happy and told me I could keep my apology."

Peter winced. He could imagine what else Cal said to the boy.

"Here are your keys." Tyler held them out. "We really thought we'd be back before anybody missed us."

He pocketed his keys. Tyler was truly remorseful, and Peter was pretty sure nothing like this would happen again. "We'll talk about it tomorrow."

"Yes, sir."

"You want me to take him home?" Jake asked.

"I'd appreciate it if you would." Peter turned to Nicole. "Why don't you let him drop you off, as well? I plan to stay here until Lori's arm is set."

"I'm staying," she said.

Nicole looked tired, and Peter said, "No, it's already past one. No telling how long it'll take."

She shifted her gaze to Jake. "Go ahead and take Tyler to the shelter. Like I said, I'm staying."

"And I'd like to stay as well," Tyler said.

Peter glanced from one to the other. When both looked determined to stay, he nodded. "Neither of you would probably get any sleep, anyway."

Jake said, "All right. If you change your mind, call me."

After Jake left, Tyler went to get a drink of water. Peter tucked a wayward strand of Nicole's dark hair behind her ear. "Thanks, but you should have let him take you home."

She leaned against him. "I was a chaperone—it's as much my fault as it is yours that we didn't see them leave."

"Let's sit over here while we wait." He took her by the hand and led her to the corner of the room. He had a feeling that after tonight, his life was going to be very different one way or the other.

CHAPTER TWENTY-ONE

LORI SHERIDAN'S ARM had a clean break and didn't take long to set. Nicole exchanged looks with Peter as Cal wheeled a subdued teenager out the door. Tyler followed behind, his shoulders figuratively dragging the floor.

"Stop a minute, Gramps," Lori said. The wheelchair stopped and the girl turned to them. "I'm sorry, Gramps. And Mr. E., thanks for calling my parents."

"An apology isn't going to get you off the hook this time, Granddaughter."

Nicole squeezed Peter's hand, hoping he'd take a softer stand.

"Your grandfather is right," Peter said. "I'm afraid there needs to be consequences for your actions." He turned to Tyler. "You, young man, are grounded for a month."

Nicole didn't think the boy's shoulders could droop any lower, but they did.

"I'm sorry, sir. Does that include basketball?"

Peter's lips pressed together in a thin line. "It includes everything. Basketball, after school activities—you think of it and you can't do it. Not for a month."

Cal nodded his approval. "Let's get you home and in bed, young lady."

After Cal wheeled Lori through the doors, Peter turned to Nicole and Tyler. "Time to get you two home as well."

They dropped Tyler off at the shelter and waited until he was safely inside, then drove to her apartment. She leaned against the doorframe. "Want to come in for a minute?"

His eyes softened, and his voice was a whisper. "I should go. You need your bed."

His words didn't match the desire in his eyes as he rubbed his thumb against her jaw. "Thanks for staying at the hospital."

Peter leaned in, and Nicole lifted her lips to his. She melted against him as his kiss sent shivers through her. That first kiss at midnight had cracked the ice around her heart, and this one set it on fire. The emotions Peter stirred up were new to her—her ex-boyfriend certainly never made her feel this way.

He stepped back. "Definitely time for me to go."

He kissed her once more before walking to his truck. "Late breakfast tomorrow?"

"Sounds wonderful." She didn't move until he was out of sight.

SUNDAY AFTERNOON, NICOLE was still remembering those kisses and the others Peter had given her. After brunch on New Year's Day, they'd spent time at her parents', and the cold hadn't stopped them from playing a game of one-on-one. She laughed, thinking how cocky he'd been going into the game. She might have let him win if he hadn't been so sure of himself.

She sighed. What a difference a few weeks could make. Everything was perfect. While it was a given that her mom liked Peter, her dad liked him as well. For the first time in her life, Nicole believed she'd found a man that measured up to her dad.

Can you really trust him? Briefly, Nicole focused on the question. It wasn't the first time it had popped into her head. Sometimes in the middle of the night doubt slithered in.

Before she could dismiss it, her cell phone rang and she answered. It was Sarah Redding from the shelter.

"Is there any chance you can help Tyler this afternoon?" Sarah asked. "School starts Tuesday and he's trying to study for that makeup test in math and not making much headway."

Nicole remembered promising the boy she'd help after New Year's. "I'll be right over."

She parked at the side of the shelter beside Peter's pickup and climbed out of her car. Peter hadn't said anything about coming to the shelter last night when they had dinner at Venelli's.

A warm feeling spread through her chest. Maybe because they'd been so busy gazing into each other's eyes. And the good-night kisses weren't half-bad. Only a couple of days since he'd first kissed her, and so far he hadn't missed an opportunity to follow up.

She practically skipped up the steps to the back door of the shelter, and Sarah let her in.

"Tyler is in his bedroom, and Peter is in my office. Go see him while I get the boy."

She hurried down the hall, slowing when she heard voices. Peter wasn't alone. She glanced in the hallway mirror, which reflected the interior of the office, and saw Allie Jefferies.

Allie was with Peter? Blood drained from Nicole's face as she watched him slip his arms around his former girlfriend and draw her into an embrace. Nicole covered her mouth with her hand and stepped back. Maybe she saw wrong.

A quick glance told her she hadn't. They still stood with their arms around each other. *Confront him. Demand to know what's going on.* But images of Stuart and his secretary bombarded her brain. With tears scalding her eyes, she turned and fled, stopping only long enough to tell Sarah she had a splitting headache and would return some other time to help Tyler.

She held back the tears until she was inside her apartment, leaning against the closed door. What a fool she'd been. She'd seen the way he looked at Allie on Christmas Day. Deep in her soul Nicole had known Peter still loved his old flame, but that he would act on it…

Nicole stumbled to the couch and buried her face in her hands. She'd been so stupid. First Stuart and now Peter. What? Did she have a sign on her forehead that said Break My Heart?

She raised her head, and the Christmas tree mocked her. He had really played her. But no more. She yanked ornaments off the tree and threw them in the box they'd come in. Once the ornaments were off, she jerked the lights, toppling the tree over.

Forget the lights. She'd buy Jake another set. Nicole wrestled the tree to the door, and stopped there. She didn't have the energy to carry it outside.

Maybe she should have accepted Jake's offer for a date New Year's Eve. At least he didn't have an old flame.

But she didn't love Jake.

More tears streamed down her face. "I don't

love Peter," she murmured to herself. *"I. Don't. Love. Peter."*

No matter how many times she said the words, it didn't make them true.

The special ringtone she'd just last night put on her phone for Peter signaled loudly. She let it go unanswered. Staring at the fallen Christmas tree, she kicked it hard. Felt pretty good. Maybe she could kick it all the way to the curb.

Her phone rang again. She could not go through hearing his excuses like she had with Stuart. Ignoring the call, she opened her door and dragged the tree outside. By the time she returned, the ringing had stopped. But he'd left her a message. She deleted it without listening to it and pulled out her vacuum. Once she had all the needles gone and the box of ornaments in her car, she felt better.

Peter had called back and left another message. Maybe she'd better text him or he might come over. After all, he didn't know she had seen him.

Feeling terrible. Will be in touch later.

There. That ought to do it. And it wasn't a lie. Her phone rang, and she was about to turn it off when she saw it was Sarah. Curiosity got the better of her and she answered, "Hello?"

"Nicole? Are you feeling any better?"

"A little, maybe."

"Well, Peter was worried that he didn't get to talk to you. And now he's driving down to the coast with a deputy to pick up two runaway teens."

Why did hearing his name make her heart hitch? "Why didn't he send someone else?"

"You know him. He just hated to ask one of the other case workers to give up their Sunday."

He was all heart. Except when it came to being true to her. "Do you know when he'll be back?"

"It's four hours to the coast and back, and then no telling how long the transfer will take."

She checked her watch. Only three thirty. "Is Tyler still there? I can come back and help him if he is."

"I'm sure he'd appreciate it, but if you're not feeling well—"

"I'm okay. I'll be there in a few minutes." The sooner she went, the quicker she could get away. She wouldn't go at all, except she'd promised the boy she'd help him.

The image of Peter with his arms around Allie haunted her all the way to the shelter. What was she going to do? Peter would want to know why she wouldn't take his calls. And he'd come up with some convenient reason for what she had seen—men always did, she thought, remembering the lies Stuart told when she found him in an embrace with his now wife.

She just didn't expect it from Peter. Jake, maybe, but not Peter. No, not even Jake. He had more honor than that. And she hadn't kissed Jake or almost told him that she loved him. Twice she'd almost said the words to Peter, but held back. What if she had told him? Would it have made a difference? She'd never know.

Pain ripped through her heart again, and she straightened her shoulders. *What doesn't kill you makes you stronger.* And this would not kill her. She parked once again in her same parking space.

"You sure look peaked," Sarah said as Nicole entered through the back.

"Headaches do that." Headaches by the name of Peter Elliott. "Where's Tyler?"

"Gone to get his math book."

She sat at the table to wait, and the boy ducked his head when he slid into his seat.

"'Lo," he said.

"How is Lori?"

"I haven't seen her, but she texted me her arm isn't hurting."

"Good." But he was hurting. Maybe if Tyler

passed the test and stayed on the basketball team, the family... No, Nicole was pretty sure it was Cal who must have put a stop to them seeing each other. Maybe he would relent. She opened his math book. "Are you ready to get started?"

"Yes, ma'am."

As they worked through the problems together, he began to grasp the concepts. "So if I remember that if two angles of a triangle are congruent, the sides opposite those angles are congruent, as well?"

"You have it. Very good." She couldn't do anything about her life, but maybe she could make a difference in Tyler's.

Tires crunched on the gravel drive, then a door slammed, and Nicole looked up. That couldn't be Peter. The back doorbell rang, and Sarah answered it.

"Come in, Mr. Sheridan."

"Afternoon, Sarah. Is Tyler here?"

"He's in the kitchen."

Beside her, Tyler tossed Nicole a panicky glance. Nicole swallowed hard. "It'll be okay."

Cal came into the room. "There you are. Mind if I talk to you, Tyler?"

"N-no, sir."

"Hello, Nicole," Cal said and took a deep

breath. "Tyler, I just wanted to apologize for the other night, son."

"Sir?" Tyler's brows lowered. "What do you mean?"

"It seems I owe you an apology. Why didn't you tell me Lori wouldn't listen to you? That you tried to get her to find Peter?"

Tyler lifted his shoulder in a half shrug. "I dunno. I guess I didn't want to get her in trouble."

"My granddaughter does a good job of that all by herself, thinking she can do anything." He held out his hand. "I apologize for jumping all over you. And thank you for getting her to the ER."

Tyler hesitated, and then accepted the man's hand. "Thank you, sir."

"She's in the truck if you want to go say hi."

Tyler shot a glance at Nicole. "May I?"

"Sure."

The boy scrambled out of the chair and raced for the back door. Nicole eyed Cal. "Thank you for doing that. You didn't have to."

"But I did. It seems I may have misjudged the boy."

"We all do that sometimes," Nicole said. Which might be a lesson for her to learn. Except she knew what she saw, and she didn't think there could be a plausible explanation for Peter and Allie's embrace.

STANDING OUTSIDE THE Harrison county jail, Peter listened as Cal Sheridan asked for leniency for Tyler, not sure he was hearing right. "Thanks, Cal. I appreciate that you called, but Tyler is still grounded because he didn't let me know about Lori's arm and he took my truck."

"Think about letting him play basketball. The team needs him, and I think he's learned his lesson," Cal said. "One other thing. I plan to vote for the youth center when we bring it up at the next council meeting. Boyd Anderson and George Bivens plan to, as well."

That meant he had enough votes to get his proposal through. The youth center was practically a done deal. The memory of how Millie and Gunner and all the others had helped decorate the building dimmed his elation. "How about Jake's senior center?"

"It wouldn't surprise me if both of them get approval, but only one of the projects will be funded."

Effectively killing the other one. It wasn't enough to get city approval. To win the contest, one of the projects had to get the twenty-five-thousand-dollar financial backing from the city.

After he thanked Cal and hung up, Peter stared at his phone. Nicole hadn't answered earlier, and she hadn't responded to the messages he left. He didn't know what was going on, but he had a sinking feeling it wasn't good.

He returned to the conference room where a social worker was processing the paper work for him to take charge of the two sixteen-year-olds he'd come to collect. Seems the girl's mom wouldn't allow her to see her boyfriend, so the two of them ran away.

Maybe on the drive back, he could help them see the mother's side. Looking at their angry faces, he doubted it. It was going to be a long two-hour trip. Not to mention he was worried because Nicole hadn't returned his texts or calls.

MONDAY MORNING, WORRY awakened Peter at six o'clock. It'd been close to ten when he and the teens returned to Cedar Grove and another couple of hours before he'd finally gotten to bed. Nicole had called him while they were on the road, but she only answered his questions in monosyllables. He'd attributed her abruptness to the election in two days, but now he wasn't so sure, and the first thing on his agenda today was discovering what the problem was.

Only it didn't work out that way. Before he could call her, he heard from the runaway girl's mother. The girl had locked herself in her room, asking for Peter. The rest of the day was spent resolving the issue.

At four, Peter speed-dialed Nicole's number, and there was no answer. He took a chance and drove to her apartment. Her car was in her parking space, so she should be home. He parked and started up her walk when her front door opened and she came out, carrying trash.

"Oh." Nicole stopped abruptly.

"Hello," he said, his heart pounding against his chest. How he'd missed her. Dressed in jeans and a pullover turtleneck, her shiny black hair in a ponytail, she looked fresh and wholesome.

"I was on my way to knock on a few more doors," she said and looked at the bag in her hands. "After I put this in the bin."

Her voice trembled, as if she was nervous.

"Can we talk?"

She looked as though she might say no, but her shoulders drooped and she nodded. "Let me take care of this. Go on in."

He stepped inside the apartment, noticing the tree was gone. Disappointment shot through him at warp speed. He'd told her he'd help take it down. Not a good sign, even if it was the fourth of January—after the last few days, he thought she'd wait for him.

"You took the tree down," he said when she returned.

"It was time."

Her gaze skittered away from him, and he studied her face. "What's wrong, Nicole?"

"Nothing."

"Look at me and tell me that again."

"We..." She chewed a fingernail. "Everything was moving too fast."

That was the problem? He'd thought she was going to tell him she didn't want to see him again. "We can fix that."

"I don't know. Right now, I think we both better focus on the election and you have that contest." Her hand flew to her mouth.

"How did you know about the contest? Did Jake tell you?"

She shook her head. "There was an affidavit in the box with the ornaments. Jake must have put it in there and forgotten."

"You haven't told anyone, have you?"

"No, of course not. But I think you should."

"Did you read it?"

Color crept into her cheeks. "I read part of it before I realized what it was." She ducked her head. "Then I read all of it."

Nicole was cute when she was embarrassed.

"Then you know we can't tell anyone, not until one of us wins."

"Well, I think it's horrid that your grandfather would do something like that."

"I'm sure he had his reasons," Peter said. "But let's get back to us."

"Can this conversation wait until at least Tuesday, after the election?"

"No. I love you and I want to settle whatever is wrong tonight."

Nicole gaped at him. She shook her head as if she'd misunderstood him. "Is something wrong?" he said.

"I can't believe you said you love me after what you did!"

Her face was bright red now, and it had nothing to do with embarrassment.

"What are you talking about?"

Her hands curled into fists at her side. "You and Allie. Embracing."

"What?"

"I saw you yesterday. You and Allie were in Sarah's office, and you were holding her in your arms."

He stared at her, understanding unfolding in his brain, right along with anger. "Too bad you didn't come into the office instead of sneaking away. If you had, you could have spoken to Matt, who was also there. You would have seen the two of us shaking hands."

"Sneaking?" Her voice rose. "What was Matt doing there?"

"He and Allie had just come to tell me they wanted to adopt Logan and Lucas." He clenched his jaw, the muscle throbbing. "I can't believe you don't trust me. That you believed the worst. Allie is a married woman. I would never—" Pain ripped a hole in his heart.

He held his hands up as if surrendering. "Never mind. Just forget it. Maybe we aren't right for each other."

Peter wheeled around and walked to the door. He should have known Nicole was too good to be true.

"Wait… I'm sorry. I—I—Stuart… I caught him—"

He shut the door, cutting off her words. He wasn't Stuart, and if she didn't know that by now…

CHAPTER TWENTY-TWO

NICOLE STARED AT the closed door. What had she done? She had just maybe let the best thing that ever happened to her walk out of her life.

All because she'd jumped to the wrong conclusion. She'd spent the night wrestling with her anger, trying to tell herself it wasn't true, that somehow she'd misconstrued what she'd seen. But the harder she tried, the more her mind insisted Peter was in fact like Stuart. Why hadn't she listened to her heart defending Peter?

She didn't blame him for being hurt and angry. Nicole winced. She should have known there was a logical answer.

Because, her head argued, with Stuart the conclusion had been correct. He *had been* seeing someone else. *But Peter wasn't Stuart.* No, but that experience branded all men capable of betraying her.

She should at least try to apologize to Peter after he had time to cool off, and if he couldn't forgive her... Nicole squared her shoulders. She wouldn't think about that right now.

She'd buried herself in work after the fiasco with Stuart, and handing out cards and brochures at the mall would get her through tonight. Tomorrow, she would try to see Peter and explain.

Monday night at the mall might not have been her best choice with only two hours until closing time and very few people shopping. Nicole didn't know why she should be surprised. It wasn't the first mistake she'd made today. Still, she dug a smile from her campaign bag and made the effort.

"Hi there," she said to a balding senior citizen. "I'm Nicole Montgomery, and I'd like your vote tomorrow in the mayoral election." She handed him a card and brochure.

"I was at the town hall meeting," he said. "Are you going to vote for the senior center?"

"I hope we can get both centers."

"But if it comes down to one or the other, which will you vote for?"

She hesitated. "If I had to vote at this very minute, I'd vote for the youth center," she replied, keeping her smile in place.

He cocked his head to the side. "At least you're honest. Young lady, I do believe I'll vote for you."

"Thank you. Get your friends out to vote for me, too."

His gentle pat on her arm warmed her heart. If she became mayor, she intended to move heaven and earth if that's what it took to get both centers. Buoyed, she turned to look for another voter and almost bumped into Jake. "What are you doing here?"

"Buying something?"

She could always count on Jake's humor. "I'm sorry. It's been a bad day."

"Have you seen Peter? He was worried about you."

The corner of her mouth turned down. "I have, and he's not worried anymore. I doubt he'll ever be worried about me again."

"What happened?"

Nicole waved him off. "It's too much to get into."

He checked his watch. "We have forty-five minutes." Then he took her by the arm and led her to the food court. "Coke?"

She nodded. Maybe she could escape while he ordered, but instead found herself waiting for him to return.

"Spill it," he said, handing her the drink.

She unwrapped the straw and stuck it through the lid. "I saw something and jumped to the wrong conclusion," she said, avoiding his eyes. When he didn't say anything she looked up. Jake was staring intently at her.

"What something?"

"He had Allie in his arms, and I thought… well, you know what I thought."

"No. Why don't you tell me?"

Jake was being difficult. "I thought he was in love with her."

"But she's married. Peter isn't the sort to do something like that."

"I know. It's just that almost the same thing happened with Stuart, except the woman wasn't married."

"So you've painted all men with the same brush."

"I was wrong, but he didn't give me a chance to explain." She propped her chin in her hand. "Do you think he'll ever forgive me?"

"I don't know. Maybe after he has time to think about it. But if he doesn't, does that mean I have a chance with you?"

Nicole glanced up at him. "Oh, Jake, you're sweet."

She liked Jake—what wasn't there to like? Handsome, kind, funny. A lot like her brothers. And that was the problem. Jake was like one of her brothers.

"Never mind," he said. "Sweet is not what I was going for, and I'm not a masochist."

Something Jake had said triggered a thought that she tried to dismiss. But it wouldn't go away. Did she paint all men with the same brush whether they deserved it or not? Had she just been waiting for Peter to betray her? Or was she looking for a reason to run because deep down she didn't think a man like Peter would actually choose her?

Her stomach sank to her knees as she acknowledged the truth. The answer was yes. That's why she was so quick to jump to the worst conclusion. And until she believed otherwise and could trust the man she loved, Peter didn't need her. But what if she couldn't change? Maybe Peter was right, and they didn't belong together.

She looked up as a soft voice announced the mall was closing. "Thanks for listening to me. Are you coming to city hall on election night?"

It was a tradition that the candidates gathered there until all the votes were counted.

"Of course I am. I'm your campaign manager."

"How do you expect it will go?"

"It'll be between you and Peter."

Another nail in the coffin. "He won't be happy if I beat him."

"He'll live," Jake said with a laugh. "And you are going to win."

NICOLE COULDN'T BRING herself to contact Peter before she went to bed. She'd hoped all evening he'd call her, so she could at least apologize. But her phone never rang. Each hour, her heart became a little heavier.

Election day, she woke with renewed purpose. She would focus only on the election today, and tomorrow, she would call Peter and see if he would talk to her. Maybe she wouldn't get in the runoff, and he'd feel sorry for her.

She opened the *Cedar Grove Gazette* and read that she and Peter were expected to be the top vote getters. Not exactly the best conditions to renew their relationship. She couldn't do anything about that, other than withdraw from the race. That wasn't happening. She had a plan for Cedar Grove, and if the voters elected her and Peter Elliott couldn't accept that, it was definitely time to move on.

Voting took place at city hall, and when she arrived, Jake was already set up across the street from the building, along with supporters for the other candidates. Betty Atkins manned Peter's table. Setting up outside city hall was a traditional last-ditch effort for candidates to appeal to the voters. Nicole felt sorry that voters had to run the gauntlet, so to speak, even though people expected to see the candidates and their supporters there.

As she pulled the lever by her name, chill bumps ran over her arms. She'd experienced the same emotion when she ran for the city council. Rebecca Caine from the *Gazette* snapped her picture as she stepped from the voting booth. If Nicole became mayor, history would be made. First woman mayor elected in Cedar Grove. She stood a little taller and smiled for the camera as Rebecca snapped another photo.

Peter was coming up the city hall steps as she descended. At least he didn't look away, although she almost wished he had, seeing the soulful hurt still in his eyes. "Good morning," she said.

He nodded. "You've already voted?"

"Yes, and I didn't vote for you." He didn't laugh, and she couldn't stand it any longer. She would like to at least be friends. "Can I speak with you? Privately."

"How about after the election results?"

"Yes. Maybe one of us will have something to celebrate." Her smile once again was met with those basset hound eyes.

As Peter and Nicole went in different directions, Jake watched Peter enter city hall. The slumped shoulders, the grim look on his face a few seconds ago. The man was hurting. He shifted his gaze to Nicole, who had stopped to speak to someone on the steps. So was she.

Peter was a fool if he let her get away. But his cousin's loss might be Jake's gain. Or not. He was afraid Nicole would never see him as anything other than a friend, and he wasn't sure his ego could handle that.

"If you only get two votes, at least we'll know where they came from," he said as she approached.

"Not. Funny."

"You're going to be in the runoff." He was 99 percent certain of that.

"With Peter. And you know who will win that race."

"Yep. You."

The look she shot him said otherwise. Out of the corner of his eye, he saw Peter reappear and head down the steps toward Betty Atkins, who waved a Vote for Peter Elliott poster. "My grandfather's attorney called this morning, and I need to ask Peter a question. Be right back, okay?"

"Going over to the enemy, huh?"

He laughed and then crossed the street. He hadn't outright lied to Nicole. Robert Corbett had called, but he was pretty sure he'd called Peter, as well. A south wind buffeted his face as he neared Peter's station. "Great day for an election," he said to Peter.

"I hope the weather encourages a big turn-out." Peter gave him a curious glance.

"Did Robert call you this morning?"

His cousin nodded. "I told him the city council should vote Thursday night on our proposals."

"Thursday night?"

"Because of the election, the council meeting was moved to Thursday. I've polled the others, and they're ready. I won't be voting on either proposal."

Jake nodded. That was the information he'd come for. He didn't want to lose control of Elliott Manufacturing, and he would if he didn't sway the city council to his side. At least he could count on Nicole's support. He started to walk away and stopped.

"You need to make it right with Nicole."

Peter stared at him as though he'd sprouted a halo. "She doesn't trust me."

"Well, she might have good reason, given her last boyfriend. Talk to her. Work this out."

CHAPTER TWENTY-THREE

THE POLLS CLOSED at seven and by seven thirty, people were shoulder to shoulder at city hall. Peter searched for Nicole in the crowd, but didn't see her. He'd thought all day about what Jake said, and he was right. Peter and Nicole were adults and should be able to at least talk.

Jake stood thirty feet from him but there were too many people to wade through, so he caught his eye instead. "Where's Nicole?" he mouthed.

His cousin pointed ahead, and Peter's pulsed kicked into overdrive when he saw her. He made his way through the crowd to where she stood with her family. Jake had beat him and was beside her already, his arm draped over Nicole's shoulder.

"Where's your mom?" Jake asked him.

"She had to return to Georgia right after she voted." Peter shook hands with Nicole's father. "It's crazy here."

"But exciting!" Nicole said.

Her eyes sparkled, but she wasn't looking at him. He missed the closeness they'd shared.

She pointed toward the stage. "Oh, look. I think they have the results."

Her excitement was contagious. He turned to see who was on the stage. Grady Smith, the election commissioner. This was it.

Grady raised his hands for quiet. "Okay, the results are in. With a little over eight thousand votes cast in today's election, this is the breakdown."

He read the list of candidates with their respective votes. Peter and Nicole were the front-runners and would face each other in the runoff in two weeks. Beside them stood her dad and brothers who cheered and hugged Nicole, then thumped him on the back.

A beaming grin lit Nicole's face. "Congratulations," she said softly, holding his gaze.

"You, too." Peter was sure his smile matched hers. The other candidates were making their way toward them, and the next few minutes were spent acknowledging well wishes all around.

A reporter from the local TV station stuck a microphone in front of him. "How does it feel to be in the runoff?"

"Great. Just great."

After Nicole said basically the same thing,

the reporter asked, "You two seem to be an item. Will that affect how you run your race?"

Nicole stiffened, a fight-or-flight look on her face, and Peter stepped in. "The race isn't about personalities. It's about who the voters think is the best person for the mayor's job." He wanted to add that it should be Nicole, but he could hardly do that.

"Do you agree?" The camera zoomed in on Nicole.

She smiled. "Definitely. And my five-point plan will give me the edge."

Nicole had recovered her poise. It should be an interesting couple of weeks.

Before Peter could ask her if she wanted to escape the rowdy atmosphere, Jake grabbed her hand and pulled her toward the outside door.

"We're going to her folks' house," he said over his shoulder. "To celebrate."

"Come over if you want to," Nicole said, her voice suddenly shy.

"I thought we were going to talk."

"Afterward?"

Peter loved being around her family, but the two of them had important things to discuss. "Just for a little while," he said.

"We can go to my apartment afterward and talk."

He nodded. That would be better than a restaurant.

Two hours later, he sat stiffly on her couch. "Your mom was gracious, once she recovered from me showing up."

"Mom's like that."

Neither said anything, and silence settled between them. An awkward silence.

"I hope we have a good turnout for the next election." Nicole's voice was shaky.

"Me, too." He wasn't sure what he was going to do about the race. Over the past week, his doubts about being the best person for the job had grown. On the drive to the coast, he'd clarified a few things in his mind. One of them was that Nicole would definitely be better for Cedar Grove than him.

"When I beat you, is that going to bother you?"

Her attempt at humor touched him. "Mighty sure of yourself. If I remember correctly, I outpolled you by three hundred votes."

"But I have a plan, and you don't." A tiny smile played at the corner of her mouth. "Jake says you got all the votes you're going to get."

"In your dreams. His, too."

Neither of them spoke until Nicole took a deep breath and said, "I want to apologize for jumping to the wrong conclusion. It was a horrid thing to accuse you of."

"It hurt." He wished he could say the hurt was getting better.

"I know, and I feel awful about it. I have no excuse except—"

"I'm not Stuart," he said.

"No, you are not, but…what he did makes it hard for me to trust anyone. You deserve someone who can trust you, someone without so much baggage."

He frowned. This sounded like goodbye. "Maybe we moved too quickly."

"That's possible, but it doesn't change me. I think you need to move on, find someone you deserve."

Wait a minute. He was angry, and he was hurt, but he wasn't ready to give up on their relationship. He turned so he could see her face. Tears rimmed her eyes. "Nicole—"

"No, Peter. Don't say anything. I'm broken, and you should have someone whole. Someone who won't second-guess."

But he wanted her.

NICOLE FELT EMOTIONALLY DRAINED. If he had taken her in his arms and told her he wanted her, broken or not, she didn't know if she could have sent him away.

But he hadn't. So it was a moot point. And he was gone now.

Once again she relived the memory of seeing him hold Allie in his arms. How in the world had she thought he was having a fling with her? *What won't kill you will make you stronger.* Her mother's words again. She hoped that went for relationships, as well. Her cell phone rang, and she jerked it out of her pocket. *Jake?* He'd been at her mom and dad's, so she didn't know what he could be calling about now. "Hello?"

"Hello, Madam Mayor."

"Don't jinx me."

"You will be the next mayor. Let's get together tomorrow and plan your strategy."

She sighed. "The only strategy I can afford is knocking on doors, and handing out cards."

"I have a freebie for you. Thursday morning, the early program on the local TV station. I'll be there to cheer you on."

"Really? That's great." Jake actually was a good campaign manager. "You aren't neglecting your job at Elliott Manufacturing, are you?"

"Things are slow right now, so I can spend a little time away from the plant. Did you and Peter talk?"

"Yeah." She didn't want to discuss it with

Jake. "I'll call you tomorrow about what I should wear for the show."

He got the message and told her good-night.

AFTER A RESTLESS SLEEP, Nicole stopped by to see her mother on her way to work the next day.

"What brings you here with such a long face?" Joyce asked. "I thought you'd still be celebrating your win."

Nicole gave her a halfhearted smile. "Do you have any coffee left?"

"I always have coffee. Have you had breakfast?"

There'd been no way she could put food in her stomach this morning. "Not yet."

"Still excited about your win last night, huh? Sit at the table, and I'll make you a scrambled egg sandwich."

Nicole wished it were about being excited.

"Peter seemed awfully quiet last night," her mom said as she cracked eggs in a bowl.

"Yeah."

"Kind of like you this morning. What's going on?"

She couldn't hold it in any longer. "Oh, Mom, I've done something terrible. I've ruined everything."

Her mom left the eggs and sat across from Nicole at the table. "Tell me what's wrong."

Blinking back tears, she spilled the whole story. "Peter thinks we can get past this, but I don't see how. I don't know *how* to trust him. I mean, if I can't trust someone who is as kind and honorable as he is, I won't ever be able to trust anyone. What's wrong with me?"

"Oh, honey, there's nothing wrong with you that faith in that man you love won't fix."

"Why did I automatically assume the worst? How could I think Peter would even do something like that?"

"Because you knew he loved Allie once, and you were insecure. It can happen to anyone."

"Did it ever happen to you? I mean—"

"Nicole, this isn't about me, it's about you. But I have learned over the years to not trust my eyes. When you love someone and there's a question, believe the best, and straightaway get the answer. And always remember—trust is a choice."

Was it possible she could change? It felt as if her whole future depended on it.

NICOLE LEFT HER mother and took the long route to the office, her mind whirling with thoughts of Peter. At the stoplight, she almost didn't see Betty Atkins trying to flag her down. Nicole lowered her window. Betty's smile could light up New York City. "What's up?"

"Nothing. Got time for coffee at Cups and More?" Betty looked as though she'd burst.

Nicole wasn't buying Betty's "nothing." She pulled her car into a parking place in front of the coffee shop and climbed out. "Okay, what's going on?"

Betty fanned herself with her left hand and a diamond sparkled in the sunlight.

"Oh!" Nicole's gasp brought an even bigger grin to the older woman's face. "You're wearing an engagement ring!" She hugged her friend. "I can't believe it, after all these years."

"Believe it. Come on, I'll buy you a latte."

A few minutes later they were sipping their coffees, and Nicole was admiring the ring. "It's beautiful."

"Hugh has always had good taste," Betty said.

Nicole wanted the kind of joy the city clerk had. "Can I ask you something?"

"Sure, go ahead."

"Why now? You and Hugh have been dating for as long as I can remember—"

"Fifteen years." Betty woo-wooed, and then she tilted her head. "After Hugh's last heart attack, something changed. Before that we were both content with just 'keeping company' as my momma used to say. All at once it wasn't enough.

"We've had some rough spots over the years and some humdinger arguments. That's probably one reason we hesitated for so long, but after the heart attack, we both knew that whatever may come, we wanted to be together. We loved each other enough to work out any problems that might arise."

"But how did you know?"

"We just did." Betty's smile was gentle. "Stuart did a number on you, but if you let what he did keep you from trusting a man like Peter, Stuart wins again. And, I bet you knew he was wrong for you long before you caught him with that secretary."

Betty's words startled her. "No…" Her protest died on her lips. "I was having doubts."

"Listen to your heart. It won't steer you wrong."

Nicole wished she believed that.

CHAPTER TWENTY-FOUR

THURSDAY NIGHT JAKE studied the five voting city council members. There would be no tie with Peter not voting. Although they didn't know it, these five people held his future in their hands. A "no" vote tonight would wrest Elliott Manufacturing from his control. He'd probably still be operations manager because if Peter won, he wouldn't want to take over the management of the company. But he wouldn't have the control he wanted and needed to make decisions.

His stomach clenched as Betty Atkins called the meeting to order and gave a positive report on former mayor Hugh Gordon. It seemed to take forever to get through the routine reports from the different divisions of the city, but finally his proposal was brought up. He moved to the front.

After a brief overview of the senior adult center for the minutes, he gave a report on the New Year's Eve get-together, and how the seniors helped decorate for the youth dance. Then he asked for questions.

"I don't have a question," Nicole said. "But I do have a bit of news. Since our last meeting, I've gone over the budget with a fine-tooth comb, and found an error that has resulted in a twenty-five-thousand-dollar surplus. Actually, Peter found it first."

"Where was it?" Cal asked.

"A debt that we will retire this month was included for the whole year. Betty will hand out the revised budget for you to go over."

Peter leaned forward. "So that means that we have funding for only one of the proposals?"

Jake noticed that Nicole barely looked at Peter. All was still not well there.

"Yes."

"Then I propose we vote," Peter said.

Cal coughed and cleared his throat. "Since most of us came into the meeting tonight thinking there were no funds, I think we need to table the vote until we have time to look over the budget and discuss it."

Jake groaned when that vote was unanimous and the meeting was adjourned. Another two-week wait. But at least he hadn't lost. When Nicole stepped off the stage, he thanked her for her support.

"It's a good project," she said.

Jake agreed. "Oh, I received a call from *Talk101*, and they already want you on their radio program again Monday morning. They even mentioned what a great job you did on this morning's TV interview."

"Thanks." She glanced toward Peter. "Have you heard any of Peter's radio ads this week?"

He shrugged. "I haven't been listening for his, just yours."

"Well, I have, and I haven't heard any. What's going on with him?"

"I don't know. Want me to find out?" he asked as the reporter from the *Gazette* approached.

"Please."

"As soon as I talk with this lovely lady." He turned and smiled at Rebecca. "Could I twist your arm to do an interview with Nicole?"

Rebecca touched her fingers to her forehead and half closed her eyes. "I see me coming to ask Nicole for an interview. Now I see you reading my mind," she said in a falsetto voice.

Jake laughed. He was beginning to really like Rebecca. "Thank you. I'll leave you two to work out the details."

He found Peter talking with Cal Sheridan and joined them.

"Do you mind if Tyler comes to dinner at my house tomorrow after practice?" Cal asked.

"That would be great," Peter said. "How do you think he's doing with the team?"

"It's like I told you before. The kid's doing well, really fitting in. With him playing we might go all the way to state."

"Is that the kid that borrowed your truck New Year's Eve?" Jake said.

"Yep, but I think he learned his lesson, don't you, Cal?"

"My granddaughter, too," Cal said with a wry grin. "See you two at the polls."

As the older man walked away, Jake said, "How about grabbing a coffee at Cups and More?"

Peter glanced toward Nicole. "Just me and you?"

"Nicole will be tied up awhile."

As they walked to the coffee shop, Jake said, "What's with not running ads on the radio?"

"I'm running ads, maybe not that many, but they are there. What made you ask?"

"Something Nicole mentioned. You aren't throwing the race, are you?"

"No, although I have thought about dropping out, except I can't do that. She'd always wonder if she would've won on her own merits."

A few minutes later, they sat across from each other drinking black coffee.

"I meant to say this earlier, but thanks for your support tonight," Jake said. "That means a lot to me."

"I've been thinking that there has to be a way to fund both projects."

"Me, too. Come up with anything?"

"I have, but you may not like it."

"Try me."

"It's possible both proposals might get approved, but only one will get the twenty-five-thousand-dollar funding and win Grandfather's contest. What if the one who wins the half million splits it? I looked over the terms again last night, and once Corbett awards one of us the building and money, it's all free and clear. If I get it, I'm willing to split it so the senior citizens can have their center, too."

He couldn't believe Peter was willing to do that. "Who are you, and what have you done with the guy who lives by the mantra that winning is everything?" he asked with a grin.

"Yeah, I know. But I've learned lately that Grandfather was right when he said that sometimes losing is winning. You didn't say what you thought of my proposition."

"I'd be willing to do the same. Do we need to run this by Corbett?"

"I'd feel better about it if we did," Peter said.

"Yeah, me, too. Tomorrow?"

"He told me he was going to be out of town the rest of the week. I'll call Monday and make an appointment."

For a minute neither spoke as they finished up their coffees, then Peter cocked his head. "We used to work together like this. Why did we stop?"

Jake slid his grandfather's knife from his pocket and laid it on the table. "Do you still have his watch?"

Peter nodded and placed it on the table, as well. "Remember what he always said?"

Jake laughed. "Winning isn't everything—it's how you win...or lose for that matter."

"Where did we go wrong?"

Jake picked up the knife and rubbed his thumb over the handle. "Grandfather would say we got too greedy."

"He was pretty wise and on target, unfortunately."

"He'd say something else right now, too."

Peter frowned. "What's that?"

"You're a fool if you let Nicole get away."

He crossed his arms. "You don't know—"

"She made a mistake."

"Nicole told you what happened?"

Jake nodded and leaned forward. "That ex

of hers? Stuart What's-His-Name? He did a number on her. Led her on for four years, until she caught him kissing the woman he's married to now."

Peter's face softened. "I'd wondered what happened there." He shook his head. "I had no idea he cheated on her. How did you know?"

"She told me some of it, and the rest I got from friends. Stuart isn't a nice man, but he made Nicole believe he loved her. I imagine it's hard for her to trust men now, especially when she saw what looked like betrayal with her own eyes."

"Even so, she could have asked me what happened."

"But she didn't. You have to work with what you have."

Peter flicked the watch open and closed it again. "I was so angry that she didn't trust me, but there's a Nicole-size hole in my heart, and it hurts. She broke it off, though, said I needed someone who would trust me. I don't know what to do."

Jake didn't realize Nicole had walked away. "Go after her, and don't take no for an answer."

Peter looked uncertain.

"Do what you want, but I'm serving you notice right now. If you're fool enough to throw this opportunity with Nicole away, I'm going after her."

A half grin curved Peter's mouth. "I thought we were going to start working together."

"We are. That's the only reason I'm giving you fair warning."

CHAPTER TWENTY-FIVE

PETER PARKED IN front of Robert Corbett's office and climbed out of his truck. After more than a week to think about splitting the money with Jake, he was even more confident this was the right thing to do. And if Corbett objected, they'd just have to find a way to bring him on board.

Jake was waiting in the reception area. He looked as nervous as Peter felt. It was evident Jake wanted this to work as much as Peter did. The senior center had become almost as important to him as the youth center. The secretary told them the attorney was waiting for them.

A folder lay opened on Corbett's desk, presumably their grandfather's will. The older man peered over his glasses. "Boys, to what do I owe the pleasure of this appointment?"

Peter and Jake exchanged glances. His cousin had designated him spokesman. "Sir, Jake and I have been talking, and we've made a decision that we're not sure you'll approve."

"And that is?"

Jake crossed his arms while Peter stared at him intently and said, "The city council is in favor of both projects Grandfather assigned to us. However, because of budget constraints, there is only enough money in the city treasury to fund one of the projects. If the youth center gets the nod for the twenty-five thousand and I win Grandfather's contest, I want to split the half million with the senior center. If Jake wins, he'll do the same with me. The building is large enough to house both projects."

"I see. Are you in agreement with this, Jake?"

He nodded. "Yes, sir."

Peter couldn't read Corbett as he sat back in his chair and rested his hands over his ample belly.

"Let me make sure I understand what you're proposing. One of you expects to be awarded funding for your project from the city, meeting the requirement of the contest. That person, in turn, will win the five hundred thousand dollars, the building and the position of CEO of Elliott Manufacturing. He will then split the winnings with the other and share the building. Is that correct?"

"Yes, sir," they said together, but somehow Elliott Manufacturing had slipped Peter's mind.

Corbett pinned Peter with his gaze. "If you win, the running of your grandfather's company will fall to you. What if you're elected mayor? How will you do both?"

"First, I do not expect to be elected mayor. As much as I hate to lose, Nicole is much better suited to running Cedar Grove than I am. But I don't want the CEO job, either. And Jake does. I'm bowing out of that. It's rightfully his."

"You're certain that's what you want to do?"

"Yes, sir," Peter said. He held the attorney's gaze. Was that a smile tugging at the corner of Corbett's mouth?

The older man slowly took two envelopes from the folder on his desk. "I know neither of you understood why your grandfather drew up this contest when he could have easily given you both the money to operate the two centers.

"But he realized he had made a grave error in continually pitting you against each other, and had, in fact, created in you an attitude of winning at any cost. Not only that, he hated that you two had become adversaries. He hoped that by giving you both deserving projects and only funding one, you would learn that winning isn't everything and would come together to work out a solution."

Corbett removed his glasses and placed them on his desk. "He had a great deal of well-placed faith in you two and fervently hoped that you would join together to get both of these projects funded."

The old attorney's chin quivered. "He would be proud of you both."

Peter's throat tightened. Next to him, Jake coughed and cleared his throat.

"He had enough faith in you that he filled out these checks and signed over the building to both of you."

He stood and handed them the envelopes. "There's a check for five hundred thousand dollars in each envelope. I'll record the title to the building later this morning."

Both men stood and accepted their envelope and shook hands with the attorney. "Thank you, sir."

The knowledge of what his grandfather thought of him washed over Peter like a refreshing rain. It had never been about receiving the money for the youth center, although knowing he'd be able to build a center and name it after his grandfather made him feel ten feet tall.

No, his heart swelled almost to bursting at receiving his grandfather's approval. A glance at Jake told him he felt the same way. Peter had never seen him at a loss for words before.

He draped his arm over Jake's shoulder.

"Come on, and we'll celebrate over a steak lunch. I need your advice about something."

"Deal."

SATISFACTION LINGERED AS Peter sat across from his cousin in Venelli's, eating their celebration lunch. He had so many plans for the youth center, and the first was to hire Clint as director.

Jake paused in cutting his steak. "You said you needed advice. On what?"

Peter laid his fork down. "I want to find a way to lose the election."

"*You what?* Why?"

"It's like I said in Corbett's office. Nicole is much better qualified to run the mayor's office than I am. She has a great five-point plan, has already contacted the CEOs of two companies who have expressed an interest in locating in this area. She has the vision. I don't."

"Just withdraw."

He couldn't do that. To Nicole, winning the mayor's office by default would be like cheating. "No. It's important that the voters choose her to lead the city."

Jake scratched his jaw. "I guess I can see that. I do know that she doesn't have much money left for advertising. Why don't you take out an ad in the newspaper listing her qualifications?"

Peter smiled. "That's an idea. I wonder if I have time to get it in the Sunday paper before the election? Maybe a full-page ad." He shot Jake a grin. "You're a genius."

"You're just now figuring that out?"

"I'll write it out and pay for it, but I'll need you to put it in the paper for me. It wouldn't be good for anyone to find out I'm the one behind it."

"Gotcha."

CHAPTER TWENTY-SIX

ELECTION DAY, AND for the hundredth time in the past week and a half, Nicole reached for her cell phone to call Peter and chickened out. He could have called her. What if he didn't want to talk to her? Or worse...

No. She had enough to deal with today. *Just get your paper, get dressed and go vote.*

She padded to her front door and opened it as the sun peeked through the early morning haze. It was going to be a gorgeous day with temperatures in the high fifties. She picked up the Tuesday *Gazette* and made a mental note to give her paper carrier a good tip for always putting the paper right at her door.

Rebecca had promised to run their last interview in today's paper, and the article should be good for a few votes. Nicole needed them after Peter's big lead in the first election. More ads would have been nice, but she didn't have the money.

Nicole had expected Peter to run more ads, but he hadn't. She slipped the paper out of the plastic wrapper and unfolded it. Her face stared back at her on the front page. She owed Rebecca big-time for her encouragement. She was as excited about her candidacy as Nicole was.

This time tomorrow she could be mayor. The thought almost staggered her and sent the butterflies in her stomach flying. She opened the paper to the inside pages, and blinked. Who...? Her mouth worked but nothing came out. She scanned to the bottom and read the signature: Concerned Citizen.

Someone had run a full-page ad with all the reasons Nicole should be mayor. She reached for her cell phone and speed-dialed Jake.

"'Lo," he mumbled.

She checked her watch. Eight o'clock. "The polls are open, and you're not up."

"Give the lady a prize," he said, sounding a little more alert. "What's up?"

"Did you run this full-page ad in the *Gazette*?"

"Huh? Oh...it finally came out." It wasn't a question. "It was supposed to run Sunday."

"So you did."

"No, I didn't. Peter did."

"WHAT!" She gripped the phone. "Why would he do that?"

"Because he's in love with you?"

"Ohh!" she growled. "What? He thinks I can't win on my own, and he has to help me out?"

"Uh-oh."

"What do you mean uh-oh?"

"Let me wake up properly before I say something else stupid. Call you right back."

She punched the phone off and paced the apartment. She didn't know who she was madder at, Peter or Jake. Because Jake knew about this ad, for sure. The phone rang again. "You better have a good reason for this, Jake O'Neil."

"I'm more awake now, but it hasn't helped me understand your problem with this."

"The problem is, neither of you asked me if I wanted the ad. Instead, you went behind my back. You have to be in control. That's what it's all about. Control, Jake. Your cousin thinks I can't get elected on my own merits so he has to help me out. You tell him this because I'm not talking to him—I don't need or want his help in getting elected. Understand?"

"Nicole—"

"All I wanted to hear was a 'yes.' Goodbye."

Tears stung her eyes. She didn't know which hurt more, that the ad was placed behind her back, or that neither of them thought the voters would choose her.

Her phone rang again. Peter. She was too hurt to talk to him and silenced the ring.

Half an hour later as she stepped out of the shower, her mother called. "Did you know Peter is handing out your cards at city hall?"

"What?"

"He's handing out your campaign literature, too. He gave me a brochure."

"Did you ask him why?"

"I did."

Nicole waited. "Are you going to tell me what he said?"

"You need to ask him yourself."

"No. I don't want to talk to him. Did you see the ad in the paper this morning? He placed it there."

"That's the sweetest thing I've ever heard."

"Mo-ther!" Was her own mother crazy? Did she think Nicole couldn't get elected, either?

"Nicole, the man's in love with you."

She closed her eyes. What if he really did love her? That still didn't excuse him from going behind her back. "I have to get dressed and get down to city hall."

ELECTION DAY HAD dawned sunny and crisp. A perfect day for voting, or at least it had been until Jake showed up. Peter stared at the full-page ad as voters walked past him on the sidewalk. The ad had seemed like a good idea. "Why did you tell her I did it?"

Jake shrugged. "I thought it would impress her, maybe score a few points for you. You sure need them."

"And now she thinks I don't believe in her, or believe that the voters will elect her. And if she wins, she'll always think it was because the ad influenced people to vote for her."

Earlier he'd envisioned a much different day. One where Nicole stood with him as they interacted with voters and then together at her victory party. Now, according to Jake, she might just kill him.

"Isn't that why you placed the ad?"

"Well, yeah." He stared at Jake. "That's it! I have to make her understand I did it because *I* believe she's the best person for the job."

"But she won't talk to you."

"Yeah." He sighed.

"You could still withdraw, even now."

Not if he ever hoped to make Nicole his wife. *Wife?* Certainty welled in his heart. Yes, wife. But at this point, he wasn't sure how he'd get her to agree, not when she wouldn't answer his calls or return any of his messages.

And whether Nicole liked it or not, he'd spent the past ten days trying to convince voters to elect her. Half the people he encountered thought it was thoughtful that he was campaigning for her. The other half thought he was crazy. And he was. Crazy in love.

"What am I going to do, Jake?"

"If I were you, I would avoid her today. Wait until the election is over, put all this behind you, and then talk to her."

At least it was a plan. His mouth went dry as Nicole's car flew into a parking space across from city hall.

CHAPTER TWENTY-SEVEN

VOTE FOR NICOLE MONTGOMERY signs greeted Nicole when she flung herself out of the car, and Peter was holding one of them. Beside him, Jake held another.

She stormed across the street and didn't stop until she was almost toe-to-toe with Peter. "What are you doing?"

"Campaigning," he said.

"But—but—"

He put his finger to his mouth. "Shh. Go vote. We're not discussing this until after the results are in." His eyes twinkled. "And I like the sweater."

Nicole looked down and suppressed a groan. In her haste to get dressed, she'd grabbed the sweater he'd given her for Christmas. He'd think she chose it purposely. If she denied it, he wouldn't believe her. "What, this old thing? I don't even know where I picked it up."

That should fix him. Except the pained look in his eyes went straight to her heart. "I—"

"Peter Elliott! What are you doing?"

They both turned as Betty Atkins marched toward them.

"I'm going to vote," Nicole said and beat a hasty retreat. She was embarrassed enough without sticking around while Betty broadcast her predicament to everyone within two hundred feet.

"New campaign manager?" Cal Sheridan asked as Nicole climbed the steps to city hall.

"Hardly. I don't know what he's doing."

"Well, did you hear what happened with the senior and youth centers?"

She shook her head.

"I'm surprised Peter didn't call you yesterday when he called me. He and Jake are combining the proposals. The centers will share the building."

Probably one of the calls she didn't answer or messages she deleted. "That's really good news."

"It's not the only good news. My wife and I are taking Tyler to live with us—we're fostering him."

She squealed and hugged him. "That's wonderful! First Logan and Lucas are adopted and now Tyler will be with you."

Cal nodded. "I think so, too. I'm glad Peter helped me see what a great kid Tyler is."

She swallowed the lump in her throat. Peter

could be a pretty awesome person when he stayed out of her business. "I better vote and get back to my table."

"I think you'll win today," Cal said. "I voted for you."

"Thank you." She hadn't expected that.

She cast her vote and hurried back to the sidewalk. Peter was gone. "Where is he?"

"He went to take care of an emergency," Jake replied.

She narrowed her eyes at him. An emergency? Or did he just not want to face her? "Why didn't you tell me you and Peter resolved the issue with the centers?"

"Peter tried, but someone wouldn't answer her phone or return his calls."

Heat flushed her face.

"Cut him some slack, Nicole. The guy is nuts about you, and you feel the same for him. So what's the problem?"

"I don't feel—"

"Yes, you do." He put his arms around her and drew her to him, patting her back.

She'd made such a mess out of everything she didn't know if they could ever get back on track. "I'm scared. What if I jump to the wrong conclusion again?"

"Like if Peter saw us right now, he might jump to the wrong conclusion?"

She stepped back and stared at the crack in the sidewalk. "But we're not... Oh, Jake, I've made so many mistakes."

"Forgive him. Forgive yourself." He lifted her chin. "He'll be back later. Tell him."

She shook her head. "I can't. Hold down the fort here. I'm going home to wait for the election results."

PETER STARED AT JAKE. "What do you mean, you told Nicole I had an emergency?"

Jake shrugged. "You did—Betty Atkins. Did you get her calmed down?"

"Yes. Where is Nicole?"

"She went home, said she couldn't stand the tension here."

"I'll be back."

He drove across town, rehearsing what he'd say when he got to her apartment. What if she wouldn't open the door?

"Go away," she called out after he rang the bell.

"Nope. Not going anywhere until you talk to me."

The door slowly opened, and she moved aside for him to enter.

"Thank you," he said as he walked past her, the sweet scent of her perfume curling around him and reminding him of New Year's Eve. The night had held so much promise.

"Can we sit down?"

She eyed the single couch, and then crossed her arms. "I'd rather stand."

"Okay." He wanted to take her in his arms and kiss her until she said she'd marry him. But from the way she glared at him, she'd knock him into next week if he touched her. "Green is your color, and that sweater looks good on you, even if you don't know where you got it."

Crimson crept up her neck. "Th-thank you." She ducked her head. "I'm sorry I said I didn't know where I got it. That was mean. I do like this sweater." For the first time, she looked uncertain. She nervously licked her lips.

The lips he wanted to kiss so bad right now it was killing him. He took a deep breath. "Look, I didn't think it would upset you if I created that ad. It's just that Jake said you didn't have the money to advertise last week. I wanted to do something nice for you."

The muscles in her neck moved as she swallowed. "You shouldn't have done it behind my back. It was like you didn't believe I could get elected, and you had to do something to make it happen."

"I know that now. But I believe in you, and I just wanted you to get elected."

"But why don't you want to be mayor?"

"Because you'll make a much better mayor than I would. When I saw your five-point plan, I realized you were years ahead of me in knowing how to move this city forward."

Her eyes softened, and she bit her bottom lip.

He took her hand. "I thought about withdrawing, but I know how important it is for the voters to choose you. I was just trying to sweeten the pot a little."

WARMTH SPREAD THROUGH her chest as she looked into his sky-blue eyes. He remembered that no one chose her as a teenager? Her vision blurred, and she blinked back tears. Now she really felt bad. What was so terrible about what he'd done, anyway?

Having him stand so close, his lips so near hers made it hard to remember why they shouldn't pursue this relationship.

The trust issue. Not his. Hers. What if something happened again? She couldn't trust herself to always believe the best about him. *Trust is a choice.* Her mother's words popped in her mind.

He pulled her in his arms. "Nicole, please don't shut me out."

Listen to your heart. It won't steer you wrong. She looked into his eyes. "I'm sorry for not trusting you. What if it happens again?"

"We'll deal with it. And apology accepted."

He was staring at her lips, and her breath hitched. "Peter—"

Her lips parted, and she leaned toward him, wanting to feel his mouth on hers.

Peter cupped her face in his hands and kissed her gently on the forehead.

That wasn't where she wanted his kiss. She slid her hands behind his neck, pulling him closer.

He took his time, kissing her closed eyes, then the tip of her nose.

A moan came from her throat as he captured her mouth, and she lost herself in his kiss. His fingers trailed her face as he released her, then claimed her lips again.

Seconds or minutes, maybe hours later, he lifted her chin. "I love you."

She smiled. "I love you, too."

Another kiss that curled her toes. When he released her, she nestled her head on his shoulder. "Hmm," she sighed.

"Double hmm," he said softly. "Will you marry me?"

She pulled away from him. "Are you sure?"

"I don't ever want to go through another week like this past one."

"I don't, either, but I always dreamed of the knee and ring thing."

"You want me to get down on one knee now, or do you want to wait for the ring?"

She gave him a lazy smile. "The ring isn't necessary. But that is how I've always wanted the man I marry to propose."

He shook his head and dropped to one knee before taking her hand. "Nicole Montgomery, would you do me the honor of becoming my wife?"

"Peter Elliott, I would love to be your wife."

"WHICH DO YOU want to do first?" Peter asked. He couldn't believe she had said yes. If he had his choice, they'd get married tomorrow. "Would you rather go to Waits' Jewelry or your parents' house?"

"Jewelry store first," she said.

At Waits' they found the perfect two-karat diamond ring and waited while the jeweler resized it, finally leaving the store around six.

As they drove to her parents' house, Nicole held her hand up. "It's beautiful," she whispered.

"I thought it was, too." Peter slapped his head. "I should have asked your father for your hand in marriage." He turned to look at her. "Do you think he'll be upset?"

She pretended to think a second, then laughed. "No."

"Well, don't say anything when we go in, and I'll pull your dad aside and ask him."

"You don't have to do that."

"I want to."

When they entered the house, Joyce looked at them strangely. "What are you two doing here?"

"We have something to discuss with you," Nicole said. "Is Dad around?"

"We were about to leave, and he's locking up his shop."

She squeezed his hand, and he kissed her on the nose. "I'll be right back."

Her dad was putting away his tools when Peter entered the shop. "Good afternoon, Mr. Montgomery."

He laid the sander down. "It's evening, and it's about time you called me Dan."

Until he had Nicole's father's permission, Peter preferred Mr. Montgomery. He cleared his throat. "Uh, I, ah...want to ask for your daughter's hand in marriage. I mean, I've already asked her, but I want your blessing."

A giant grin split Daniel's face. "Are you sure? She's quite the handful."

"Oh, yes, sir. And that part about her being a handful? I wouldn't want it any other way."

"Good. Then you have my blessing. Now, let's go see if Joyce has ferreted this information out of Nicole."

Tears streamed down both Nicole's and her mother's faces when the two men entered the back door.

"I thought you were going to wait," Peter said.

"She saw the ring." Nicole wiped her eyes.

"I can't believe it," Joyce said, blotting her lashes. "My little girl is getting married, and maybe getting elected mayor."

Peter and Nicole stared at each other.

"The election!" they cried in unison.

"Polls close in thirty minutes," Peter said. "We better get down there."

"We'll be right behind you," Dan said.

AT SEVEN FIFTEEN, the election commissioner emerged from the room where the votes were being counted. Nicole's heart fluttered. Standing by Jake was Rebecca, who gave her a thumbs-up. No matter which way the election went, she'd have to thank the reporter for all she had done. Peter squeezed her hand. "You're going to win," he whispered.

She wasn't so certain. And if the voters

didn't choose her, she would live. And whether he believed it or not, Peter would make a good mayor.

Nicole held her breath as the commissioner spoke.

"The results are in and this is the vote breakdown. Peter Elliott 3,450 votes."

Her stomach sank to her knees. Someone had told her the turnout was lower than the first election, somewhere around six thousand votes. She turned to congratulate Peter.

"G. Nicole Montgomery 4,324."

Nicole's heart sang.

She'd won!

Peter lifted her off her feet in a crushing bear hug. "Congratulations, darling!"

When he set her down, her family mobbed them, congratulating her on being mayor and Peter for snagging Nicole. As soon as there was a lull, her mom announced that there'd be a party at their house and everyone was invited.

Jake stopped before he left and kissed her on the cheek. "I'm happy for you, kiddo."

"Thanks, Jake. And thanks for being my campaign manager. You're pretty good at that."

He gestured at Peter. "I had a little help." Then his eyes lit up. "Now will you tell me what the *G* stands for?"

"No way." Nicole pointed toward Rebecca, who was chatting to Betty. "But your favorite reporter might."

"Becky knows?" He glanced toward her. "I'll have to weasel that out of her on the way to your folks' house."

When they were alone, Peter took her in his arms. "Have you thought about a date? We could elope next week. Or have you always wanted one of those big weddings?"

She closed her eyes. She'd never had girlfriends to dream about her future wedding with when she was a teenager, but she had always wanted to be married in a church with family and friends around. "Nothing huge. A church wedding, though," she said. "And how does June sound?"

"Like a long way off."

She laughed. "It'll be here before you know it."

He kissed her. "June it is, then. The first of the month, I hope."

"June first sounds good."

"By the way, what *does* the G stand for?" When she didn't give him an answer, he said, "I'll find out when we get the marriage license."

She took a deep breath and released it. "It stands for Giselle."

"That's beautiful. And it fits you." He traced his finger along her jaw to her lips. "We'll name our first daughter Giselle."

But what if their daughter was a tomboy like Nicole?

Giselle.

It *was* beautiful, and Peter thought it suited her. Maybe it was time to embrace the fact that the person defined the name, not the other way around. With a contented sigh, she nestled her head on Peter's shoulder. "I like that."

* * * * *

LARGER-PRINT BOOKS!

GET 2 FREE LARGER-PRINT NOVELS PLUS 2 FREE MYSTERY GIFTS

Love Inspired®

Larger-print novels are now available...

LARGER-PRINT BOOKS!

GET 2 FREE LARGER-PRINT NOVELS PLUS 2 FREE MYSTERY GIFTS

Love Inspired®

SUSPENSE
RIVETING INSPIRATIONAL ROMANCE

Larger-print novels are now available...

YES! Please send me **The Montana Mavericks Collection** in Larger Print. This collection begins with 3 FREE books and 2 FREE gifts (gifts valued at approx. $20.00 retail) in the first shipment, along with the other first 4 books from the collection! If I do not cancel, I will receive 8 monthly shipments until I have the entire 51-book Montana Mavericks collection. I will receive 2 or 3 FREE books in each shipment and I will pay just $4.99 US/ $5.89 CDN for each of the other four books in each shipment, plus $2.99 for shipping and handling per shipment.*If I decide to keep the entire collection, I'll have paid for only 32 books, because 19 books are FREE! I understand that accepting the 3 free books and gifts places me under no obligation to buy anything. I can always return a shipment and cancel at any time. My free books and gifts are mine to keep no matter what I decide.

263 HCN 2404   463 HCN 2404

Name	(PLEASE PRINT)	
Address		Apt. #
City	State/Prov.	Zip/Postal Code

Signature (if under 18, a parent or guardian must sign)

Mail to the **Reader Service:**

IN U.S.A.: P.O. Box 1867, Buffalo, NY 14240-1867
IN CANADA: P.O. Box 609, Fort Erie, Ontario L2A 5X3

MMLPBPA15